THE CHAMELEON

I0549301

CHAMELEON

by

Janice Olson

Lyndon Publishing
P. O. Box 382380
Duncanville, Texas 75138

This book is a work of fiction. References to real people,
establishments, organizations, or locations are intended
only to provide a sense of authenticity and are used
fictitiously. The names, characters, places, and incidents
are the product of the author's imagination or are used
fictionally to provide a sense of authenticity. Any
resemblances to actual events, locales, or persons, living or
dead are purely coincidental.

Other novels by Janice Olson

Texas Sorority Sisters Stand Alone Series
Serenity's Deception
Lethal Intent

Coming Soon New Releases

Run ... But You Can't Hide ~ 2014

Romantic Comedy

Mr. What's His Name ~ 2014

Non-Fiction

Springs of Mercy
A 30-day Devotional

Coming Soon Audio Books

Serenity's Deception
Lethal Intent
Chameleon

Many thanks to all who have helped ...

My novels undergo copious edits and are read and reread many times for editing purposes before the final draft goes into printing to catch my numerous errors due to my dyslexia. The reason I mention this, it takes a lot of people to read my novels before publishing.

A very special *thank you* to Jacqueline and Jewlene, two of my beta readers, for all the time and effort you have put in reading my novel to keep me on track. You ladies are amazing.

Also I wouldn't be able to write my novels if it wasn't for my *No. 1 cheering fan*, my husband, Harry. Your love and encouragement makes me feel I can conquer the world.

I mentioned my dyslexia earlier to encourage others who may suffer from dyslexia. I am evidence there is hope. We dyslexics are creative people, but we need help to recognize our potential. If you or someone you know has dyslexia and needs help, please visit: http://www.american-dyslexia-association.com/ or http://www.interdys.org/.

I pray you will enjoy Chameleon, Roni's story. And if you haven't read my other novels, please do.

Blessings,

Janice

CHAMELEON

PROLOGUE

April, 1995—Houston, Texas

"Veronica, please gather your things and go to the principal's office." Mrs. Davis gave Roni a strange look. The note delivered by the student monitor seconds before dangled from her teacher's fingertips.

Fear snatched Roni's gut. Of all the kids in school, why would she be called to the principal's office? She could understand Tommy Rafferty being asked, he was always in trouble ... but her? *No way!*

The snickers and whispers of her classmates went around the room quicker than a dog treeing a cat. She stuffed her things into her backpack, slung one strap over her shoulder, and then without glancing at her classmates, rushed out the door to escape all the prying eyes.

In the hall, Roni met silence and the eerie feeling she was in big trouble and she didn't know why. Her blood pumped fast and furious in her ears. Her feet pounded loud, matching the cadence in her head—*I won't throw up. I won't throw up, I ...*

The chant did nothing to stop her stomach from rumbling. As she passed the gym, Roni gagged on the odor of BO and sweaty feet colliding with the smell of cafeteria food from down the hall. Her breakfast made its way up her throat. A pucky, metallic taste filled her mouth as she gulped air to force the awful gunk back down.

Hugging her stomach, she refused to disgrace herself by up-chucking on the tile floor. She'd never live it down. Every Hostler Junior High boy in eighth grade would call her by some looser name like *barf-face* or *bait-breath*. She'd be ruined for life unable to show her face in school again.

Her gaze traveled to the front office looming straight ahead. The room looked like a prison with its grey, metal doors and wire-meshed windows. Standing just inside were two uniformed policemen talking with Principal Hadley.

Roni's heart skittered to a stop and then kicked in violently hammering against her chest. She could barely catch her breath and her feet felt encased in cement. Reaching out with a sweaty hand, she grasped the handle and pulled.

Mr. Hadley swung around. "Here's Veronica Reeves now."

The two officers, in dark navy uniforms, turned in unison. Their badge glinted from their shirt pocket. One was a woman. By the look on their faces, something was wrong—*terribly wrong.*

The sight of their gun hitched to their belt had Roni quaking. A picture flashed before her eyes—arms behind her back, hands in cuffs, classmate's faces plastered to the windows jeering as the police hauled her off in the squad car, sirens blaring.

She wanted to turn and run but the principal's stare nailed her in place.

"Come into my office."

Squaring her shoulders, Roni looked at him. "Sir, w-what did I do? I ..."

Mr. Hadley waved her silent.

What little courage she had deserted her. She forced her marshmallow legs to move. She did her best to act as if the laughter of the two students sitting in the front office didn't bother her.

The officers shut the door behind them closing Roni off from her junior high world. She rubbed her sweaty palms down the sides of her pant legs.

"Sit down, please." Mr. Hadley motioned for her to take the middle of the three oak chairs in front of his desk.

The toast and cocoa from breakfast continued to swim and gurgle. And that didn't seem to be the worst of her problems either. She had a most urgent need to go to the restroom. And right now, she wasn't sure which she would do first. Vomit on Mr. Hadley's clean carpet or ... wet in his hard oak chair. If she did either, she'd never live it down. She'd be too mortified to show her face in school again.

Gulping down the knot that seemed to be stuck in her throat, she eased back into the chair, her fingers fidgeting in her lap as she waited.

What had she done that would take two officers to handle—two officers sitting on each side to keep her from escaping?

Mr. Hadley cleared his throat. "Veronica, this is Officer Meeks—" He motioned to the woman first. "—and Officer Roman. I need you to listen carefully to what they have to say." He cleared his throat again, nodding for the officer to begin.

Their hot stare bore into her. Her throat stung and tightened and tears pricked her eyes. Something was wrong, *bad* wrong. She could feel it in her bones.

Officer Meeks scooted to the edge of her chair and faced Roni. "Hi Veronica."

Coffee breath fanned Roni's face causing her stomach to revolt even more. She never did like the smell of secondhand coffee, and she held her breath to avoid it now.

The officer's uneasy smile made Roni's knee want to bounce, but she wouldn't let it.

"I'm afraid we have some bad news."

The skin under the woman's chin rolled as she talked and swallowed. "Your mother and father were in a bad car accident."

The tatty-tat-tat of Roni's heel hitting the floor sounded like a jackhammer. And though she tried, there was nothing she could do to keep her knee from bouncing. The feel of tiny gerbil tracks skittered across her skin as stinging nettles attacked her armpits. This was much like the time Goober jumped out of the girls' restroom stall and scared her spitless.

"Are they in hospital? Will you take me to them?" She swiped her cheeks with the back of her hand.

Officer Meeks shook her head. "I'm afraid not, sweetie. Both of them were killed in the accident."

Everything in the room seemed weird-like. A loud scream filled the room, hurting her ears.

You're lying. I want my mom and dad. Take me to them. No! Don't touch me. I want my parents.

The words raced through her head as Roni shrank away from the woman's touch. She wanted nothing to do with the officers. She jerked up out of the chair with every intention of running out of the office.

The woman grabbed her arm, stopping her. "Veronica, honey, listen to me. What I've told you is true. Your parents died early this morning."

Roni covered her ears. "No! I won't listen to you. I don't believe you."

Just like the time she and her friend Beth Sue held their breath until everything turned black, Roni felt a tingling sensation spread upward through her body. Her head felt light. The room swirled, fading into darkness, surrounding her with a world of nothingness, then …

Mama smiled.

Daddy waived.

Roni ran into their arms. The warmth of their hug took the chill away.

Why would Officer Meeks tell such an awful lie?

CHAPTER 1

Present day—Athens, Texas

Veronica Reeves took a deep breath of country fresh air, glad to be home, even if for only the weekend. She moved up the small knoll to the deserted canopy away from the rest of the guests and main festivities hoping for a few minutes of privacy.

Her jeans that had long lost their crease, felt hot and confining. Roni reached around to pull her blouse away from her sticky skin. A bead of sweat trickled down the hollow of her back, pooling at the base of her spine causing a momentary chill to cover her skin.

The scorching heat of summer showed no signs of relenting, making late September warmer than usual. From the south, a tall threatening bank of clouds moved toward the Triple Cross Ranch. The huge oak trees, along with the white tent canopies peppering the lawn were starting to whip and snap with the rising wind.

The stir of air felt good against Roni's clammy skin, but she feared the impending storm would put an end to Marcus Peters' sixty-fifth birthday celebration.

Samantha and she had picked a western theme for Marcus's party. And by the turn out of the two hundred or so guests, the majority of them wearing cowboy boots, rhinestone shirts, and Wranglers, they had achieved success.

Roni slid her glass of tea on the table and sat down wishing she could free her feet of her boots and sink her toes into the thick, green grass. At the ripe old age of thirty and holding the esteemed position as the Peters' attorney, there came a certain self-imposed decorum. For her, bare feet were not an option—maybe later.

Her gaze traveled across the grounds that encompassed the house and a small portion of the Triple Cross Ranch. The guests milled around under tents set up to prevent them from baking in the sun.

All-in-all, the birthday barbeque took place without mishap, if she didn't consider Drake Peters' earlier entrance with a gorgeous brunette hanging on his arm, laughing. Since their arrival, Roni made certain she was too busy to care what Drake and the beauty might be doing at this moment.

A movement down a little ways and to her right caught Roni's attention. *Well speaking of …*

She shook her head as her gaze continued to follow Drake. He crossed the lawn with the grace of a panther eyeing his prey. Unlike most of the guests, he wasn't wearing a cowboy hat which allowed the wind to whip his sandy-colored hair about his ruggedly handsome face. Starched dark denim jeans rode nicely just above his hips. And his tight abs and muscles strained at the fabric of his white shirt.

What he did for a shirt and jeans could only be described as *pure male magnetism.*

No one would call Drake drop-dead gorgeous, but he had a rugged quality with his chiseled Nordic features that caused women to stop and take another look and then … fall at his feet.

Roni let loose a snort of laughter at the picture in her mind.

Drake stopped at the table where the model-like brunette sat alone. She was the epitome of elegance. He bent to speak into her ear, then stood back to watch the woman's reaction. *Immediate.*

Her face glowed and he joined her bubbly laughter, drawing the attention of those nearby. The young woman looked full in Drake's face and gave him a captivating smile. He turned on the charm and gave her one of his *you won't be able to forget me* looks.

Roni didn't want to feel jealous, but she might as well call a spade a spade. She wished she hadn't noticed the little byplay and gave herself a good mental scolding for doing so. She moved her gaze to the children playing beneath the trees.

Drake was a good friend, always had been since she'd moved to the Triple Cross. She knew better than to expect more.

And though she knew she shouldn't, she envied the brunette's long legs and designer body, something she'd never have. The woman had style and beauty. Roni knew she lacked both. With her short, petite frame she wouldn't be mistaken for a model or, in her opinion, beautiful either. And apparently blondes with olive complexion weren't the rage this year, if Drake was any judge.

If only he would look at me like that instead of settling his gorgeous green eyes on Ms. Legs.

"Watch out, Sweetie, the little green monster is showing." Throaty laugher rang out at Roni's expense.

She snatched her gaze away from Drake and his latest conquest and directed it on his sister adding a disgruntled look as she entered the tent.

Samantha pulled out a chair, slid her generous curves into the seat next to Roni with an all-knowing grin. Her friend even had the gall to laugh at her expense.

"Was I that obvious?" Roni lowered her gaze, feeling her cheeks burn, closing off all visibility to her thoughts.

Giving Roni a playful nudge, Samantha shook her head, merriment dancing in her emerald eyes. "Don't be silly. You were only obvious to me *and* ... a hundred or so guests. But other than that, *nawh.*" She gave another deep throaty chuckle before pulling Roni into a hug. "Just teasing, sweetie. No one noticed."

Roni pursed her lips, then gave in to Sam's good-natured teasing, hugging her back.

"*Whew,* sure is hot and sticky." Samantha pulled at her shirt fanning the material. "Thankfully, the wind came up to keep it from being unbearable. Maybe the storm will give us a reprieve from this scorcher."

"Not likely. It'll just get hot 'n' muggy. You know how Texas is after a summer rain." Roni's gaze rested upon her companion who was more like a sister than a friend. The burnt-red, curly strands glisten with the brilliance of early fall leaves—a color Samantha hated and Roni loved.

Where Drake looked more like Marcus, tall, commanding, and dark blond, Samantha, except for green eyes like her father's and Drake's, resembled her mother Elle—fair skin, that burned even with tons of suntan lotion, and refined, reddish-brown curls. Though the same height as Roni, Samantha's petite frame carried full womanly curves partially due to her three adorable children.

"Why is it none of the men I date don't quite match up?" Secrets were none existent between Roni and Samantha since the day Roni arrived at the Triple Cross seventeen years ago.

"*Mmm,* could be my brother inherited the Peters' charm and he's a hunk. When I met Geoff, he had that same appeal, to me." She shrugged. "But since we're an old married couple now, marriage seems to have a way of mellowing one's outlook." Samantha glanced over at Geoff talking with

Marcus. A hint of color deepened her cheeks as she dipped her head.

Roni wondered what was going on. She'd never heard Sam even hint of trouble in their marriage. Maybe they'd had a tiff before the party.

Geoffrey Hansen, shy of Drake's six-one by three inches, wasn't Roni's idea of a hunk, not even when he was younger. But now, with a slight graying at the temples of Geoff's curly brown hair and a little paunch above his belt, he didn't come close. He lacked the Peters' charm and the magnetic personality of his brother-in-law, Drake.

For some reason when Samantha met Geoff at UT, he captivated her. They dated through college, and when they graduated, they got married immediately. Marriage and three children later seemed to have mellowed them both, but unlike Geoff, Samantha had grown more beautiful.

Roni noticed Geoff looked a little on edge. The discussion was getting heated, if Marcus' gestures were any indication.

By the pallor on his face, Roni knew Marcus was getting tired. His first round of chemo on Monday had hit him hard and the affects still had a hold on him. She wished he would sit down to rest and quit discussing business, but knew it wouldn't happen unless someone intervened.

Roni raised her brows and gave a slight nod. "I believe you'd better step in and referee. Marcus might hurt Geoff's feelings again. It looks pretty intense over there." She nodded at the two men.

By Sam's taunt, compressed lips and Geoff's belligerent posture, Roni figured they would have a heated discussion when they got home, if they waited that long.

"You're right. They shouldn't be discussing business today, if that's what they're doing. Especially since Drake is in charge of the company now. Geoff knows better." Sam huffed then softened. "And Daddy … well you know Daddy."

Roni's fond gaze fell on her former guardian. "Yes, I know Marcus."

Both men looked heated, but Marcus' body language was aggressive and in Geoff's face, which shouldn't be happening in Marcus' present condition.

"I bet daddy started the conversation. He just can't let go. It's in his blood." Sam pushed out of the chair, frustration plan on her face. "I better go separate them. I'll see you later."

She walked out from under the canopy, stopped, then turned with a mischievous grin. "Oh, Roni, I believe there are several eligible bachelors here today. Come to think of it, I've noticed a couple of them ogling you. I suggest you take a look at the meat market to take your mind off what ails you."

"Take care of your business. And I'll take care of mine." Roni waved her off, shaking her head smiling, yet a little peeved with Sam's suggestion.

"What business are you going to take care of squirt? And what's this about a meat market?"

Drake's deep baritone voice startled her, but at the same time, sent chills of pleasure reeling through her body and her nerve endings on alert. Then she remembered he had just come from flirting with Ms. Legs.

CHAPTER 2

Nick Holdum stood on the hill beneath the shade of a tree overlooking the gathering below. Not likely he'd be a welcomed guest at the Triple Cross Ranch. The odds were more probable once he concluded his business with Marcus Peters he'd be given the boot.

The old man is in for a rude awakening. He chuckled as envy and hate mingled. The thought of *getting even* gnawed at his gut.

Which one is Marcus? From this distance it was too hard to tell.

He spotted a couple of men talking. The tall, thin, white-haired man seemed to be domineering the conversation. From the pictures he'd found on the Internet it could have been Marcus.

Continuing to scan the crowd, a petite blond in fitted blue jeans and a white shirt caught his attention. His gaze followed her as she strolled off from the other guests and angled up a small knoll to one of the little white tents dotting the grounds.

The graceful sway of her hips as she sauntered toward the shade, natural, yet sensual, made him wish for a closer look. Too far to see her face, he couldn't tell for sure, but Nick bet she was a beauty. What he could see, didn't look bad.

Not bad at all. Maybe I'll get a chance to meet the little Texas filly after I speak with the old man. He chuckled, yet little humor was involved.

Nick moved across the front lawn towards the entrance of the house. He took in every aspect of the Peters' home, or should he say mansion? His old rented apartment in New York would take up one small corner of the white-stoned dwelling.

He may not have been raised with money, but he knew how to mix with the influential, and often did at his last job. However, he figured he wouldn't fit in here, which really didn't matter. What he wanted to accomplish was to rattle their cage a bit, shake up their self-important lives, and leave a little something behind they weren't expecting.

His long legs made short business of the twenty or so steps up to the wide, wraparound porch. His heart beat double time as he stared at the ten-foot, oak double doors barring his entrance. He figured they would stay closed to him if he didn't play his cards right or lost his cool.

In the center of the doors, a brass plate etched with a lone star and a triple cross held a brass knocker. The shiny brass didn't dare show a smudge or finger print. Everything around the Triple Cross Ranch was tidy, neat, and clean, unlike the dirty laundry he was about to unload once he got inside.

Another glance around riled his temper. His mother could have used some of the wealth of the Triple Cross. Instead she died in poverty.

He reached for the brass longhorn head, held it in midair for a few seconds, feeling its smooth warmth, and then lowered it with a *rat-a-tat-tat*. He allowed the knocker to drop from his fingers, which caused another tat, before he stepped back.

It might be too late for his mother but just in time for what he wanted, if what he read in the papers were true.

CHAPTER 3

Roni's humor dried up and heat crept into her face. The familiar, deep, resonating voice could always turn her insides out, and today was no different. How long had Drake been standing there? Had he overheard what Sam and she were discussing? *Goodness*, she hoped not.

"My name's not squirt." The fear Drake had heard their discussion, along with his choice of childhood endearment, precipitated the sharp edge to her voice.

Would the man never think of me as anything other than a child or his sister's playmate?

"And furthermore, what Sam and I were discussing is none of your business. Don't you have somewhere you need to be?" She inclined her head toward the tent where she'd last seen him.

Of all the dumb things to say.

"*Whoa!* Down girl, down." He held his hands out in front of him, teasingly.

His irresistible smile did a number on her overheated senses. "I'm sorry, Drake. This Texas weather has addled my brain."

"Apology accepted." He gave an all-knowing look with a slight nod in the direction of the house as he slid down into the chair next to her, his elbow bumping hers.

"My business, as we speak, is on her way to see her fiancée, which you might remember is my best friend, Tom, from UT. He's coming into town tonight and she had to rush home to greet him. So you see I have no business except for you. Now tell me, what were you and my sister up to?"

His warm skin next to hers made her uncomfortable in a good way. Roni cleared her throat, giving him a sunny smile. Her brain worked feverously to come up with something plausible. She drew a blank.

"I should make sure the candles on the cake are lit." Why had she turned into a blubbering adolescent? Roni moved to stand.

Drake stopped her from rising. "You don't need to leave. They've kept you busy all afternoon. This is the first I've been able to talk with you."

"I really should be going. And, if you've a mind to, you could help Sam with your father. Marcus looks extremely tired and he's talking shop, which as you know, is a no-no. He should be resting, not getting all riled up."

Drake shook his head as he looked over at his father. "I'm not stupid enough to enter that fray."

His glance went to the large dining tent where the cake blazed brightly before shifting his sparkling gaze back to Roni.

"And it looks like the candles are being lit at this very moment. Is there anything else I may help you accomplish?" He chucked Roni lightly under the chin with his knuckle. "Let me see that gorgeous smile that melts my heart."

"Don't be silly." Roni slapped at his hand. "Go away and stop being such a pest."

Drake clutched his chest, slumped next to her, dropping his head on her shoulder. "You've wounded me deeply. Here I trekked all the way up this mountain to take care of my best girl—"

"It's not even a small hill, more like an incline." His nearness did odd things to her stomach.

"—then you to treat me like this. I'm wounded."

"Drake, behave before everyone begins to stare." Roni shoved him off her shoulder, instantly regretting the absence of his nearness. The smell of outdoors and spicy musk lingered, causing an overwhelming desire for something she couldn't have.

Drake gave her a hurt little boy look. "I'd rather sit here and keep you company. You're more enticing and delectable." His brows moved up and down comically.

If only you were serious.

"If you insist in keeping me company, then come along." She stood. "It's time to sing "Happy Birthday" to your father. Hopefully, that will keep Marcus from arguing."

Drake stood, latched onto her hand to stop her from leaving. "I have complete confidence someone will start the song without us."

Continuing to hold on to her, he played lightly with her fingers. His touch warmed her and caused her to long for more than he was capable of giving. She tried to extract her hand but he held on.

"I have something I've been meaning to ask you for some time." Drake's green eyes darkened and his gaze swept over her face.

His look she couldn't discern, making her uneasy. Her nerves already on edge, her whole body on alert from his continued touch, she opted for humor.

"What do you want to ask me? Jump through a fiery hoop—I refuse to. Put my head in the mouth of a lion—no can do. Wrestle a rattlesnake—not on your life." Her grin faded and she stopped her teasing monologue when she saw Drake wasn't playing along.

His serious demeanor, which wasn't like him at all, caused Roni concern. "Drake, what's wrong? Is it your father? You know I'm willing to do what I can."

His brow wrinkled in confusion, then a crooked smile appeared. He interlocked their hands, pulling her closer to him. "No, this has nothing to do with my father and everything to do with—"

"Sir?" Charles, the butler and all-around man, walked under the canopy looking troubled.

Roni tried to free herself, but Drake wouldn't allow it. He held on as he turned to face the older man, dragging her with him.

"Your timing stinks, Charles, what is it?" He nailed the man with an intense gaze.

Plainly flustered, Charles cleared his throat. "I-I hate to disturb you and Ms. Roni, but there is a man asking to see your father. I don't know quite how to handle him."

"What man? What is there to handle? Just show him to the party."

"Well, you see Sir, when I asked him if he was invited, he said no, but Mr. Peters would want to see him. I told him Mr. Peters couldn't come to the door because a party was being held in his honor. That's when the young man said he had a present for him. I didn't see anything except a manila envelope."

Charles took a deep, nervous breath, wiping his forehead. His behavior unusual for the unflappable servant who was well-respected and loved by everyone at the Triple Cross.

"Do we know the man?"

"Well, that's just it. I don't believe anyone has ever met him."

Charles' agitation spilled over affecting Roni. Her lawyerly instincts came to the forefront. She wanted to jump in and get to the bottom of what was making Charles so skittish.

"Out with it. Just tell me what he said." Drake, clearly exasperated, shook his head.

"Well, you see Sir, I would have brought him out to meet Mr. Peters, but when he told me who he was, I thought you had better come talk with the man first. I showed him to the library."

"Who. Did. He. Say. He. Was?" Drake's voice rose in frustration.

The kindly old servant cleared his voice and looked a bit harassed and embarrassed. "Mr. Peters' s-son—y-your brother."

CHAPTER 4

Drake stormed off toward the house leaving a stunned Roni with a ruffled Charles behind.

"Ms. Veronica, I don't like this at all. I fear what Mr. Drake will do when he sees the man. I'm worried."

"Don't be. Go back to the house. I'll follow Drake and see if I can get to the bottom of the man's claim. And please, don't mention this to anyone, not even Samantha."

"Very good, ma'am."

They both struck out toward the house—Charles to the kitchen entrance—Roni to the veranda and library.

When she reached the French doors, Drake had already entered and heated words were coming from inside. She rushed into the room and saw a standoff between the two men. With Drake's back to her and the other man angrily staring at Drake, she took a moment to assess the stranger.

He had broad shoulders and much the same size of Drake. His hair, a little darker brown but greatly in need of a trim, rested at the edge of his collar. In blue jeans and a pullover, he could have fit in with the guests at the party. However, his combative stance—legs apart, hands balled into fists—told her he was ready to spring into action with the slightest provocation. The man's angry words drew Roni's attention and nearly knocked the breath from her chest.

She gasped causing both men to turn and stare at her with almost identical angry eyes. When the man, about the same age as Drake, looked at her, his gaze softened.

Drake recovered quickly and gave her a sardonic smirk. "Come in and shut the door, Roni. Meet Nick Holdum. He *claims* to be my half-brother." Venomous sarcasm dripped from Drake's voice.

She shut the door and crossed the room to where they stood.

Mr. Holdum gave her an engaging smile so identical to what Drake often gave her, she felt a little off kilter. His slow assessment of her body made Roni uncomfortable and a little steamed. A scathing remark sat on the tip of her tongue, but she held back knowing it would only add fuel to the already hot tempers.

His perusal of her didn't go unnoticed by Drake and added to the charged atmosphere, if that were possible.

Roni moved closer to Drake, needing to show a collective front, and to let Drake know she stood beside him in this fight. Her allegiance was to the family who took her in when she had nowhere to go.

The half-brother, yet to be proven, watched her like a hawk ready to pounce. The game he played, was it to gain access to the Peters' fortune?

Unsure if the anxiety was due to the two combatants in the room or what she overheard upon entering the library, she decided to see what, if anything would transpire. Seeing the need to infuse friendliness into the already cold, charged atmosphere, Roni held out her hand.

"Mr. Holdum, I'm Veronica Reeves the attorney for the Peters' family." She wasn't sure why she added her title, but maybe he'd take it as a warning.

Nick grasped her hand, holding on longer than necessary. He grinned down at her then he allowed her fingers to slip from his grasp. "Well, hello, Attorney Veronica Reeves. Nice to make your acquaintance. You have perfect timing, I might add."

He turned his cold stare on Drake. "Since you have your attorney present, I'll make my demand again. I want to speak to Marcus Peters. And I won't leave until I do. He needs to know he has another son."

CHAPTER 5

"Why you—"

"Nick, is it?" Roni stepped in front of Drake to stop him from lunging. She hated the ploy of using the man's given name, knowing Drake would think her a traitor, but she had to try to defuse the outbreak of tempers.

Nick smirked and inclined his head.

Drake's heated breath fanned her neck as he grasped her waist to move her out of his way. She resisted, adding slight pressure to Drake's hand, hoping he wouldn't ignore her gesture. He didn't, but he moved next to her facing his opponent.

"I'm sorry but your request is denied. A party is being held in Mr. Peters' honor at the moment. So as you can see he can't be disturbed at this time."

"I believe you better rethink your decision. He'll want to see me, especially since I understand he's sick. Cancer is it? What a shame." Nick's snide inflections showed he was less than sympathetic.

"You scum." Strained and barely audible, Drake's voice was filled with hate. Once again he gave pressure to her waist to shove her out of the way.

She turned to face Drake, her eyes pleading. Under her breath she mouthed, "Please let me handle this. Think of your father." She saw his instant resignation.

Turning all business, she stared at Holdum, her savvy lawyer face in place. "Then you will understand why I say, this isn't the best time or the best way to bring up your claim."

"It's not a claim. It's a fact."

"To be proven." Drake shoved through clenched teeth.

She prayed Drake would let her take care of the matter instead of fanning the flame.

"I think you can appreciate, we want to shield Mr. Peters from becoming unduly upset until we've researched the matter. Why not give me your information and allow me to do my research, and then in a few days I'll give you a call. If the facts are true, we will break the news to Mr. Peters."

"I would rather speak to the old man myself *now*. I want him to hear what I have to say, then he can call me a liar to my face. He'll …"

Drake inched closer to Holdum, not willing to be put off any longer. "You can either do what Ms. Reeves has suggested or not, your choice. Either way, you're not speaking to *my* father, and that's final. Hand over the proof and get out of here. *Now!*" Drake's rigid body was proof he was ready to force the issue of Nick's leaving.

Roni positioning herself between both men with hardly room to breathe, then held out her hand.

"Mr. Holdum, give me the documents and allow me to do my job. As the attorney for Mr. Peters, I assure you; I will give this matter my full, undivided attention."

Nick glanced over her shoulder to Drake. She could tell he was weighing her words and judging Drake's reaction to whether she had the Peters' authority.

"Sure." He handed her a manila envelope along with a smile that could melt a spinster's cold heart.

"Drake, would you give me a pen please." While she waited, she kept her gaze on Nick, her best lawyerly smile in place.

She held out the pen. "Mr. Holdum, please write down where I may reach you. I assume your birth certificate is among your proof along with your previous address." She hoped he would say no.

"You bet." His brows arched upward, his gaze confident. He took the pen, gave Drake a cocky sneer, and then leaned over the desk to write his information. When he had completed the task, he looked Roni in the eye and gave her a warm gaze. "Is there anything else you need, *Roni*?"

"Why you—"

Roni placed her hand on Drake's arm to calm him. Barely under control, he stopped.

Ignoring Nick's familiarity at the use of her nick-name, she grabbed a notepad. "I don't have my business card with me, but I'll write down my office number. If you should have any questions don't hesitate to call."

She picked up the envelope, looked at the written information. "I see you're from New York. How long do you plan on staying in Athens?"

He gave her a teasing smile. "Well, now, as you might say down here in Texas, *I don't rightly know, ma'am*. I s'pose I'll be here until I see my father. And then again, I just might like Texas so well I decide to stay." He directed a hard glare at Drake.

When he looked back at her, she saw his determination. Roni knew he was an adversary—one she would work hard to defeat.

"How soon may I expect to hear from you?" The glint of steel she'd witnessed earlier in Holdum's eyes was gone, a spark of humor in its place.

"Give me a few of days to check your information. Once I have, I'll give you a call. But, I must insist you do not contact Mr. Peters regarding this matter, or any matter. All inquiries are to be directed to me from this point forward."

Seeing an obstinate flicker in his eye, she added, "Mr. Holdum, let me make myself perfectly clear. If you don't heed my advice, I *will* file a restraining order against you." She knew the order wouldn't do much to keep him away if he was determined to see Marcus, and her warning didn't seem to faze him.

"Let me add, you will find the folks around here don't look kindly at someone who won't take note of the law. I would hate to see you hauled off to jail for a minor infraction."

Drawing herself up to her full five foot two, Roni fixed her eyes on him with a look most opposing counsel hated to see directed their way.

"I would hate to file a restraining order, but please take note. I won't hesitate to do whatever it takes to keep Mr. Peters from being unduly disturbed or dragged into a useless legal battle. And then it won't be him you'll be facing, but me and a judge."

"Warning duly noted, *Roni*."

He drew out her nickname tantalizingly slow, irking her and goading Drake further.

Holdum folded the note, slipped it in his shirt pocket, and then turned to leave the room. He stopped and looked back at her and Drake.

"By the way, if you want irrefutable evidence to my antecedents, I'd be more than happy to take a DNA test to prove up."

Roni didn't display the shock she felt. Instead, she moved toward the door to the hallway doing her best to usher him out before Drake plowed into the man taking him down.

"If it comes down to that, you may rest assure I *will* request a DNA test. May I show you out?" She looked at Drake. "Wait for me please. I'll only be a moment."

Nick walked to the library doors then stopped. "See you later, bro, and tell daddy I said hello." He gave an insolent salute and a mocking laugh before sauntering out of the room.

Drake's long stride had him already halfway to the door when Roni pulled it shut behind her.

"I don't think my brother likes me very much." His laughter rang out, echoing in the hall.

"This isn't a game or a joke to us. You must know what a shock your claim is to Drake. But he's a reasonable man. If what you say is true, he'll come to terms with it." Roni opened the front door.

Nick stopped short of the threshold and turned toward her, sneering. "*Come to terms with it*, is that what he'll do? *Hmm*. I'm not so sure. It's been a few months since I found out I'm the son of Marcus Peters, and as of yet, I haven't *come to terms with it*.

"I'll give you time to do your research, Roni, but I warn you, if you take too long, I will see the old man and nothing you can do will stop me."

"You may expect my call as soon as I have thoroughly checked out your claim." Roni gestured toward the porch, hoping he would get the hint and leave.

He grabbed her hand, holding on as he watched her with a devious smile.

She tried to extricate her hand, but he wouldn't allow it. Something passed over his face. *Uncertainty?* Slowly, he released her, his fingers caressed her palm, his eyes bright with mischief.

Roni felt heat travel up her neck, but did her best to turn it to her advantage with stern words. "Mr. Holdum—"

"Nick, please. Mr. Holdum is so old fashioned. And I love the way you say my name with your Texas drawl."

She ignored him. "Mr. Holdum, as the Peters' attorney, I warn you again. No further contact with *any* of the Peters family, including Drake. Any questions or matters you think you need to get off your chest must come through me." She stepped back. "You have my number."

"Yes, *ma'am*" He patted his pocket. 'Right here over my lit'l ol' heart."

His playful manner and mocking accent bought out her temper more. She wanted to slam the door in his face, but didn't. When she closed the door, she met resistance—his foot.

"Have dinner with me?"

"I beg your pardon?" She was unable to hide the shock.

"I said, have dinner with me ... tonight. You name the place, the time."

"Is this to discuss your claim?" She wasn't about to play his games.

"No. Just you and me, a man and a woman having dinner together. I'd like to get to know you better. How 'bout it."

"Mr. Holdum—"

"Nick"

"*Mr. Holdum*, I'm flattered you would want to ask me out to dinner, but—"

"It's only dinner. And, we don't have to bring up my claim. You and I can get better acquainted, see if the draw between us is worth pursuing. Who knows, you might find you're attracted to me more than you are to my brother. I know I'm attracted to you."

Roni's blood boiled and not from the Texas heat. "Under the circumstances, having dinner with you would be highly unprofessional, which I am not." She took a calming breath.

"Does that mean no?"

"You know exactly what it means. Now, if you will excuse me."

"*Chicken.*" His laughter stopped her retreat. "Are you and Drake an item?" He looked her squarely in the face.

"I beg your pardon?"

"You heard me."

Why was she standing here listening to the man? "In the first place, it's none of your business, and—"

Deep mocking laughter rumbled in his chest. "I'm going to have fun giving my ol' bro a run for his money. You're worth it, Attorney Veronica Reeves." He sauntered across the porch and down the steps. "I'll be waiting for your call, *sweetheart.*"

CHAPTER 6

The insufferable man. Of all the nerve.

Returning to the library before she simmered down wouldn't be a smart move. It would just incite Drake more.

Roni waited in the hall while willing her temper to calm. She took several slow breaths that seemed to work. Maybe the added few seconds would give Drake time to get over being displeased with her for stepping in and taking charge. Yet staying out here in the foyer might cause him to come looking for her and incite his temper more.

She might as well face him and get it over. *What a mess.*

Bracing herself, she ran her sweaty palms down the sides of her jeans and entered the library.

Drake stood in front of the full-length portrait of his mother, Elle, hanging above the cadenza. Roni knew he wasn't studying her painting, but he was contemplating what he'd have to do to get rid Nick Holdum. His stance, rigid, shoulders squared, head tipped back, was much like she'd seen Marcus do often when weighing heavy, unpleasant matters.

His mannerisms reminded her of a crisis she faced years ago in this same room. Only back then the problem had been of her doing.

Five months after her parents' death and her arrival at the Peters' home, a girl at school taunted Roni calling her the *Peters' charity case.* One word led to another. Before long, Roni hit the girl square in the face giving her a bloody nose and a black eye.

Samantha wanted to be with Roni as she faced Marcus, but Roni knew the humiliation and the punishment was hers alone. When she entered the library like a doomed convict on the way to the gallows, she found Marcus standing in almost the exact same position as Drake now. And the same as that day, the feeling of loss, guilt, loneliness, and being a true outsider overwhelmed Roni once again.

Drake must have sensed her presence. He swung around, his face full of ... *contempt?* For her or Nick Holdum?

"Why did you interfere? I wouldn't have given that imposter the time of day."

The blinding rage he directed her way had nothing to do with her but everything to do with Holdum.

"Drake, this has headlines and insurmountable damage control written all over it, not only to your father, but for the Peters Corporation. The way you were handling—"

"I would have thrown the fraud out of this house, out of our lives."

"Yes, I can pretty well guess how you would've handled it. You would have showed him to the door, leaving your Wheeler boot imprint on his backside." She paused hoping for her next words to sink in. "And where would that have gotten us?"

The question hung between them.

He gave her a rueful smile. "At least I would have received a little satisfaction for what his claim will put us through. As it is ..." He glanced off shrugging before turning his hard gaze on her again. "As our attorney, you should've backed me up."

"What exactly do you think I was doing? *As your attorney,* I was and am backing you up. I have to take any and all threats—"

"Stop right there, that guy's proof is bogus. My father would never do something so careless as to *impregnate a woman and callously throw her aside* as that jerk so succinctly put it."

"You are probably right, but ..."

"Probably? But?"

The sneer and the cynical arch of his brow had Roni reeling. She didn't deserve his look of contempt nor his scorn.

"There's no *probably* or *but* about it. My dad *isn't* his biological father, nor is he my half-brother." He pointed at the envelope setting on the edge of the oak desk. "*That* you can trash, or do whatever you want, but there will be no more said about this. The matter is closed."

Roni picked up the envelope, stuffed it in one of the credenza drawers. "I'll take care of this after the party. But regardless how you feel about my actions, I owe it to your father, even your family, to look into the matter, if for no other reason than to disprove his claim. Surely, you know this is the only way to make the problem go away."

She lifted her hand in supplication. When he turned his back on her, she let her arm drop to her side, the wound of his dismissal cutting her deeply.

"Drake, do you want your father's name emblazoned across the headlines or the six o'clock news? I owe it to Marcus to check out his allegations and nip them in the bud before they mushroom into a full blown nightmare. I need to make sure what he says *isn't* true."

He glared at her. "There isn't an ounce of truth in his statements. I don't care what the imposter has to say."

"Then let me do my job. Let me prove him wrong. As your father's attorney and as yours, it's my obligation to research this man's claim and prove beyond a shadow of a doubt what is true and what isn't. But let me make myself perfectly clear. I will do the research with or without your permission because of Marcus."

She watched Drake carefully. She could see her words had struck a chord. He needed to know the validity of Holdum's claim as much as she did.

"It looks like no matter what I say, you are going to do it anyway." He glanced out the window to the grounds below with a clear view of the festivities.

"Yes. I plan on putting these accusations to rest."

"If I can't stop you, then whatever you do, I don't want my father getting wind of this. Understood?"

"Certainly. You should know by now I would do nothing to cause pain or disruption to Marcus or this household, especially at a time like this."

"Until you have thoroughly dispatched the matter, it's business as usual. And, Veronica, I know you and my sister are close, but not a word to her about any of this. Do I make myself clear?"

"Perfectly. But as the family and corporate attorney *and* friend, your warning is totally uncalled for and unnecessary."

The use of her given name and his stinging retort caused her to wish she had chosen a different profession or, at least wasn't the Peters' lawyer. But she was, and she would do what she did best—her job.

Without another word, Roni moved to the door leading to the party, then pulled it open.

"Roni?"

She stopped without looking back, head high, bracing her shoulders, her emotions too raw to speak.

"I'm sorry. What I said was thoughtless. I know better. Will you forgive me?"

"Yes." She slipped through the door not wanting to further the conversation. If she stayed a moment longer, she just might tell Drake what she really thought.

Roni made her way to the refreshment tent, picked up a bottle of water, and then looked for a place to nurse her wounds. She found a canopy a little ways from the other guests—the perfect place to cool her temper and sooth her injured pride. For Drake to rebuke her angered her more than she wanted to admit.

She gazed at the party and noticed many of the guests had left, leaving a handful of stragglers who were still milling around talking.

Placing her bottle of water on the table, she allowed her mind to wander, willing her damaged heart to release the pain. The vivid memory of her first sighting of the Triple Cross, made Roni smile. She freed the hurt and anger, grabbing hold of the beauty around her.

As a twelve-year-old, city-bred, newly made orphan, the ranch made quite an impact. Seventeen years ago she thought the Triple Cross Ranch to be at the very edge of the world, the last jumping off place before hell. Everything seemed foreign and in the middle of nowhere—solitary confinement at its worst. She felt she had been uprooted and planted in a strange, ugly land, and wondered what she had done to God for Him to give her such a punishment.

There were no high rises, no malls, no shopping centers, and McDonalds' was over ten miles away in the small town of Athens, Texas. She was surrounded with rolling hills covered with huge gnarled oaks and frightening enormous longhorns standing in the shade seeking a little reprieve from the relentless heat.

Come to think of it, when she arrived everything at the Triple Cross was disagreeable to Roni, except for Samantha who became her best friend.

Now, Roni couldn't seem to get her fill of the Triple Cross or her adopted family. Living in the city gave her a deeper appreciation for the rolling hills and countryside.

Dallas had its appeal, but didn't compare with what the ranch had to offer. She'd still be living here if the seventy-five mile one-way commute hadn't made it impossible.

Who was she kidding?

She could make the trek back and forth. But she had stopped the frequent visits sometime last year. And though she loved visiting with Samantha, being treated like Drake's kid sister didn't sit well.

Living away from the ranch was best. Even though she called the Triple Cross and all it stood for *home*, she didn't have the constant reminder of what she could never have—Drake's love.

CHAPTER 7

Drake watched through the window as Roni made her way down the steps and headed for the refreshment tent seemingly avoiding Samantha and his father. He felt terrible for making her the brunt of his frustration. Something she didn't deserve. The blame rested solely with him and … *Holdum.*

Holdum … he had to be an imposter. Nothing else made sense. Otherwise, his dad would have said something about another son, especially since his illness.

Deep down Drake knew when it came to his father his own reasoning could be slightly bias. And if he were perfectly truthful, Holdum held a striking resemblance to the Peters' side of the family.

Could it be possible his dad did have an affair? No. It couldn't be true.

Maybe one of his dad's brothers was Holdum's father. His uncles weren't as well-off as his father and maybe Holdum knew it and was looking for someone with deeper pockets.

How old was this guy anyway? Drake thought he looked to be close to his own age or could even be older. Maybe this happened before his folks met.

Drake disliked all of the disquieting thoughts of the man claiming to be his brother. But Roni was right. Someone needed to check Holdum out, if for no other reason than to prove him an imposter *or* the real thing. There was no need to say anything to dad until they were absolutely certain one way or the other.

He ran his hand over his eyes trying to rub out the memory of what took place minutes ago. This day hadn't turned out at all like he'd planned. After he'd worked up the nerve to finally talk with Roni, the imposter ruined the chance of telling her what was really on his mind. And now he didn't dare speak for fear of Roni's contempt.

Drake kept his attention on Roni, not because he didn't trust her to keep quiet, but because he loved watching her. If Charles hadn't interrupted him, he would have asked her to a movie later this evening, just the two of them *alone*. He wanted Roni to know exactly how he felt and hoped she'd be receptive to his love.

Since she'd moved to Dallas last year, it hadn't taken him long to appreciate how much he missed her. At first, when she wasn't around, the house seemed quiet and empty. He knew he had to give her space, solo on her own for a while, before he could convince her to be his wife and come home.

When Roni's visits to the ranch became less frequent, it began to sink in. She had actually moved for good. He had to talk with her, tell her how he felt. But when? The timing always seemed to be off.

Drake smiled. He wasn't sure when he had recognized he had it bad for the slip of a girl he'd watched grow into a beautiful woman with a kind and generous heart. And just like a few minutes ago, he knew she would fight to right the world for those she loved.

The horrible thought occurred to him. What if she wasn't interested in what he offered? What if she couldn't get past thinking of him as a friend or worse yet ...*brother?* He prayed she wouldn't be repulsed when he spoke with her.

What if she had someone in Dallas she was dating? The thought twisted his gut and made his physically ill. Samantha had never mentioned Roni's interest in another man. If she was, surely his sister would have told him. But if Roni did have someone, he'd have to convince her he was a far better match for her in every possible way, as she was for him.

He shook his head trying to dislodge the picture of Roni with another man, which soured his mood further.

Her friendship, her company, even the sparks of fire in her eyes when he teased her, there was so much more to Roni. She challenged him to be a better man.

He knew her likes, dislikes, knew when she was troubled or agitated, as she was right now with him. Knew when she needed space, and when she needed to be with those who understood her. He also knew when she was funning and trying to goad him into believing her when she was actually telling a whopper of a story.

He smiled again. *Man*, he had it bad. What if he couldn't convince her?

A couple of men saunter up to Roni and engaged her in conversation. They were laughing, having a good time. And of all things, the men were his friends. He was going to give them a heads-up—*Roni was off limits*. Or at least he hoped she would be if he could ever get her alone long enough to broach the subject without a major crisis taking place.

Drake strode out the door with purpose, heading in Roni's direction. When he moved up next to her, he noticed her stiffen, and then relax. Both men brought Drake into the conversation, yet he was more aware of Roni than what was being said.

In the library, he hadn't handled the situation well. He owed Roni more than an apology for being such a jerk. He hoped he hadn't ruined his chance of making her see him in a different light, as a man who cared about her and loved her with all his heart

CHAPTER 8

Roni felt Drake's presence long before she heard him. Somehow she always sensed when he was around. At first, she stiffened, then relaxed. She knew she had done nothing to deserve his censure. And she also knew that he wouldn't broach the subject of Holdum in front of his friends.

When she looked at Drake, she saw the remorse in his eyes and softened toward him. It was always so, even at twelve when she fell madly in love with him. He was a college freshman home for spring break. He'd tease and make her angry, but she couldn't stay irritated for long, especially when he'd give her one of his smiles. She'd forget why she had been upset with him in the first place.

Roni listened to the men, smiled where appropriate, but had little interest in what they were saying. Gazing around the grounds she saw Marcus. She could tell by the way his normally straight back and shoulders were slumping, he was exhausted.

When there was a lull in the conversation, Roni touched Drake's arm to gain his attention. "Drake, your father looks worn out. I think you need to convince him to go inside."

He laughed. "I believe you would have more influence on him than I would." He turned to his friends. "If you will excuse us, I believe Roni and I need to speak to my father."

Drake took her arm and led her over to where Marcus stood in a heated conversation. The warmth of his touch melted her insides. Why couldn't she stay mad at this man?

When Marcus noticed who had joined them, he smiled benevolently at Roni. "Where were you two? You weren't here to wish me well on my sixty-fifth. Business?" He raised his brows in a playfully manner. "Or pleasure?" He winked at Roni.

"Neither. Happy Birthday, Dad." Drake clapped his father on the back and then gave him a hug.

"Thanks, Son."

Roni slid her arm through Marcus' and snuggled up next to him giving him a sweet smile. Rising on her tiptoes, she placed a light kiss on his cheek. "Happy Birthday, Marcus. And I pray you have many, many more years to come."

He gave Roni a hug. "Thank you, sweetheart."

She could tell by his pallor, Marcus was failing fast and needed to rest, but wouldn't unless she forced him too.

"And now gentlemen." Roni gave all the men a beguiling smile. "If you will excuse Marcus, I need a private word with my guardian."

The men laughed, saying their goodbyes before they sauntered away. Drake walked next to his father while Roni still held Marcus' arm, his weight leaning into her. She led him to a cushioned chair under a canopy where he could catch a nice breeze.

"Now what was so all fired important to haul me away from my friends?" Marcus stared at them, but he lacked conviction in his tone.

Roni slid a chair closer to him, patting his arm. "Nothing. I just wanted some time with my favorite guy."

"And you don't think I know what the two of you are up too." Marcus threw them a challenging look. "You maneuvered me away from my guests so I would sit down and rest."

"Guilty as charged, Judge." Roni's chuckle brought about laughter from Marcus. His face brightened.

"You scamp."

Roni always played the fixer in the family. She had a second sense when something wasn't quite right. Just like when she convinced Marcus to see a doctor. If she hadn't pushed and then pushed some more, it might have been too late. As it was, he had a slim chance he'd beat the disease. But Marcus was a fighter, and he wouldn't give up easily.

"*Humph.*" He shook his head eyeing his son then he looked back at Roni. "When are you going to come to your senses and move back home where you belong?"

"Marcus, you know I can't. I have a partnership in the firm and—"

"Yes, and I shouldn't have given you my business. That Dallas law firm knew a good thing when they talked you into joining their firm. But they would have never recognized your potential as a partner if you hadn't brought such a big client with you. Not that your work isn't well worth a partnership … it is." He shook his head emphatically. "But those big city boys wouldn't have had the sense to recognize how good you were without my business."

His words stung, but she realized he was fighting for what he wanted—her back at the Triple Cross. He was becoming more adamant about her return, especially since his illness. She gave him a cheeky smile.

"But you did, for which I am eternally grateful. Now you must come to terms with the fact my place is there, not here."

"You'd have more of an inducement to come home if I give my work to a firm in Athens. Of course, with the proviso, you were made partner and had full control of my affairs."

She laughed at his machinations, but knew he was quite serious. "You won't do that. From the beginning, you've told me to stand on my own two feet. And we both know you would never pressure me into anything I didn't want to do."

"*Humph.*" He looked at Drake. "She's using my own words against me. Help me out here, son."

"What can I say?" Drake shrugged. "The woman has a mind of her own."

Roni shook her head rolling her eyes. "Marcus, you would never force my hand at doing something I don't want to do." She gave him a stern look. "So put all the scheming aside and just be glad I enjoy city life."

"City life, *my foot.* One of these days you'll wake up and realize your place is here at the Triple Cross. I hope it's sooner than later."

By the look in his eyes, Roni knew Marcus was still plotting how best to convince her to move home. Maybe because he was sick, or because he thought she belonged here at the Triple Cross, but whatever it was, she knew he wouldn't give up so easily.

"If you married Drake you would be home where you belong."

CHAPTER 9

"Marcus, *really!*" Roni's laughter sounded strained. "I'm beginning to think you're mind has become confused by your meds. You know Drake and I are like brother and sister. Best friends. It takes more than friendship to make a marriage."

Roni's words jabbed Drake hard, especially about the brother-sister reference. With his father sticking his two cents in, he didn't dare speak with Roni. She'd probably think he was pursuing her to placate his dad.

"*Pooh.* You aren't brother and sister. Never have been. And if you'd get that foolish notion out of your head you would see Drake and you are perfect for each other. Drake's—"

"Dad, I think you've said enough." Drake wanted time alone with Roni to explain his feelings, not this open forum his dad seemed determined to have.

"Don't dad me. I'll speak my mind. If you'd both be truthful, you would know what I say is true. Marriage to one another would be the best thing for both of you and for me too."

Drake could see this talk wasn't sitting well with Roni. He could practically see the hackles rising on her back.

"You could marry Roni and she'd come home where she belongs, son."

"Dad, please. Drop it."

Though he believed Roni had feelings for him as he did her, if his Dad continued to push, she'd become belligerent, which wouldn't serve his purpose well.

He wanted time alone with Roni to show her how he felt. Not now and not with his father's interference.

"I'm sure if and when Roni wants to come home she knows the door is always open."

"Nonsense." His father gave them a disgruntled look. He emitted a small moan, closed his eyes, and then bowed his head, holding his forehead.

"Marcus." Roni move out of her chair and down on her knees looking up at him with concern. "Are you all right?"

Drake hoped his father wasn't faking it to gain Roni's sympathy. It would be just like him to use his sickness to his advantage.

"Dad." His stern tone gained his father's attention. And though he looked pale, he didn't look ready to expire.

"Drake, your father's not well." By her puckered brow he knew Roni thought him heartless. "Take him up to the house. He needs to rest. No, I'll take him up myself."

The alarm in her eyes made him want to tear into his dad for giving Roni such a scare.

"I'm fine." His father gave a watery smile as he patted her hand. "I just want to see you both happy before I die."

"Don't say that." Roni took hold of his arm. "You're getting treatment. And miracles still happen. I'm praying you'll beat this thing."

"You're such a sweet girl. Who knows, you may be right." His eyes watered. "But I'd like to see you settled. Whether you want to believe it or not, and though I might be a tad prejudice, Drake is the perfect man for you. Make me happy and say you will at least think about what I've said."

"Dad, why don't you let Samantha walk you up to the house while Roni and I talk."

His father's narrowed gaze told him he was aware of what Drake was up to—to get rid of him.

"Oooh, all right." He patted Roni's cheek. "Roni, you know I love you, don't you?"

"Yes, Marcus, and I love you. You're like a father to me."

"Then please give my words some thought. I really want to see you happy and settled. And right now you're neither." His father stood along with Roni and gathered her in his arms. "I would love to see you back home where you belong."

Roni didn't answer him, but allowed him to kiss her forehead before leaving and heading in Samantha's direction.

Drake knew he had to try to patch up the damage his father had done.

"Roni, I'm sorry—"

"Why, Drake? Why?"

He recognized how crushed and deeply affected Roni was by his father's words, but now she looked angry. How to explain?

If he told her how he truly felt it would sound like he spoke to appease his father. However, if he kept quiet …

Either way, he was doomed if he spoke, and doomed if he didn't.

CHAPTER 10

Drake told him to leave, and he had every intention of doing just that, but curiosity got the better of him. Nick wanted to see which man was Marcus Peters. He knew if he waited long enough, he'd have his answer.

Leaning against the same tree he had earlier before he entered the house, he observed the dwindling party. Many of the guests had left and others were in various stages of leaving.

Roni had walked down the hill but didn't join the others. He smiled. In his opinion, her nickname suited her better than Veronica. Veronica was staid and reserved and unapproachable. Roni was feisty, full of life, and ready to tackle a rabid dog if those she loved needed protection. Nick smiled picturing Roni's stern, challenging face. He knew she perceived him as a threat.

A few minutes later Drake sauntered over to where she and a couple of men stood talking.

He was going to give his brother a run for his money where Roni was concerned, or at least give it a good try. She was worth it.

Roni and Drake moved to another group with the same tall gray-haired man he'd figured earlier was Marcus. Were they discussing him? If they were, he knew for sure they would have plenty to say now and in the days to come.

What a shocker. A son no one knew about—except the old man, of course.

When the three of them moved under one of the white canopies, he had his answer. He'd picked out the right man. Marcus Peters. The man who got his mother pregnant then left her to fend for herself. The same man who hadn't owned up to his responsibility but would now pay dearly for his mistake.

If Drake thought to slow down the process of proving Nick was a Peters, he'd face a rude awakening. Nothing they could do or say would keep him from contacting Marcus, even if he had to bust the door down to gain access. The old man wasn't going to die before he saw the son he tried to overlook.

Retribution. The word screamed in his head. Nothing short of making Marcus Peters suffer would satisfy. The man would pay for leaving his mother destitute.

Resentment festered and roiled. He shoved away from the tree, heading for his car.

In the next few days, he'd do more research on Marcus. He'd ask around town to find out what the good people of Athens, Texas, had to say about his *dear ol' papa.* And, if he let a few hints slip here and there about his own ancestry, so much the better. Not much big brother could do to stop him now.

CHAPTER 11

"You know Dad. When he gets something in his head, well, there's just no stopping him."

Drake seemed as frustrated as Roni. And right now, she'd like nothing better than to clobber someone, namely the man standing beside her for not speaking up.

"You could have stepped in at any time and stopped him. Instead you said nothing, which gave him hope. Your father thinks we will magically get together and I will return home to marry you because he wishes it so."

She took a deep breath trying to calm her temper without revealing how she really felt. "You're going to have to fix this, Drake. I'm not moving back. My work, my life, is in Dallas now."

Roni looked away. She was disgusted with Marcus for talking about marriage. And she was equally disgusted with Drake for not trying to stop his father from making an uncomfortable topic more so. But mainly, disgusted with herself for having the horrible misfortune to love a man who could never love her back.

She felt like she had been the brunt of someone's horrible, sick joke. Drake couldn't have known the damage his father's words or the lack of Drake's own concern had caused her emotionally. Fortunately, neither father nor son knew the truth.

Hunching her shoulders forward, she wrapped her arms protectively about her waist. She gazed out to the pasture and the longhorns grazing peaceably. If only the same tranquility would come to her heart and ease the pain.

For years she had hoped Drake would see her as someone more than a friend. But she knew her hope was in vain. And though she loved Drake dearly, apparently he would never be able to return her love. And to enter into a marriage, as Marcus suggested, where both people weren't passionately in love just because they were a good match and good friends, would never work for her, no matter how much she deeply loved Drake.

"Roni, listen to me, please." Drake touched her arm. When she looked at him in disgust, he dropped his hand to his side. "I'm sorry about dad. He means well."

"Oh, I know he means well." She shook her head in frustration. "Drake, you know there can never be anything between us, at least as far as marriage goes."

He looked at her strangely. "Why not? We're not related. Am I that repulsive?"

"No, but ..."

He moved to the corner of the canopy, reached up, resting his hand high on the metal tent pole as he looked out over the pasture to the east, his posture unyielding. "I believe we are two healthy adults who are capable of love."

Drake sounded angry ... hurt. *At her?* Roni didn't know what to think or how to react. Would he really be willing to go along with his father's crazy idea? In stunned silence, she watched him wondering, what next?

When no more words came she said, "Yes, we are both capable of love. However, I'm not willing to sacrifice my life on an altar just because Marcus Peters believes it's a good idea. I know I owe your family a lot. Your parents were more than generous to take me in. But really ... don't you think that's asking a bit much?"

She moved to where Drake stood, touching his back to gain his attention. "Drake, don't do this. Don't be angry with me because I can't agree to your father's plan. It has nothing to do with you, but everything to do with me."

Drake shrugged off her hand without looking at her. "Don't worry, Roni. I'll speak to dad and tell him the subject is closed." He lowered his arm from the tent pole. "I think I'll go see about him. Sam may need some help." Drake left the tent eating up the distance to the house and out of sight.

Tears pricked Roni's eyes. How could the day that had begun so beautifully go so impossibly wrong?

She stiffened her back and her inner resolve. Self-pity had nothing to do with what she knew was right. She wouldn't go into a loveless marriage ... regardless how much Marcus or she wished it could be so.

CHAPTER 12

Exhausted but delighted to see the last of the guests gone and the wait staff in the process of removing the remnants of the festivities, Roni headed in the direction of the veranda and library. She had waved Samantha and her family off over an hour ago, assuring Sam she would see to the stragglers, and for her to go home and take care of her family.

Roni's throbbing headache shot pain to the back of her eyes and across her forehead. Her fingers kneaded the area over her brows. Making it to her room for a quick shower and early evening, held more appeal with each step. Right now, nothing would feel better than to crawl into bed, pull the covers over her head, and not come out for a couple of days. *Or at least until the horrible remnants of this day disappears.*

Drake hadn't been seen since their conversation earlier, not that she wanted a continuance of this afternoon. She was concerned he might still be angry with her. Why was it whenever her heart was involved she couldn't say what she truly felt?

Prayerfully, Drake had turned in for the night. And with any luck, Marcus was already asleep, which suited her on both counts. She didn't want to encounter either man in her present condition. The way she felt, to have a discussion—namely the idiotic idea of marriage to Drake that Marcus thought was a cure-all for her problems and his—wouldn't bode well for either party. She's apt to say things she'd regret.

Not one to run from the distasteful, Roni knew she would eventually face the problem, but just not tonight. And then there was the matter of Nick Holdum.

Roni groaned. Her headache started with Holdum's appearance, got worse with Marcus, and became a full bloom killer when she squabbled with Drake, if she could call their conversation a squabble. At this moment, she would be at a definite disadvantage, and it wasn't like she was going anywhere. She planned to stay the weekend and return to Dallas Sunday evening.

If it weren't for the matter of Holdum's envelope in the credenza drawer and fearing someone, namely Marcus, would find it, she would have bypassed the library and gone straight to her room.

Roni feared Holdum's claim was viable but knew she wouldn't know for sure until she did more investigation. A trip to New York might be in order to see what the neighbors had to say about Holdum and his mother. Why hadn't he mentioned the whereabouts of his mother? What role did she play in all of this?

She opened the library door hoping she could get in and out and to her room without meeting anyone. The moment she stepped inside, she knew her hope was in vain.

Drake sat at the desk, his forehead resting in his palms, reading a document. Before she could back out the door, he glanced up, blinked several times as though he didn't believe she was standing in the room.

"Roni? You still here?" He leaned back continuing his puzzled stare.

"Yes. I'm staying until tomorrow evening. I assumed that would be okay." Surely he wasn't still upset with her. From this distance she couldn't tell.

"This is your home too, you know. I was just afraid you had left for Dallas without saying goodbye since ..." He waved then let his hand drop to the desk.

He didn't have to finish the sentence for her to know what he meant. She moved further into the room then stopped. "No. I had planned on going to church with you and Marcus, if he's not too sick."

He nodded and then motioned. "Come in. Have a seat."

She didn't move.

"Please, just a few minutes. Like old times."

His tired, sad gaze had her accepting his suggestion. "How's Marcus? Hopefully, in bed?"

"Yes. He was worn out. I think the party was too much, too soon."

Still wishing she could head to her room, she witnessed the misery in Drake's eyes, and moved to the couch instead. "I was afraid today might be too exhausting for him." She removed her boots and then tucked her legs beneath her.

"Roni, I'm sorry about earlier. Today didn't turn out at all like I had hoped for."

Baffled to his meaning, she narrowed her eyes. "I don't follow."

He took a deep breath. His troubled demeanor had her concerned.

"With Dad's sickness, and then ..." Drake leaned back in the chair, his head resting on the headrest. He closed his eyes briefly, and then stared at her oddly. "I had expected so much more from this day. I wanted it to be different, special."

Now he was really scaring her. *Was it Marcus? Did he know something she didn't?*

"I was looking forward to spending some time with you. I rarely see you anymore. And whether you believe me or not, I miss you. I miss having you around the house. I miss our talks, even our healthy arguments." He chuckled. "This place is lonely and quiet without you."

The fine lines around his gorgeous eyes were a little more pronounced. Her heart tightened. She didn't want to fight this battle here and now.

"Drake, you know why I left. My work is in Dallas. The drive is grueling."

He nodded. The silence in the room wasn't unsettling. It never was with Drake. Before she moved to Dallas, they sat many nights, just like now, in companionable silence, each working or reading or in their own little world. Words weren't necessary between them. But if the need arose, they would talk or hash out a particular problem, or sometimes discuss recent happenings. She loved those times, and like Drake, missed them too.

"Come home."

His words, a mere whisper, startled her. Her breath caught in her throat, and her heart nearly stopped. She couldn't have heard him correctly. "What?"

He leaned forward, elbows on the desk, tired eyes intent on her face. "Come home, Roni, please."

She stood, not sure if she would leave or pace around the room. To look at Drake was impossible. His words confused her. He sounded hurt, lost, almost pleading, which tugged at her heart, making her want to do his bidding

"Is it Marcus?" She looked at him intently hoping to detect the truth of the matter.

He moved from behind the desk and stood in front of her and tenderly gripped her by the shoulders looking deep into her eyes.

"No. Yes." He swallowed. "I'm asking for him ... for me. We ... no, I need you. I'm not sure I can handle what's coming without you here. I need your steady assurance everything will turn out all right. Dad has some major hurdles to cross, and I'm afraid without you, he won't make it. I know I won't."

She had never heard Drake talk like this, or act in this manner. His vulnerability affected her as nothing else could.

"Roni, what if he dies?" He released her, then slipped his arms around her back, pulling her to him.

Hers hands went around his waist, her head on his shoulder. A natural response, nothing more. Roni knew their embrace was one of mutual need—giving and receiving—the need to connect with someone who also felt the fear of uncertainty and of possible loss.

They stood locked in each other's arms for some time before Drake breathed in a deep shuddering breath. He released her, and then stepped back, directing his gaze out the window.

The comfort she felt in his arms turned to a feeling of emptiness.

Drake cleared his throat, reaching for her hand. "Come, sit with me for a little while." He led her to the couch where they often sat together.

Roni took her position on one end of the sofa, Drake at the other end.

"The last few weeks have been miserable, a nightmare without you here. I think Dad felt it too. No excuse, but possibly the reason for his outburst this afternoon." He shrugged and gave a rueful smile.

"The cancer tests and then Monday with the chemo, the uncertainty … all of it was tough on him. He's a lot weaker than he wants to admit. I've seen him when he doesn't think I'm around to notice. I believe he's scared, and unless the chemo works he knows he's going to die."

Concerned, Roni said, "Marcus has always been strong and so positive. Once he gets his strength back he'll be his old self again."

Drake shook his head. "I'm not so sure. He's been saying odd things. He's tired. He'd like it all to be over and done. He even said he wasn't going to take anymore treatments. He's pushed Sam and me away and won't let us close to him."

Drake ran his fingers threw his hair, looking everywhere but at Roni. When he did, his eyes were pleading.

"I hate to ask this of you. But do you think you could take off some time, maybe come back to the ranch for a few of days? I think it would help cheer him up."

She knew time off wouldn't be a problem for her. As a partner of the firm they would allow her as much time as needed.

"What if Marcus thinks I'm coming home to stay, that we'll do what he asked?"

"If you'll come back for a week or two, I'll make it perfectly clear you are here only for a short visit—vacation only. I'll also make it clear, he is not to mention anything about you staying permanently. Will that work for you?" He appeared hopeful but guarded.

"I have a few weeks I can take. And what work I need to do I can handle over the phone or Internet. And if something does come up, I can always make the trip into Dallas."

"Any time you could spare would be a blessing." His appearance changed radically, almost excited. "How soon do you think you could come home?"

The word *home* struck a chord of longing in Roni. She couldn't let Drake know she wanted to be *home* more than he wanted her here.

"I'll go back to Dallas tomorrow night, pack a few things. On Monday I'll arrange my schedule at the office. I should be back at the ranch sometime Monday evening." She didn't believe her return would affect Marcus' outlook one way or another, but if it did, so much the better.

"Drake, I'll do what I can to cheer him, but don't expect a miracle just because I come home for a few weeks."

Drake's relieved smile gave her assurance she was doing the right thing.

"Thanks, Roni. Your being here will make a big difference. And—" He held her hand in his warm palm. "—I can't tell you what this means to me. Since his sickness, he's constantly mentioning how much he misses you." He glanced down at their joined hands then back up at her. "I think he worries about you more than he does Sam or me."

"Unlike you two, I was his ward, a responsibility thrust upon him. He just hasn't figured out he doesn't need to protect me any longer."

"That might be part of it, but not all of it. He loves you, Roni. We all do." Drake's look softened. "If I didn't know better, I'd say he loves you more than any of us."

Roni smiled, thinking about Marcus and Elle after her parent's death. They both worked so hard to make her feel welcome and a part of their family, and they had succeeded.

"No. You and Sam stayed around close, didn't move off. I wanted to spread my wings, so I moved away. That's why he talks about me and wants me to come home. Marcus will always believe everyone should be right here with him or at least in easy reach."

Drake's warm chuckle and touch caused doubts to surface. Returning to the ranch might be the wrong thing to do. It would be easy to believe Drake actually cared for her, only to find he didn't. And if that happened, she'd be left with a broken heart.

"You may be right on that score." His glanced turned her insides into a quivering mass of uncertainty.

"Thank you, Roni. I know I've asked a lot of you. But until Dad is over this rough patch—this cancer thing being so new and all—your being here will make him feel better."

Roni's heart twisted. She wished for so much more from Drake yet knew it could never be. "No thanks necessary. But don't put too much stock in my return bringing about miracles. "

Just like his hug early, Roni knew holding her hand was Drake's way of connecting. She warned her heart to take no notice, but it didn't want to listen.

"I just wish you or Sam would have called and told me about Marcus' state of mind before now. I could have arranged to be here at least part of this week, which might have made a difference."

"Until Wednesday, he seemed to be taking everything in stride, but then, well, he started talking crazy like mentioning Mom, going to see her, and other strange things. We thought it might be the meds, and then today ..." A crooked smile appeared. He gave her hand a squeeze then released her. "Well, you got a small taste of what he's been like."

"I did. I'm sorry."

"No, don't be. You being here will help his outlook tremendously."

Roni stood, needing to put some distance between her and Drake for her emotion's sake. "Well, I'll do what I can. But for now, I've got a headache that won't quit. I'm going to take some tablets and go to bed." She moved to the credenza, pulled out Nick Holdum's envelope before heading for the door.

"Roni."

She stopped, glancing back not sure what to expect. His sweet but serious smile tugged at her heart.

"Whether you want to believe this or not, Dad may just have the right of it. Together we make a great team. I'd be proud to have you as my wife."

CHAPTER 13

After his last outburst, Drake feared Roni would change her mind about staying at the ranch. But for some reason he couldn't hold back how he felt, even though what he said was a small portion of what he really thought. He knew it was too soon to speak of love, especially after what his father had done this afternoon.

Though their hug was anything but passionate in nature, when he held her in his arms, he knew more than ever he wanted her as his wife. Roni was the essential part of him that was missing. From the moment she walked in from outside, the room lit up. Just having her around him thrilled him beyond reason, making him feel whole, able to take on the impossible.

Man, you've got it bad. And what if Roni doesn't see it your way?

He didn't want to image Roni with someone else. He'd have to convince her they were meant for one another.

The first time he saw Roni, he was a brash, boisterous college freshman home on spring break and too full of himself. She stood back withdrawn. Her timid, curious gaze never left him while Samantha ran squealing to jump into his arms.

When Sam finally let go of him long enough to introduce the new member of their family—*Veronica Reeves, Roni for short*—his longing to protect her tugged at his heart.

From the first day they met she belonged to him. He didn't realize it then, but he did now. All he saw was a cute, sad kid still mourning the loss of her parents. The overwhelming desire to protect her, to make the hurt go away, to be near her was so strong he sought her company anytime he was home.

Drake smiled at the remembered and endearing image.

Almost overnight Roni changed from a sad, gangly teen into a beautiful, mature woman heading off to college. He teased Sam and her about steering clear of the college men. He even said he might drive to Austin to make sure the men knew the two of them were off limits.

Samantha punched him on the arm, warning him he'd be sorry if he showed his face on campus. Unlike his sister, Roni shook her head, gave him a strange look, and then ignored him.

Though Drake dated other women while she was in college, none of them quite measured up to Roni. He was always anxious and waiting for her next visit home.

Her smiles warmed him. Her playfulness delighted him. Her impassioned banter, even how she spoke her mind holding nothing back, made him desire her more. And when he teased her, she gave back as good as she got. He loved their times together, and missed her when she wasn't around.

Many times, while in her company, he would catch her studying him, then look away as though distracted. She never seemed more than friendly toward him. But he wanted more and hoped she did too.

He had his work cut out for him and hoped his own stupidity of not speaking his true feelings hadn't cost him the opportunity to win her affections. Even now she could already have someone in Dallas she didn't talk about.

His heart tightened painfully over the thought of Roni with another man. If there was someone, he'd work doubly hard to convince Roni the guy wasn't for her, or die trying.

Drake moved back to the desk, picked up the top sheet determined to get through a few more documents before going to bed.

His father had asked him to take care of anything pending. He'd been putting it off for a week now and it needed to be done. Too restless to sleep, he figured mind numbing paperwork might do the trick anyway.

The stack of papers didn't seem to diminish and the words began to run together. Drake stood and stretched, hoping to clear the fog in his brain. He sat down again and reached for the next paper on top of the slowly dwindling stack of work. The document looked like someone had balled it up, then smoothed it out again.

Thinking it strange, Drake flipped to the last page and saw the signature was John F. Reeves—*Roni's father?* He couldn't be certain because he didn't remember her father's first name. Except for the college pact and then later their wills agreeing to raise each other's children if something drastic were to happen to either of them, he'd never heard of any other dealings his father had with Roni's dad.

The letter dated February 4, 1993, was filled with scathing remarks, listing accusations of bad faith, bogus investments, and fraud against Pioneer Drilling Company, naming his father as principal shareholder. The man called his father the worst kind of scum and crook he'd come across—and ended with … *to think I called you friend. No more.*

The summer before his senior year in high school, Drake went with his father to west Texas a time or two to observe the drilling of some of the wells. That was about the time the Peters' Home Improvement Stores were beginning to really grow. Also about the time his father had started his drilling company.

With a quick glance at the clock, he knew he should be in bed otherwise, he'd be in no shape to go to church with Roni and his dad.

He folded the letter to take to his room, and then cleared off the desk. Tomorrow, with his mind fresh and his father available, he'd ask him about the matter and if John Reeves was Roni's father.

Drake figured as tired as he was, he'd fall right to sleep. But when he crawled into bed, his mind wouldn't settle down. He turned on the lamp, grabbed the letter off his nightstand, and began to read it again. He didn't believe his father had conned this Reeves fellow out of all his money to the point of bankruptcy. There had to be a more logical explanation to the story.

A tap on the door had Drake placing the letter on the nightstand. He was in the process of scooting out of bed when his dad poked his head into the room.

"I saw your light on and thought I'd check. Something troubling you?"

His father looked better than earlier this evening, yet his skin still held a slight washout look. Drake knew this wasn't the time to ask about the Reeves' letter. He'd wait until tomorrow when his dad was more rested and he was too. If he mentioned it now, neither of them would get any sleep.

His father's gaze landed on the letter and he turned pale with a look of concern. Drake knew the discussion wouldn't wait.

He prayed the man wasn't Roni's father, and his dad could explain. If not, it could drive a wedge between Roni and them, especially if she was unaware of what took place.

CHAPTER 14

Roni's groggy brain couldn't quite grasp what caused her to wake up, but something had pulled her from a deep sleep. Disoriented to her surroundings, she remembered she wasn't at her apartment but at the ranch. She strained to listen but didn't hear anything.

She gave her pillow a few good punches to fluff it up, then rolled over to go back to sleep. A shout had Roni up and out of bed and pulling on her robe. Though indistinguishable, the heated words got louder. She recognized the instigators, Drake and Marcus.

When she walked out of her room the hall fell silent. She had almost convinced herself she had imagined the shouting, when another bout of angry voices erupted.

Rushing down the hall, she stopped at Drake's room and raised her hand to knock as the door was thrown back on it hinges. Marcus, his face modeled with rage, stood in the opening and stared at her in shock.

"Roni." He stepped back, a little shaky. "How long have you been standing there?"

Drake stood behind his father, the remnants of rage draining from his face.

Thinking Marcus' question odd, she answer, "I heard raised voices and came to see what was happening. I was about to knock when you opened the door. Are you all right? What's going on?"

Marcus turned to look at Drake. "Everything is fine." He glanced back at her. "We were just discussing some company business."

"This late at night?" She gave them both an incredulous look. "Surely it can wait until morning. You need your rest, Marcus." She threw a disgruntled glare in Drake's direction. "And you should know better than to get your father all riled up over business at this time of the morning. One fifteen isn't a time to discuss *anything.*" She extended her arm to Marcus. "Come on. Let me walk you back to your room."

Marcus hesitated only a moment before grabbing her arm and giving her a wide smile. "We'll talk tomorrow after church, Drake."

"You can be sure we will. And I want answers. Do we understand each other?"

"Completely. Tomorrow."

Leaning on Roni a little more than normal, Marcus laughed as they walked. "Drake thinks he runs the company. But I let him know I'm still in charge."

Roni figured she'd stop back by Drake's room once Marcus was settled in and give him a good piece of her mind. She felt sure it was one conversation he wouldn't enjoy.

"You know you *did* put Drake in charge. He's good at it too. So let him do his job." She patted his arm good-naturedly, wanting him to know she had his interest at heart. "What you need to do is to pretend you are on vacation." She smiled fondly up at him. "In fact, I'll tell you what I'll do."

"What's that?" His steps became a little slower.

She worried he might be weakening. *He shouldn't have been out of bed.*

"I'm going to take some vacation time and come back to the ranch for a couple of weeks. I'll make sure you behave."

"And little missy, do you think you can keep me in line?"

His rumble of laughter made her feel better about her decision. He almost sounded like the old Marcus again.

"Yes, I do."

"Now that'll be something to see."

"And I'm just the one to do it too." She reached for the door knob. "Now go inside, get in bed, and get some well needed rest."

When he hesitated, she asked, "Do you need some help?" Knowing good and well, he'd say no.

"No. I'm not some baby who's in need of tending. I can get in my own bed." He gave her a kiss on the cheek, then walked away grumbling under his breath.

"I heard that."

"That's not all you're gonna hear if you keep standing in my doorway." He waved her off. "Shut the door and let a man have some privacy."

"Goodnight, Marcus. Sweet dreams."

"You too, sweetheart."

She pulled the door shut, but stood for a moment listening. Once she heard him moving about, she headed back to Drake's room.

Roni lifted her hand to knock, but like earlier, the door swung open. Drake stood there like an avenging angel ready to take on the world if need be. But much like his father earlier, he seemed shocked to see her standing outside his door in the hall.

"Did you get him settled?" Drake leaned against the doorjamb, arms crossed over his chest, looking too cavalier and none too happy.

"Yes. But you shouldn't argue with your father, especially this late at night. He's in no condition to be upset." Roni gave him a no-nonsense glare. "You know better."

"If you noticed, he was in my room, not me in his. I didn't go looking for a fight." He grinned sheepishly. "He threw down the gauntlet." He shrugged. "I picked it up."

"You're not a medieval knight fighting on the field of honor." She breathed in deeply doing her best to control her temper. "Furthermore, he's your father, Drake."

She touched his arm hoping he would realize she cared about him also. "In his condition you shouldn't be arguing with him. He's weak and vulnerable. He feels like he has no control over anything—his company, the cancer, you, me … you name it. His former way of life is slipping out of his grasp. And since he feels he doesn't have control, he's going to lash out at those he loves, mainly you. You're where he wants to be—viable, full life, and doing his job at the company he started."

Drake covered her hand with his. "I understand what you're saying. However, what we were discussing goes beyond …" He shook his head. "Oh, never mind." He lowered his hand and stepped back. "I think we both need some sleep."

His abrupt manner hurt. Apparently he didn't need or want her opinion.

"Goodnight then." She turned and headed for her room. Before she entered, she looked back and saw Drake watching.

He nodded, waved, and then stepped back. The soft click of Drake's door caused Roni's heart to ache. She wanted to cry with frustration. How had her world gone so terribly wrong? Or worse yet … how long will she continue to love Drake knowing he could never love her?

CHAPTER 15

The tense atmosphere between the two Peters' men made the drive from the ranch to the church uncomfortable. Anxious to get out of the highly charged car, the large colonial church building with its tall steeple was a welcomed sight.

When they stepped inside the sanctuary, Marcus and Drake, barely cordial to each other, maneuvered Roni between them on the pew. She prayed their mood would improve during the service.

It didn't.

Whatever had riled them in the early morning hours continued. Neither man would budge an inch in his stance. They were acting like children on a playground, willing to stay mad for not getting their own way.

What irked her most, they didn't seem to be the least bit repentant or ready to settle matters. And neither seemed to think Pastor Johnson's wonderful sermon on "Love Covers All" was for them, which made Roni even more determined to get to the heart of the matter.

She released a derisive chuckle under her breathe. What made her think she could unravel what was taking place between father and son? She couldn't even unravel why she loved a man who wasn't remotely interested in loving her?

"What's got you smiling?"

The deep timbre of Drake's voice jerked her back to her surroundings. Her cheeks flamed when she realized he was watching her closely.

She averted her head. "Nothing. Just private thoughts."

The sound of their footsteps on the sidewalk, the muted voices of others leaving church, even the slight rustling of leaves in the warm breeze filled her ears as her heart beat erratically. Drake's nearness and smell of his cologne brought sensations she didn't want to explore.

Roni looked around to see where Marcus might be and saw him standing at the bottom of the church steps talking to one of his friends. She figured he'd be a while. Touching Drake's arm, she motioned for him to move off the sidewalk and stand beneath the tree to wait for his father.

"What's going on between you and Marcus? Surely, it can't be so horrible you'll barely speak to one another."

He moved to stand facing her, his green eyes darkened. When she saw the muscle in his jaw twitch, she knew it was much worse than originally thought.

"Drake, I don't know what's been said, but please, pull down that wall you've erected and apologize. Whether he's right or wrong, you need to make things right with your father. He's ill and has more on his plate than he can handle at the moment."

"You don't know the half of it." He looked away disgusted.

Worried it was something more than a tiff over turf, as Marcus led her to believe, she touched his arm giving it a slight squeeze.

"Talk to me, Drake, let me help, please. I hate seeing you and your dad at odds, especially now."

By the look in Drake's eyes she knew her plea was useless, but she had to try again.

"If not for your dad's sake, then do it for me." Her words seemed to incense him more, yet not as much as their petty grievance was beginning to anger her. She removed her hand.

"Well, I'm telling you here and now, I won't live one day under a roof with the two of you acting like polecats ready to tear into each other at the least provocation. So don't count on me coming back Monday evening." She turned, thinking she'd go back to get Marcus.

Drake caught her by the arm. She stopped and faced him, her temper barely under control.

"Roni, please."

The pleading of his voice caused her to soften even though her anger was great.

"I can't explain the why right now. *Shoot!*" He rammed his fingers through his hair causing some of the strands to stand up. "I'm not certain I understand why. I'm still confused, but I'm trying to sort through the details. Suffice it to say, some of my lifelong beliefs about my father were shattered. And the worst of it is I'm not sure I will ever get to the bottom of the truth."

He glanced down the street then back at her. "But I promise you this. If you'll come back home tomorrow night, before you return from town, the matter will be taken care of and everything will be settled ... *one way or another.*"

Though Drake said the last under his breath, Roni heard him and it worried her. In the last seventeen years of being a part of the Peters' family, she'd never seen Drake and Marcus this badly at odds.

"It's not about the Holdum matter, is it? We don't know yet if his claim is valid. I have it slated to begin the research first thing tomorrow morning."

"No. But that's one more thing against him. I'll bring that up also when I meet with him later this afternoon."

"No, Drake, please leave the Holdum matter to me until we know more conclusively your father is involved. The man's claim could be bogus and there's no use in worrying him unnecessarily over the matter until it is proven otherwise."

"All right, I'll leave Holdum's claim to you. But please, I really need you to come home for at least a few days ... a week or two would be better. I'm sorry I can't give you my reasons, but until I know more of what I'm dealing with, it'll have to remain that way."

He shoved his hand into his pant pocket, fidgeting with his keys. "As to your earlier plea to make amends, I believe the best you can expect until a few things are settled is that I'll be civil toward him. It'll be hard but ..."

"Did you hear yourself? *Civil?*" She shook her head. "I hope you will be more than civil. This is your father we're discussing. He's due your respect regardless what your disagreement."

"I know. But this ..."

"Drake, where were you when the sermon was being preached this morning?"

A guilty grin appeared. "I know. And I'll work through this. But right now my feelings are too raw on the subject. And until I get to the bottom, I don't see my temperament improving a whole lot."

He looked pleadingly at her. "Please don't let this stop you from coming back tomorrow night. I can't promise everything will be worked out. Things still might be a bit uncomfortable between dad and me. However, I'll promise to do my best to hold on to my temper."

"Well, are we ready to go?" Marcus came up alongside Roni, linking his arm with hers. He glanced at his son, but Drake avoided Marcus by looking over at the parking lot.

"Yes." She smiled brightly at Marcus. "I don't know about you, but I'm starving."

"I'll go on ahead and pull the car around."

Before anyone could even say *boo*, Drake struck off across the parking lot.

Marcus' eyes twinkled down at her. "So, when are you leaving for Dallas, and when will you be back?"

"If I didn't know better, I'd think you were trying to get rid of me."

"Nonsense." Marcus patted her hand. "If I had my way, you'd come home for good. I miss you more than you'll ever know."

Roni looked ahead at Drake knowing she wouldn't go back on her plans. "I'm leaving after lunch but I'll be back tomorrow night around eight or nine."

"Great. Maybe you'll come to your senses and move back home for good."

"*Marcus.*"

His face lit up. "You can't blame an old man for trying. And hopefully Drake's ill wind will have blown over by then." Marcus gave her a wink.

"What's going on between you two?" Roni hoped he'd open up to her.

He avoided looking at her. "Let's just say, Drake and I don't exactly see eye to eye on some things. But don't you worry. Everything will be over and done with by tomorrow night."

Marcus' words should have brought relief. Instead, the worry lines in his face made Roni a little uneasy and concerned.

CHAPTER 16

The Uptown trolley bell clanged loudly while it maneuvered the corner, then began the ascent up the hill to the Dallas Museum of Art. Roni closed her iPad and slipped it in her briefcase knowing she had reached her stop.

She hoped her day would go better than her night. Troubled over Marcus and Drake hadn't been conducive for a good night's rest. Maybe coffee would get her past the wrung out feeling.

When she exited the trolley, she felt someone bump her. Though a little irritated, she ignored it and moved on up the street, then turned the corner heading for her office.

"Fountain Place is a unique looking building, especially when all the fountains are up and running."

The familiar voice was too close for comfort. Startled, Roni jerked around to glare at Nick Holdum. "What are you doing, following me?"

His laughter and the fact he was close enough for her to see the fine lines at the edge of his eyes, unnerved her. It was his good fortune she wasn't a man. Otherwise his reception might have been more than heated words, more like a punch in the gut.

"I thought I'd check out the lawyer who's checking me out. Seems only fair." He shrugged, titling his head to one side, grinning as he fell in step with her.

The sparkle of his green eyes made her think of Drake. She shoved the thought aside. Not the time to be distracted.

They waited at the light for a car to turn the corner before they crossed.

"Our offices don't open until 8:00. I suggest you find a place to have a cup of coffee." She pointed to the Starbucks directly in front of them, which was attached to the Fairmont Hotel.

"I'll buy you one. How 'bout it, counselor?"

His drop-dead smile unnerved her. And, she didn't like the fact he had followed her.

Normally, she stopped at Starbucks before going on to the office, so what the harm. Maybe this small window of opportunity would give her a chance to learn a little more about Holdum the man, if she could hold her temper together.

"I'll buy my own." She knew her tone sounded churlish, but he had caught her off guard. *How did he know I would be on the trolley and at that precise time?*

Moving past Nick Holdum, Roni pulled on the door handle to the hotel and Starbucks entrance. Nick reached around her and held the door open to allow her to pass through. Before she could open Starbucks' door, he beat her to it.

"After you."

The guy agitated her. In so many ways he was too much like Drake, yet dissimilar, and it disturbed her.

The line to order coffee was short. She moved up to the counter and said, "Hi, Jamey. My usual, please."

"And just what is your usual?"

His minty breath fanned her cheek. His voice, a deep, soft whisper, made her extremely uncomfortable.

"And yours, Sir?"

Jamey's request enabled Roni to step aside and not answer, and helped to keep distance between her and Nick.

"I'll have a Grande Caffè Americano." He flirted shamelessly with Jamey, which the girl didn't seem to mind. Then he sauntered over to where Roni stood waiting.

She wanted to ignore him but decided being obstinate wouldn't work in her favor. Information is what she needed from this guy, and friendliness was the best way to achieve her goal.

"How did you happen to catch me on my way to work?" She stared at him wanting to see if he would be truthful.

He shrugged nonchalantly. "A hunch which paid off. I waited for you."

His answer took her aback, yet she did her best not to show shock. "How did you know I would be passing in front of the Dallas Museum at this time of the morning?" *This guy was too slick by far.*

He leaned his shoulder against the wall, crossed his leg over the other looking quite smug, or was it devious? "To be honest, I wasn't sure what time. However, I followed you from Athens to your apartment yesterday evening."

Anger hit her full force. She was ready to take someone's head off—namely Nick Holdum. "You stalked me?" He had no right. She felt violated.

He shrugged again. "Not stalked exactly. More like chance and circumstance. I was leaving Athens yesterday for Dallas when you breezed past me, so I followed you. I wasn't sure, but I figure it was worth a shot that you rode the trolley to work, since you took it to the deli on McKinney last night. What did you buy ... pastrami?" He raised his brows smugly.

She smiled without answering, gritting her teeth. He knew where she lived. What type of man was she dealing with? Dangerous? She'd be more careful in the future.

"And the trolley? You just looked to be the type who would be early to work." He gave a confident shrug. "Especially, since I knew you were going to do research on me and wouldn't want anyone else in your firm to know. And with New York being a full hour ahead of Dallas, well, it looks like I assumed correctly."

She was itching to wipe the smug arrogance off his face. He was too cocky and too good at logic. She wouldn't make the same mistake of underestimating him again.

"Your coffee's ready."

Jamey cut off what she wanted to say to Nick, which was just as well. Roni grabbed her cup, moved to the coffee condiment bar. Before she put her lid back on her cup, Nick was beside her.

"Shall I walk you to your office so we can talk more?"

"Thank you, but no." Roni smiled sweetly. "I have a meeting first thing this morning. I'll have my assistant book you in at nine-thirty."

"That'll work. I'll see you later then." He nodded his goodbye before heading in the direction of an empty table.

Roni left Starbucks, her teeth worrying her bottom lip. How best to deal with Holdum? By all appearances, he was a Peters, but that didn't mean he wasn't a threat.

When she arrived at her office, she shut the door and turned on her computer, and then pulled out the documents Holdum had given her. Everything looked authentic, but there were forgers for a price who could make documents look real.

After several phone calls, one of them being to Frank Thornton, the PI Phillip Bradley recommended, she was as prepared as she could be to face Nick Holdum.

Promptly at nine-thirty her legal assistant announced Holdum. His confidence preceded him while his gaze took in her office. Seeing her name on the door, he was no doubt measuring whether she was truly a partner or a woman who was in a token position to fill a quota.

"Well, did you learn much in two hours?"

Holdum's to-the-point approach didn't bother her. In fact, if anything, gave Roni confidence. This was her world he'd entered.

"Have a seat, please." Roni took a quick look at her notes while he strolled to the chair in front of her desk. She picked up a sheet of paper and held it out.

"What I need from you is written on this list. And for the blood sample, you will need to personally appear at the clinic address provided, show your picture I.D at check in, and present this sheet to them. They will take a sample of your blood, and later send the report to me. All the written instructions are on that sheet along with some questions you will need to answer. You may mail all I've requested to me in this envelope."

She passed the envelope to him. "Do you have any questions for me?"

"*Hmmm.* Quite efficient. Yes, one."

"Yes?" His calculating gaze gave Roni pause.

"Will you have dinner with me tonight?"

"No. And if you don't intend to take this matter seriously, then this meeting is over."

He shrugged. "Had to give it another shot. What happens once you get the results back?"

"Once I have evidence one way or the other, I will contact you. We will proceed from there." She witnessed a sparkle in his eye. Was he toying with her? Maybe his claim was false after all.

"Will you then?"

"Will I what?"

"Go out to dinner with me? You might find you like me more than my brother. Unlike him, I know how to show a woman my true feelings."

He hit a sore spot. Roni forgot about keeping her cool. She stormed around her desk to the door, swinging it open.

"The answer is still no. I believe we are finished." She waited for him to move.

When he was slow to respond, Roni saw red. "Mr. Holdum, I believe we are at an impasse. If you won't take this matter seriously, than neither can I. I'm sorry, but I have another appointment." She motioned at the outer room hoping he would take the hint.

"Oh, but I do—" He walked toward her, then stopped. "—take this matter very seriously."

Roni didn't like him in her personal space but she stood her ground without retreat. His cologne was heady, but irritating.

"In fact, I take this whole matter of my parentage so serious, Marcus Peters is about to find out what happens to a man who doesn't take care of his obligations."

"Am I to perceive your words as a threat, Mr. Holdum?"

"No. Just a fact. Peters will answer to me for what he did to my mother."

Roni held down her animosity not wanting to show the man he had gotten under her sink. "Let me remind you, Mr. Holdum—"

"Nick."

"*Mr. Holdum*, until I have had a chance to have your documents carefully researched, and until you provide a blood sample proving you are indeed Marcus Peters' son, my warning still stands. You are not to contact Marcus Peters. Do I make myself clear?"

"Crystal." A cocky, all-knowing grin appeared.

He ran the edge of his forefinger along her jaw. When she stepped back repulsed, he lowered his hand to his side.

She didn't like how Nick Holdum made her feel. He was too much like Drake and it would be easy to transfer her repressed sentiments for Drake to him, even if it was counterfeit.

~ 85 ~

"Know this, *Veronica*, if you think to stall for any length of time, I'll not hesitate to talk to the old man. And a puny restraining order won't stop me."

CHAPTER 17

The sun hung low in Roni's review mirror as she approached the town of Athens. The thick clouds were rose tinted and outlined by gold making it a beautiful close of day—the kind Texas was noted for. Yet the scene did little to lift her spirits. Nick Holdum occupied much of her thoughts and spoiled the trip.

She departmentalized all of the information she'd looked at and had received so far. Everything seemed to be pointing in Holdum's favor. Roni figured this news would greatly affect Drake.

True, she had a long way to go to acquire additional research and findings, the blood tests the defining factor. If Holdum went today, the results wouldn't be back for several days.

Frank Thornton's call earlier hadn't been what she'd hoped for either. But she hadn't held out any great expectations. His preliminary check on Holdum's claim looked viable. Though Frank's man, once he flew to New York, would dig deeper to see if neighbors, relatives, or friends could corroborate or refute Holdum's story. The report could differ.

Unless Drake asked, she wouldn't mention Holdum or give a report, at least not yet. No sense of getting him worked up before all the results were back.

Nick Holdum—now there was a man to steer clear of, but knew she couldn't because of Marcus. She would have to keep an emotional distance though. He had a certain magnetism a lot of woman would find hard to resist, and she was no exception.

He had a definite charm and easy manner, if one could get past the anger directed at Marcus. And truth be told, he looked too much like Drake for Roni's comfort or sanity. Thankfully, she recognized his appeal for what it was—displaced attraction, one brother for the other, which would be an easy thing to do, but detrimental also.

What was she thinking? Of all the stupid ideas floating around in her head, thinking of Nick Holdum in that way was the dumbest. She didn't know Nick, but she knew Drake. Besides the facial similarities, the two men were nothing alike. Hands down, Drake was a far better man than Nick. He was forthright, honest, and courteous, not many men could stand in his shadow.

The gate opened as her car swung into the drive. By the time she reached the house the sunset had faded and darkening shades of dusk cloaked the land. For some people this was a peaceful time of day—closure. For others, a time of unsettling and melancholy. Tonight, hers was the latter.

The Triple Cross Ranch held a special place in Roni's heart, and more so since she no longer lived here. And though it hadn't always been so, it didn't take long for her mindset to change.

She relished the quite, serene familiarity of the countryside where a sound could travel for miles unhindered and the beauty went on forever. This was home. No city smog. No high rises blocking her view. No bumper to bumper traffic to contend with. *Well, at least for two weeks.*

The faint smell of cattle, fresh mown hay, and the scent of someone barbequing drifted through her open window. The aroma of grilled meat triggered her hunger pangs, a reminder she hadn't eaten dinner, and lunch had been a quick snack.

Roni drove around the side to the five-car garage. By the time she had parked the car and turned off the ignition, Charles was waiting at her door with a grateful smile.

"I'm so glad you came back, Miss Roni." He went to the trunk of her car and grabbed the two larger bags before heading to the side entrance of the house. "I'll come back for the others after I put these in your room."

"There's no need. I've already got them." She hefted the briefcase strap over her shoulder and grabbed the small bag. "How is Marcus doing?"

"Things will be much better now that you're here again."

Not sure what Charles meant, she hoped Drake and his father weren't still arguing. If they were, she would give them both a piece of her mind.

They walked down the side hall and through the foyer. Charles and she were on the half landing making the turn to the second floor when raised voices came from the library. Placing her things on the landing, she turned and said, "Charles, once you've taken the suitcases to my room, please come back for these. I'll see what's going on."

She headed back down the stairs to investigate. The library door stood slightly ajar. Roni could see Marcus sitting behind the desk and Drake standing in front glaring angrily at his father.

"You *will* come clean with her, or I'll tell her myself. I won't allow this matter to be shoved under the rug any longer. What happened has to be told. She has every right to know." Drake noticed Roni in the doorway.

"How long have you been standing there?"

Drake's angry tone and glower had her cringing. Did he think she had been eavesdropping? She felt a flush travel up her neck to her face which brought anger.

"I heard you yelling halfway up the stairs. Would you like to explain what's so all-fired important to raise your voice to your father when he's sick?" She advanced further into the room, glared at Drake, giving back as good as she received.

Marcus offered a tentative smile. "Welcome back. I'm so looking forward to our time together."

Muttering under his breath, Drake rammed his fingers through his hair before turning his back on Roni and his father. He stared out into the blackness beyond the window.

Drake's troubling attitude and Marcus' drawn appearance riled Roni all the more.

"Drake! What's going on? Marcus?" She was hot enough to tear into both men. They were acting like children, not like rational adults.

Drake tipped his head back, his eyes closed. The heavy breath he expelled was filled with pent up frustrations. When he turned and faced her, she could see he was plainly troubled, yet he stood silent.

"You two are worse today than you were yesterday. Drake, I told you to settle this matter before I returned." She gave both men a disgusted look. "What were you arguing about? Who is she, and what does she need to know that is so all-fired important that you two are at each other's throats?" *Simmer down.* She tried, but she couldn't, she was too keyed up.

Drake starred at his father, then opened his mouth.

"Drake." Marcus shook his head, voice pleading, his face ashen. He appeared weak and vulnerable.

"That's enough. Whatever it is, can wait until tomorrow." She walked around the desk to stand beside Marcus, resting her hand on his shoulder.

"Come on, you're going upstairs to bed." She stood back and waited for Marcus to comply, then stared pointedly at

Drake. "And if you need help getting ready for bed, Drake will assist you."

"I'm fine. I can get to my room on my own." Marcus grumbled under his breath as he stood.

Roni allow him to pass in front of her. She followed behind to ensure he was indeed stable enough walk without assistance.

"I'm not a baby, Roni. I can make the stairs just fine on my own. Been doing it for years." Marcus waved her off. "You go have dinner. I'm sure you didn't eat before you left town, probably haven't eaten all day. I had Charles order up a steak for you. I'm sure Hazel has everything ready by now."

His steps were slow and careful. He complained the whole way, which made her smile. His mutterings about how he was being treated like a baby could be heard as he climbed the stairs.

"I heard that." Roni wasn't about to budge until he got to the top landing and out of sight.

"And you'll hear a whole lot more if you don't take yourself off to dinner."

She chuckled, then sensed Drake behind her. Roni swung around giving him full view of her anger.

"Roni …"

"I'm starved and I'm going to find that steak. If you have something to say to me, you can join me while I eat." She stormed off toward the kitchen only to find her dinner waiting for her in the dining room along with Drake's.

So he hadn't eaten either. Probably too busy harassing Marcus.

She walked to where she normally sat at the oak dining table that could accommodate eight or twenty, whatever the occasion called for. The many dinners that had taken place in this very room had been fun and memorable. Drake's mother Elle had decorated the dining room with light green stripped and muted flowers wallpaper above oak, beadboard wainscot shortly after Roni had arrived, and nothing had changed since.

She glanced around the room. It was comfortable and inviting, yet elegant. The serving buffet, that would be full to running over at Sunday dinners and Saturday breakfasts, was empty except for a few crystal pieces for decoration. The room had an inviting, stay-awhile atmosphere. Elle had often mentioned her dinners were to be a time for talking and bonding as a family, to learn about everyone's day.

No bonding would take place tonight. Roni was too angry to even be halfway cordial.

Drake pulled out her chair and stood next to it, waiting for her to be seated. She mumbled her thanks, and then felt churlish. His thoughtfulness didn't deserve her snarly attitude.

Without looking in his direction, Roni bowed her head for the blessing. Drake's deep voice and prayer caused more of her anger to dissipate. Yet she wasn't ready to let it all completely go. Not until Drake explained what was going on.

The food, though delicious, set hard on Roni's stomach as the unsettling silence prevailed. She placed her fork and knife on the edge of her plate, a little heavier than normal.

The clink of metal on china caused Drake to glance up. His face showed his turmoil was as great as hers.

"Now you're scaring me, Drake. What's going on?" When he didn't answer, she figured she'd start the conversation and see if it wouldn't loosen his tongue.

"I wasn't eavesdropping earlier, you know. With the door open and your voices raised, it was difficult not to hear. Who is the woman you were talking about?"

He wiped his mouth with his napkin, but still held the cloth as he rested his forearm on the table. Like her, he'd only eaten a portion of the food on his plate.

"I can't say, at least not now. It's not my story to tell. However, if my father doesn't speak with you by tomorrow and explain the situation, then I will. But first, I'll give him the opportunity to disclose the nasty business. He should have done it years ago instead of ignoring it and thinking it would mysteriously disappear."

He stood and threw his napkin on the table, something so uncharacteristic of Drake.

Roni knew he was about to leave and she wouldn't be any the wiser. "Drake, you're beginning to scare me. Please talk to me."

Sorrow filled his eyes as he shook his head and pushed the chair under the table. "If you'll excuse me, I have some work that has to be done before tomorrow. I'll say goodnight."

He walked away but stopped at the door and glanced back. "Roni, I know it doesn't look like it, but believe it or not, I am happy you've come home." Drake gave her a sad, weary smile, fatigue showing in the lines of his face. "If for no other reason ... to keep me from strangling Dad."

CHAPTER 18

Roni threw her files on the small writing desk in her bedroom, her mind rehearsing Drake's last words. In all the years she'd lived under the Peters' roof, she had never heard Drake talk in that manner about Marcus. Something was terribly wrong to divide father and son who had always been close.

She pulled out the chair and plopped down, weary to the bone. But she had to get the report done and emailed off to her assistant before morning. To spread her files out on the large study desk in the library like she normally did, would have been more conducive to working. But she knew Drake was using the library and she didn't want to be with him in his present mood. Instead, she plopped the numerous files on the bed, retrieving the one she needed.

Her mind kept drifting to the argument of earlier. To say Marcus and Drake had never argued would be a lie. Throw two grown men together, have them living under one roof and running a business, they were bound to incite differing opinions and heated arguments. Especially, when one had old ideas and the other had new, and neither able to give. She had seen many passionate debates in the past, but never this caustic, and never at such an impasse.

Kicking off her sandals, Roni pulled her fuzzy socks on, dreading the thought of working when her mind was so distracted. Maybe once she started, work would keep her mind occupied and off of Drake and his father.

A tap on her door had Roni nervously answering.

Drake stood in the hall wearing jeans, a faded t-shirt, and a silly grin. He held a cup of tea and a small plate of Sock-it-to-Me cake she'd passed up early. A jolt of love for the man who could be so thoughtful and caring had her shoving her earlier disgruntled thoughts out the window.

"A piece offering and an apology, if you'll accept it."

"How thoughtful. Thanks."

He glanced inside her room and saw the files on her bed and paper scattered across the desk. "Why didn't you come to the library to work?" He gave another sheepish grin that could turn her determination to mush.

"I wouldn't have come down either if I had come home to the welcome you received. I'm sorry, Roni." The stark realization of his behavior earlier accompanied the sincerity of his apology. "Please forgive me."

Her heart wasn't a match for his plea, or for that matter … him. "You're forgiven. But I'm not the only one, you know." She gave him a pointed look.

His face clouded, and he glanced briefly in the direction of his father's room before looking back at her.

"You're right, of course. And I will. But not tonight. Tomorrow." He paused, searching her face. "Come downstairs. Eat cake with me, please. Cake never tastes as good as when it is shared with someone you love."

His grin was infectious, yet a pang of regret filled her knowing the love he spoke of was of friendship.

"And bring your files. You can do your work while I do mine, just like old times. My work seems to go faster with you in the room. *Please.*"

Though she knew she should keep her distance, the moment she saw him—cake in hand—she couldn't.

"*Oooh,* all right." She pointed to the cake and tea. "Take those to the library. I'll grab my files and be right down."

"Thanks. Right now, I need your company in the worst way."

He stared at her like a hungry man who couldn't get his fill, then gave her a dashing smile making her heart beat erratically. His gaze confused her. If she didn't know better she would believe he loved her as she loved him. But she knew different.

She stood watching Drake saunter down the hall balancing the cup and plate. Barefoot, his t-shirt hanging out, his hair tousled as though he'd ran his fingers through it several times. He was eye candy to her starving soul.

Roni wished he wanted her company because he loved her, but she would settle for being a close, personal friend to Drake and make it suffice ... for now. One day she would find a man she could love and who would love her back. But until such time, she'd remind herself—Drake and she were friends, longstanding friends, and after all was said and done, that meant something ... *didn't it?*

When she entered the library, her cake and tea, along with his, were on the coffee table in front of the couch where he sat waiting.

Roni placed her things on the library table. She ran her hand along the smooth wood, remembering Elle had insisted in moving the desk into the room in front of a window specifically for her. Most times when she came home from law school, Roni could be found right here bent over her books or staring out at the view working over a problem. Often Drake would be sitting at his father's huge desk going over business files as they worked together in companionable silence. The memory of those moments was dear to her.

"A penny for your thoughts."

Startled, she jumped slightly. She hadn't realized Drake was watching her and felt a little foolish he caught her daydreaming.

"A penny isn't near enough for my thoughts." Laughing, she continued toward the couch. "In fact, I don't believe you could afford them." She sat down, pulling her feet up under her before taking the cup of tea Drake offered. "Haven't you heard?" She kept her face serious. "I'm a big-time attorney now and my thoughts are petty pricey."

He laughed. "Well, Miss Big City Lawyer, drink your tea and eat your cake while I enjoy your company then." Drake's gorgeous eyes sparkled.

"Roni, I miss you. I wish you would take Dad up on his offer and move back home."

"Not you too." She rolled her eyes as she placed her cup down and grabbed the plate of cake. "You know my work is in Dallas. The drive is too long and grueling, especially when I have to spend late nights at the office working, which happens on a regular basis."

"You could move to Athens, partner with a firm here, or open your own practice. You're a good lawyer. And with your corporate expertise, you would only need a few more clients to earn as much as you do now."

His reasoning gave her nothing to counter unless she just out-'n'-out lied.

"Don't say, no. Give it some thought." He picked up his cake and took a bite. He grinned after swallowing. "If you did, it would mean I could see you every day, which would make me ... and everyone else happy."

"I wish I could say I was placed on this earth just for the sole purpose of making you and everyone else happy, but I wasn't." She took another bite of cake then returned the plate to the table.

The reality she would do just about anything to make him happy if he loved her, made the cake taste like paste in her mouth. She grabbed her cup, sipped the warm tea willing the glue to move down her throat as she watched Drake over the rim of the cup.

"I understand."

She couldn't tell if he was disappointed or what he thought. Lately, Drake, someone she believed she knew so well, was proving to be more of an enigma, and one she'd be willing to give up a lot to understand.

When had their friendship changed and become strained?

When I realized he would never love me. I changed and erected the wall between us, not him.

She touched his knee hoping to infuse normalcy back into the awkward moment. "Drake, I would love to live here all the time, but it's just not possible." She didn't dare tell him why or their friendship would become even more awkward than it was now.

"I eventually want to get married. And you know as well as I do, the pickings in Athens are slim around here for a single woman lawyer in her thirties." She opted for humor. "My choices are either old Judge Timmons, who has one foot in the grave, or that lawyer who just recently divorced his fourth or was it his fifth wife—what's his name?"

"Gilley. And I wouldn't let you near either one of those woman chasers. I could fix you up with one of my friends, or—" He hooded his eyes while watching her. "—you could marry me."

She glanced away not wanting him to see how his words hurt. "Don't be silly."

Taking a breath, she gave him one of her best smiles and then heaved herself off the couch. "I don't know about you, but I've got work to do. Sitting here won't get it done."

Taking her cup of tea, she moved to the library desk feeling his gaze. She wanted to turn around and tell him how she really felt, but knew she would never have the nerve to do something as foolish as laying her true feelings out in the open.

At the library table, in the window's refection she watched Drake at his father's desk. She knew he was unaware of how impossible he was making it for her to keep her mind on her work.

With her gaze back on the document in front of her, she heard every little move he made. The shuffle of papers. The scratch of his pen. The thumping of his fingers while he thought over a problem, even his foot rubbing his leg. All of it had lulled her mind into thinking of him and not her work.

Outside the window everything was pitch black like her thoughts. She wondered how she'd extricate herself from the spell Drake had woven around her heart. When she saw his reflection in the window behind her watching, an odd expression on his face, she was jerked out of her thought and back to reality. As their eyes connected, Roni believed she saw sorrow, or maybe regret. She turned to look at him

"My mind isn't on work, so I'm calling it a night. I'll see you at breakfast."

"Sure. Goodnight, Drake."

"Roni—" He hesitated, a flitter of uncertainty in his eyes. "Thank you for coming home. I know it's been tough on you, and I won't make it tougher by begging you to come back home to stay. However, I want you to know the house is always open to you, whether permanently or otherwise. It's up to you."

Drake walked from the library, leaving behind a stunned and worried Roni. She chalked up his strange behavior to the problem with his father. And their argument tonight probably bothered him more than he let on. If their quarrel involved a legal matter, Roni knew they would eventually turn the problem to her for handling.

Her thoughts returned to Drake's offer of marriage. For him to ask her to marry him just to ease his father's mind, meant matters were worse than she originally thought.

CHAPTER 19

"Is Marcus upstairs?" Geoff stood in the doorway of the breakfast room.

Roni set her cup of coffee down.

Drake laid his newspaper aside. It was plain his brother-in-law was out of sorts. Lately, that seemed to be his usual attitude. He was going to have to talk with Geoff and get to the bottom of his dissatisfaction before it spilt over into the company.

Maybe Geoff was upset because his father had given Drake full reign of the company and he had stayed in the same position instead of rising to take Drake's job. Whatever, he'd have to get over it, the sooner the better.

The early morning sun glinted off the bay window into Geoff's eyes. He raised his hand to shield his face, moving further into the room, out of the sun's glare.

"He hasn't come to breakfast yet, but he should be down soon." Not too sure why his brother-in-law was here, Drake asked, "Is something wrong? Are Sam and the kids okay?"

"Yes, they're fine. And no, nothing's wrong." He shifted his weight. "Marcus called last night. Said he wanted to see me first thing this morning, but didn't say why. It appears he's forgotten." Geoff rammed his hands inside his pant pockets looking frustrated.

Drake wondered if his father had been so upset with him he called Geoff. No, that's foolishness. His dad wouldn't involve Geoff in this mess. The fewer people who knew the better.

"Have a cup of coffee and sit down. He should be here any minute now. Or would you like some breakfast?"

"I ate at the house." Geoff moved to the coffee server, filled a cup, and then leaned his hip against the buffet. He took a sip then placed the cup back on the marble top.

Drake glanced at his watch. His father must have spent a restless night after their argument. He felt bad, bad enough to give the matter a rest this morning. But if his dad didn't tell Roni by this afternoon, he would.

Geoff sat down across from Roni.

"How's Sam and the kids?" Roni gave Drake a questioning look, seemingly as confused as Drake over Geoff's behavior. "I thought I'd call her later to see if she would want to meet me for lunch."

Geoff wrinkled his brow as though he'd just noticed her. He gave a distracted nod. "She'd like that. How long are you here for?" He glanced at the empty doorway.

"For a couple of weeks. Marcus asked me to come for a visit. I took some time off." She wrinkled her brow, watching Geoff. "I brought some work with me. May have to make a trip or two into town, but—"

"Give Sam a call. She'd love to have lunch with you." Geoff stood, glanced around the room. "I have a few things to take care of at the office before a meeting, so I'll head out. Tell Marcus I came by. Have him give me a call if it's still important."

"I'll make sure Dad knows you dropped by. I'll see you a little later."

After Geoff left the room, Drake turned to Roni.

"I need to be leaving too, but I'll check on dad before I go. It's unusual he would sleep this late, especially with you here. Maybe he isn't feeling well after all."

He chuckled. "Or maybe, he doesn't want a repeat of last night and is waiting until I leave before he comes down."

"Drake, what's driving a wedge between the two of you?"

"I'll give him the chance to tell you first. But, I promise, if he doesn't say something to you by the time I get home, then you and I will sit down and have a nice long talk. I'll explain everything." He shoved his chair back to stand.

"I'll walk up with you." Roni stood. "I left my work in the office, but I need to grab my cell phone just in case one of the partners or my assistant needs to get in touch with me."

Drake waited for her to catch up.

"I left Dallas so quickly, I think everyone was a little stunned. They'll probably be calling with questions about some of my clients. It's been a while since I've taken any time off. We've been so busy. But I promised Marcus and you."

She passed in front of him. He walked beside her through the hall and up the stairway. The scent of her freshly washed hair, her light perfume—*flowers*—filled his senses. No other woman affected him as she could.

He loved to hear her smooth, silky voice, her laughter, even enjoyed her silence. Come to think of it there wasn't much he didn't love about Roni.

When they reached the landing, she turned the opposite direction. "I'll meet you back downstairs."

Drake stood watching the gentle sway of her hips and the golden strands of wavy hair bounce around her shoulders until he felt foolish gawking like an adolescent.

He struck off toward his father's bedroom and knocked softly. When his dad didn't answer, Drake put his ear to the door but didn't hear the sound of the shower or movement in the room. He tried the doorknob and stepped inside.

"Dad?"

His father was still in bed, eyes closed. When his father didn't move or answer, his heart twisted with apprehension.

Drake rushed to the bed, touched his dad's face. His skin was cold, his lips bluish in color. He felt for a pulse but didn't find one.

Drake ran out of the room and saw Roni coming toward him.

"Roni! Call 9-1-1!"

CHAPTER 20

The medic's had come and gone, taking Marcus' body with them. They didn't say much to Drake or Roni. She kept hearing in her head, *I'm sorry. There's nothing we could do.*

This was too much like the time Roni's parents were killed and the officer said they were dead. She didn't want to believe the woman back then, just like she didn't want to believe the medics now.

Though she tried to hold it together for Drake, Roni couldn't keep back the tears. Her heart felt like it was being ripped apart. Everything seemed surreal. Any minute now, she expected Marcus to walk into the room and say something funny, or ask when she was moving back home.

She would never hear his voice again. She'd never hear his sage and *sometimes* awful advice. She'd never hear his silly jokes, the ones she'd heard a hundred times or more, but always managed to laugh. He'd never give her another hug. He would never …

Her breath hitched in her throat. The severe ache wouldn't go away.

Marcus' passing had brought back all the haunting memories of her parents' death and the remembrance of being alone—just like now. It seemed like she couldn't escape the memories of the past, at least not today.

Drake and she had moved into the living room to wait for Samantha. Even this room was filled with memories. Roni chose to sit in the loveseat with an easy view of Drake.

Marcus' overstuffed chair, bearing his imprint, unclaimed, deserted, flanked the two small sofas. Elle's chair, or at least that's how Roni always thought of the flowered chintz chair, sat at an angle with easy view of the room and entrance.

Solitary and hurting, Drake stood guard at the front bay window overlooking the drive. Outside, thick clouds masked the sun causing a gloom to settle in the room that was normally bright and cheery.

Silent, hands clasped at his back, Drake seemed to be holding it together a little better than Roni. Even though she'd had good practice at holding in her feelings, she wasn't doing such a good job at the moment.

Seeing Drake quietly mourning, Roni wished she could go to him and give him comfort. Yet she didn't know what to say without sounding trite.

What does one say at a time like this? Words, even if spoken from the heart, seem to sound commonplace and empty.

Drake leaned his head back, drew in an anguished breath, and then let it out before returning his vigil to the window. He had drawn away from her after he had talked privately on the phone with Samantha. His polite treatment of her was more like a stranger, not a friend.

His silent grief was tearing her apart. "Drake, please talk to me."

When he turned, his face showed the torment he suffered. She stood, swiped at the tears running down her cheeks, wishing she had the nerve to go to him, collect him in her arms, and drive away the hurt, but she didn't.

He walked to her instead. When he opened his arms, she slipped into his soothing embrace willingly. She prayed he would receive the comfort he needed as she was receiving comfort from him.

Drake pulled her up close, holding her head against his shoulder. His chest heaved with the grief he'd repressed since finding his father. He mingled his sorrow with hers. They stood locked together in their heartache, giving and receiving what little encouragement they had to offer.

"Roni."

His choked, muffled cry went through her like a searing iron, piercing her heart with his pain. Yet, only time would heal his lost.

"Our last words …" He swallowed. "Our last words were angry ones. How will I ever forgive myself? He died remembering my anger, not my love." He pulled away and moved to the window, his back to her again.

She felt empty and alone and unable to answer. His loss and hers were one and the same, only her last words were not angry ones

He breathed out loudly. "Forgive me. I shouldn't have burdened you with my guilt."

She moved to where he stood, slipped her arm through his, leaning her head against him.

"Drake, you could never be a burden to me." She willed him to turn to her, but he didn't. "There isn't a doubt in my mind Marcus loved you and he knew you loved him too, no matter if your last words were bitter. His pride for you was evident. I saw it last night in the midst of the squabble, even if you didn't."

Drake swiped his hand across his eyes. "I pray it is so. But how do I reconcile myself to the fact the last few days we were at odds with one another—hardly speaking except to argue?"

Taking a few moments to will her thoughts and words in order, she prayed by some small measure she could bring peace to Drake's troubles soul.

"We all have regrets. Things we didn't say and wished we had, but in time you will come to realize your father knew how you truly felt about him. Though you may have been angry and he with you, Marcus knew you loved him and you had not stopped loving him."

"I pray you're right. But ..." He lifted his shoulder then dropped them in defeat, doubt weighing him down. He backed away, breaking contact with her. "Samantha is here."

They were both in the foyer by the time Samantha burst through the front door, her face red and blotchy. In her arms, a bewildered little Ellie on the verge of bawling.

"Oh, Drake." Sam's cry sounded more like a wounded animal than a grown woman. Little Ellie howled in earnest not understanding what was taking place.

Roni knew brother and sister needed some time together.

"Hi Ellie, come to Auntie." She held out her hands and the toddler flew into her arms sobbing. Ellie nestled her face in the hollow of Roni's neck. She felt the little one's tears on her skin. Her clean baby smell began to sooth Roni's aching heart.

Sam threw herself into Drake's arms. Brother and sister commiserated each other over their mutual loss and heartache.

Ellie gave a hiccup, breathy cry looking over at her mother, and then at Roni.

"It's all right, baby girl. *Ssh-ssh*. Give Auntie another hug."

The baby latched her arms around Roni's neck again, squeezing tight, letting out a small sniffling sound.

"Auntie loves you, Sweetie-pie."

The little one grabbed Roni's cheeks. "Mommy crying." Huge tears filled the toddler's eyes and rolled down her face. Her bottom lip trembled, then she buried her face in Roni's shoulder, hanging on tight again.

Roni breathed deeply of the toddler's sweet scent, finding a solace in the little one's love and affection. Something she needed.

The foyer was filled with sounds of mourning, quiet words of consolation that did nothing to erase the pain or loss. They stood suspended in their own world of grief and misery, until it got quiet.

Samantha pulled away from her brother, staring from one to the other. "When did it happen? Was anyone with him? Did he say anything last night that made you believe he wasn't feeling well?"

Drake slid his arm around Sam's waist. "Let's go into the living room. We'll talk there." He pulled her along with him, matching his stride to his sisters.

Not sure if she should go with them or take Ellie to the playroom, Roni made up her mind and headed for the back of the house.

"Roni."

She glanced back and saw Drake standing in the entrance of the living room looking needy and unsure.

"If you don't mind, please ask Hazel to watch Ellie, and ask Charles to bring some coffee to the living room. And hurry back. I need you here." The last was barely above a whisper.

"I'll be right back." Knowing Drake wouldn't have asked if he wasn't in desperate need of her, she rushed to find Hazel.

When she returned to the living room, Samantha and Drake were sitting opposite of one another on the loveseats. Sam seemed a little more in control. She embraced Roni before slipping her shoes off. Sam sat back down again, stretching her legs out on the cushions. Picking up one of the decorative pillows, Sam hugged it to her chest and sniffled.

"Come sit down." Drake patted the cushion beside him, waiting for Roni to comply.

She joined him on the loveseat, a little flustered yet didn't know why. Drake and she had sat together like this many times before, but somehow today was different. Maybe, because today Drake needed her.

"I'm so glad you're here and not in Dallas. Drake told me how you took charge and saw to everything. Thank you." She fisted the shredded tissue in her palm then began pulling it apart. "Did you arrive in time to visit with Daddy before he went to bed last night?"

Roni felt Drake stiffen beside her. "Just for a moment. I arrived around eight. He'd already had a full day and was tired. In fact, I insisted he go to bed. Surprisingly, he did."

"That is a surprise. But then, you always did have a way with him." Sam sat in reflection. "In fact, I often teased him that he loved you more than Drake or me."

"You know that's not true." Roni didn't want either of them thinking Marcus didn't love and dote on them. She was his responsibility, someone to watch over. They were his flesh and blood.

"You and Drake were his pride and joy. After I moved out and came back for visits, all Marcus could talk about was how well you and Drake were doing, how your children were so smart and beautiful."

"I know." Samantha nodded swiping at her cheeks. "But Daddy always thought of you as one of us. And he couldn't stand it when you moved off to Dallas to work." She laughed. "I'll never forget the day you left. He told everyone *she hasn't learned where she belongs yet. I'll give her some time to find her way, then I'll make her come home.*"

A gurgle of poignant laughter erupted from Sam. "He actually thought he could tell you to come home and you would." She picked at the fringe on the pillow a sad smile in place. "He didn't realize you had become so headstrong after you received your degree and started practicing law."

Sam glanced at Drake all levity gone. "Who found him?"

Roni knew Samantha would have to be told, nothing but the details would satisfy her. Again Drake tensed beside her, this time he reached for Roni's hand and held it on his lap.

The discussion of Marcus' death and what needed to be done next followed until the room fell silent. Brother and sister both caught in their own world of memories.

"Drake, when will we be able to have Daddy's funeral?"

"I won't know until I hear back from the coroner. The medic said to call later this afternoon. We'll know something then."

Drake rubbed a hand over his eyes and released a heavy sigh. "There's something else you don't know, Sam. Something that you must know."

Charles walked into the front room with the coffee tray. Everyone sat silently while he served the coffee, then left.

"What?" Samantha questioned.

"Saturday afternoon, during Dad's party, we had a visitor."

"Who? I didn't see anyone."

"You wouldn't have. He didn't come to the party, he came to the house." He glanced at Roni. "Roni and I met him in the library."

"What did he want?"

"He wanted to see Dad, but I wouldn't let him. He claims to be our brother, Dad's son."

"Our *what?*" Sam's legs swung off the cushion, her feet slapped the floor. She glanced at both of them as though they had lost their minds. "And you didn't think I would need to know this? Why wasn't I told? And why are you just now telling me?"

She shot to her feet, sparks of anger radiating from her red, puffy eyes, fists on her hips.

"Until Roni is through researching his claim, I thought it best to keep it between the two of us."

"Did Dad know about it?"

"No. With Dad's sickness and all, I didn't want him upset. I wasn't going to mention it until we were certain if this guy was truly our brother. Then, and only then, was I going to tell you or Dad."

"Well, what changed your mind and why tell me now?" Sam was hurt as if they had purposely kept her out of the loop.

"He might show up once word gets out Dad is dead." Drake gave Roni a meaningful stare. "Would you like to explain?"

Roni motioned for Sam to take her seat before she began.

"I believe what Drake is referring to is your father's will." She glanced at him to make sure she was thinking along the same lines as he.

Drake nodded.

"First off, I need to explain, the authenticity of Nick Holden's claim is very probable."

CHAPTER 21

Drake's hiss filled the silence. He withdrew his hand, leaned forward, his elbows on his knees, and then stared at the floor.

"Nick Holdum? Is that his name? Where has he been all this time?" Samantha didn't seem as upset about the man's claim as Drake.

"New York. At least that's what he claims." Drake's anger was evident.

"What have you learned about him, Roni? Is he really Dad's son—ou-our brother?"

"Everything seems to points in that direction. However, I am still in the process of checking him out. So far, the proof he offered has proven to be legitimate."

"*Humph.*" The muscle in Drake's jaw ticked like a time bomb.

Roni turned to Drake. "I didn't have time to tell you last night, but I have hired a PI, Frank Thornton, to dig deeper into Holdum's claim." She glanced at Sam. "He was recommended by Phillip Bradley, Madison's husband."

"Was he the same one that was involved in Madison's stalker?"

"Yes. And Phillip said he was a great help in bringing that Angelo character justice." Roni cleared her throat. "Frank, or one of his men, will be flying to New York today or tomorrow to check into Nick's relatives, neighbors, job, anything that will help to prove or disprove his claim."

Drake didn't say anything, he didn't have to, she could feel his anger.

"Do either of you know where your father's will might be?"

"I know Daddy had one." Sam moved the charm back and forth on the chain hanging around her neck. "William Thompson in Athens was the one who drew up Mama's and Daddy's will. He would have a copy, wouldn't he?" Sam directed her question to Drake.

"I would think so. There might be a copy at the office in the safe also."

Drake sat back, rolled his tight shoulders a couple of times. "I'll check this afternoon when I make the trip to the office. We need to make the staff aware of what has taken place. And though they may have already heard, we need to make a formal announcement."

He turned to Roni. "Can he claim one-third of the estate?"

She didn't have to ask who. "I won't know until I get a look at the will." She hoped Marcus had set it up to protect his estate for Drake and Samantha. But if Holdum was his son, he had a right to some of the estate also.

Drake shook his head. "What a mess."

"Why borrow trouble until we know for sure." Roni hated what she needed do, but with everything so delicate concerning Holdum, she forged forward. "Drake, I'll go with you to pick up the will."

"Is that necessary?" He nailed her with a puzzled stare.

"Yes."

"What's going on, Roni. Why the cloak and dagger routine?" Samantha studied her intently.

Roni tried to laugh it off. "There's no cloak and dagger. I haven't read Marcus' will and I don't want any surprises. I need to know if Nick was mentioned in his will. Plus, Mr. Thompson or I will have to present the will to probate."

"This is all too much to grasp. First, daddy's death, and now, I have another brother."

"I know, but Drake needed to tell you. With your father's death, Holdum may appear and make claims. I need to be prepared to head off a disaster. Nick Holdum is way too clever by far."

"What do you mean?"

Drake's scrutiny had Roni doing her best not to show she was holding back Holdum's surprise meeting yesterday. "The man seems to know a lot about your father and his business. He also has a ready answer for just about everything."

"You've spoken to him since Saturday?"

Roni knew she couldn't lie to Drake. "Yes."

"And you didn't think it important enough to mention?"

"Drake, I didn't have time last night, and then this morning … well."

"Where?"

His question threw her off-kilter. "What do you mean?"

"Where and when did you speak to him?"

"He dropped by the office yesterday. I gave him the forms to get a DNA test."

"I thought you said his claim was good." Drake countered.

"I did. However, until all the facts are in, I'm treading cautiously. We've got to wait for the DNA test."

"He took one?" Drake sounded skeptical.

"Yes, yesterday, after he left my office. I should have the results this week. Until then, well let's just say I'm reserving my judgment of the man."

When Drake gave her a questioning look, she said, "You know as well as I do, while he was here Saturday, he showed signs of animosity toward your father, way beyond the norm.

In fact, I would say he came here with the express intent of making your father's life miserable. At least Marcus has been spared that indignity."

"Excuse me Mr. Drake." Charles stood in the living room entry, plainly upset. "A Detective Jeffers wants to speak to you."

"Is he on the telephone?"

"No, Sir." The old man was flustered. "They're waiting in the entry."

Everyone stood.

"What do you think they want?" Samantha grabbed her chain, holding tightly to the charm.

"I don't know, Sam. Probably a formality. I'll go see." Drake's sharp answer didn't do anything to calm his sister.

Roni's heart twisted. The police coming to the house wasn't a good sign. They wouldn't be here on a routine death, but she wasn't about to mention that fact.

They were met in the entryway with two men wearing suits and ties, with several dressed in jumpsuits carrying cases marked forensic.

Sam hung back by the living room entrance, anxiously watching.

Charles stood to the side out of the way.

"I'm Drake Peters. May I help you?" He walked up to the man standing in front of the others.

"Are you the son of Marcus Peters?"

"Yes."

Roni knew by their demeanor this wasn't a routine visit.

"I'm Detective Luke Jeffers and this is Detective Will Timmons. These other men are from Athens' forensics."

Jeffers, a little older than Drake, was all business with his dark astute eyes and black hair cut military style. He took stalk of the room with one sweeping glance, including poor Samantha.

He held out a folded paper to Drake. "This is a warrant to search the premises. We are here to collect evidence in the murder of Marcus Peters."

CHAPTER 22

Sam's gasp drew everyone's attention. She moved up next to Drake, latched on to his arm, trembling. "That can't be right. Daddy was sick. Had cancer. Drake, tell them."

"And you are?"

"This is my sister Samantha Hanson." Drake put an arm around Sam pulling her into his side.

Detective Jeffers nodded, his glance swept over to Roni, then back to Drake. He pointed to the paper Drake held. "The search warrant gives us the right to search these premises. Would someone like to show the team where Mr. Marcus Peters' room is?"

"May I see that, please?" Roni held out her hand as all eyes turned to her.

Drake gave Roni the document. She skimmed over the pages quickly to note where the search would be conducted, then folded the document.

"And you are?" asked Detective Jeffers.

His penetrating gaze would have unnerved most people, but not her. Roni figured she was in for some small town law enforcement charm of putting the little lady in her proper place.

"I'm Veronica Reeves, of Danton, Purser, and Reeves, Attorneys at Law. I represent the Peters family."

"Were you called to be present because of Mr. Peter's murder?"

"No. We were not aware Marcus was murdered. We were under the impression his death was due to cancer."

"Well, Ms. Reeves, you will find the search warrant is in order and signed by Judge Ferris. Is there somewhere we may talk while my men go over the crime scene? I have a few questions to ask."

"Certainly." Roni smiled sweetly, knowing men often underestimated her ability in her capacity as a lawyer because of her young appearance. "Will the living room do?"

"That will be fine." He motioned to those behind him. "And my men?"

"Charles will take care of your men."

She moved to where Charles stood waiting. "These men are here for the *sole* purpose of searching *Mr. Peters'* bedroom for evidence." She gave him a direct, meaningful look. "If you will show them to his suite, I would appreciate it. And, Charles, please wait in the room while they make their search. The search is for *his suite only*. Do you understand?"

Charles nodded, worry imbedded in his brow. "Yes, Ms. Veronica."

"Good." Roni patted Charles on the shoulder to sooth his concern. She wanted him to know she was depending on him to follow her orders implicitly. Then she motioned to the men standing by Detective Jeffers. "If you'll follow Charles, gentlemen, he'll take you to Mr. Peters' room."

Seeing Samantha's blanched face, Roni knew this would be tough on her. "Shall we?" She motioned toward the living room.

Detective Jeffers and Drake waited for Roni and Samantha to pass. Roni hooked her arm in Samantha's as they moved into the room.

"What's going on?" Sam's words were barely audible.

"Nothing to worry about. It's purely a formality." She hoped she was right. But a coroner rarely made the mistake of calling a death from natural causes, murder. Something was terribly wrong.

"Please, Detective Jeffers, have a seat." Roni sat across from him, while Drake slid in beside Samantha. "How may we help you?"

"I have a few questions." He turned his attention to Drake. "I understand Marcus Peters was a widower. Is this correct?"

"Yes. My mother died two years ago."

"Are there other children besides you and your sister?"

Detective Jeffers didn't miss Drake's hesitation nor his questioning deferment to Roni.

"Is there a problem—something I should know?"

Roni figured he'd find out on his own, might as well tell him up front. "At the moment we are in the process of proving up a claim brought up by Nick Holdum. On Saturday he showed up at the house claiming Marcus was his father, which claim is still in the investigative phase."

"Would you say this Nick Holdum was angry with your father?" He directed the question to Drake.

Drake didn't hesitate. "Yes. However, I'd say he was more upset with me for not allowing him to see dad."

"I see." He turned to Roni. "I will need Holdum's contact information."

"I'll get it to you before you leave. I have it upstairs." She noticed the Detective's curiosity, yet surprisingly, he returned his attention to Drake.

"Mr. Peters, when your father retired for the night, who was in the house?"

"Please call me Drake, Detective. And in answer to your question, the only people in the house were Ms. Reeves, Charles, our all-around man—the one who answered the door and is upstairs with your men—and Hazel, our cook and housekeeper, and of course, me."

The Detective's dark stare swung back around to Roni. "How long did you stay last night, Ms Reeves?"

"I never left." If she hadn't been watching the officer closely she might have missed the spark of interest.

"Do you live here?"

"No."

"But you stayed the night?"

"Yes." Roni knew what he was thinking, but if he wanted to know why, he would have to ask.

"Were you here on business?"

"Partly." She could see the Detective was getting irritated.

"Isn't it a bit unusual for an attorney to do a sleepover at a clients' house?"

"I wouldn't know, Detective, is it?" She wanted to laugh.

His hard gaze locked with hers. "Would you please explain the nature of your *sleepover* last night? Were you here to discuss business with Mr. Peters or his son Drake?"

"Neither." She smiled sweetly. Not wanting to get on the bad side of the Detective, if there was one, she figured she'd assuage his curiosity. "Mr. Peters gave me an invitation to stay at the ranch as his guest for a couple of weeks. And since I had some vacation time, I thought it might be a nice change from Dallas."

"Which Mr. Peters invited you?"

"Marcus."

"Does he do this often?"

"To me, yes." She showed no reaction to his questions. "To dispel your suspicions, Marcus and his wife Elle were my guardians for over nine years. When I moved to Dallas and became a partner in the firm of Purser, Danton, and Reeves, I had a standing invitation to come home anytime."

"I see. And do you live here?" He directed his question to Drake

"Yes."

"And you were here all night?"

"Yes."

"Did either of you hear anything out of the ordinary during the night? Or see any signs of a break in?"

"No." Both Drake and Roni answered.

Detective Jeffers continued his questioning. He even asked Samantha a few. Though visibly upset, Sam took his inquiry quite well. When he asked if they knew of any reason someone would want to kill Marcus, Samantha began to cry in earnest.

Drake wrapped his arm around his sister's shoulder. "We have no idea who would do this. And I can't imagine how anyone got into the house without waking us. Only family members and staff have a key and know the security code."

"I'll need a list of those people, please."

Roni mentally ticked off each name Drake gave Detective Jeffers. The question of who and why gnawed at her gut, but she couldn't come up with an answer.

"At this time, that's all the questions I have for you. But I would like to speak with—" He flipped back the pages of notes and stopped, the tip of his pin making a checkmark. "—Hazel."

Roni stood. "I'll be happy to take you to her. But first, I have a question for you, Detective Jeffers."

Jeffers watched her closely, a little surprised. "All right."

"If Marcus didn't die from natural causes, what was his cause of death?"

He glanced around the room at its occupants. "By suffocation."

CHAPTER 23

Reeling from the detective's report, Roni wondered who would suffocate Marcus and why? It would have to be someone with strength enough to hold him down while he fought off his assailant. Though he was in a weakened condition, she knew Marcus would have put up one remarkable fight.

"Samantha, why don't you come with us so you can take Ellie home?"

When she saw the question in Detective Jeffers' eyes, Roni answered, "Ellie is Samantha's three-year-old daughter, named after her grandmother. Hazel is watching her in the playroom."

She waited for Sam to stand. "I think it would be a bit disconcerting for the child to see all of your men traipsing about. It would be better if she were taken home, less unsettling for the child. Unless you have more questions for Samantha."

"Not at this time."

They all moved to the doorway. "If you need me any further, Detective Jeffers, I'll be in the library." Drake motioned to the room across the foyer.

Entering the playroom, Ellie ran to her mama. Samantha scooped her up into her arms and gave Ellie a big hug and kiss.

Hazel stood to leave the room.

"Hazel."

"Yes?"

"This is Detective Jeffers from the Athens' Police Department." Seeing the woman's worried look, she added, "You have nothing to worry about. He wants to ask you a few routine questions. If you would please, show him to the breakfast room and offer him a cup of coffee."

Roni glanced at the officer. "I'm sure, Detective, you could use some. And the breakfast area is as good a place as any to ask your questions. Hazel will be happy to offer you some of her Strawberry Dream Cake too."

"Thank you. I'll take you up on the coffee." He patted his flat stomach. "I'll have to pass on the cake."

His smile made him look almost friendly, but Roni knew he was anything but. He was here ready to jump on anything he thought to be a clue to Marcus' murder. He'd ask questions until he found his suspect, which suited her fine.

When Hazel and Detective Jeffers left the room, Sam rounded on Roni. "What's going on? Why is he questioning everyone?"

"He has to eliminate all of us as suspects so he can move on to find the person responsible for your father's death. And since we don't know who that person is, and he doesn't either, he's working on the process of elimination."

"Why would he think we were suspects? None of us would do such a thing."

Ellie fidgeted in her mother's arms straining toward Roni. When she reached out to Ellie, the child virtually jumped into her arms.

"We know that, but Detective Jeffers doesn't. So we answer his questions truthfully, and hopefully, he moves on." She squeezed Ellie. "Give Auntie a kiss before you go."

Ellie gave her a big, wet, sloppy kiss, squirmed to get down, and then ran toward the foyer.

Ronie walked with Samantha to the front door. "Don't worry. Everything is going to be all right." Her gut told her otherwise. "Go home. Get some rest. I'll call you if we hear anything."

"You better."

"I promise. Give my love to the boys."

She waited for Samantha to drive off before she stepped back inside. Charles and the other men were coming down the stairs. She wished she could be privy to their thoughts as they filed out the door and to their vehicles.

Detective Timmons, balding, in his fifties, and not as buff as Jeffers, stayed behind. "Do you know where I might find my partner?"

"Certainly, I'll take you to him."

When Roni and Timmons stepped into the breakfast room, she heard Jeffers' voice.

"Would you say he was violently angry, enough to harm Mr. Peters?"

"I don't think so. But I've never seen Mr. Drake so upset with his father before."

"Do you know what the fight was about?"

"No sir, it's not my business to listen. I just heard raised voices."

"Detective Jeffers, Detective Timmons is here to see you." Roni stepped aside to allow the man to pass.

Timmons nodded for Jeffers to step out of hearing range.

"Oh, Ms. Roni, I hope I didn't cause trouble, but ..." Hazel, in tears, looked worried.

Roni soothingly rubbed the woman's shoulder. "No need to be concerned. Just tell the Detective what you know. All I ask is you tell the truth and don't speculate on what you don't know. Okay?"

Hazel sniffled, nodding. "He asked me how Mr. Drake and Mr. Peters got on. When I hesitated, he asked if they'd been on the outs lately. I told him about their fightin' for the last couple of days. The policeman seemed very interested. I tried to tell him this wasn't normal. They rarely had words. But he didn't seem to listen." She wiped her cheek. "He kept asking about the fight they had yesterday evening." Hazel gave Roni a pitiful look. "Did I do wrong?"

Continuing to rub Hazel's shoulder Roni said, "No, you did nothing wrong. Everything will be all right."

The men stepped back into the room and Detective Jeffers directed his gaze pointedly at Roni. "I need to speak with Charles. Would you mind asking him to come to the breakfast room?"

"I'll go find him." Poor Hazel was practically over the edge, way past her endurance. "If you are through with Hazel, I think she could use some rest. I believe she has reached her capacity for distress."

At first, Roni didn't think Jeffers would agree, but when he saw the woman, he nodded.

"If I have more questions, I'll come back tomorrow when things are a little more settled."

"Thank you." Roni gave an appreciative smile. "Hazel, why don't you go lie down for a while?"

"What about lunch?"

"I think we know where the kitchen is and it won't be the first time we've made our own sandwich."

"Thank you, I do feel a might under the weather. I'm plum frazzled out."

"Take the afternoon off. And don't worry about dinner. We can fend for ourselves."

All during the exchange she could feel Detective Jeffers' eyes on her. When she glanced up, he had a strange expression. Maybe he couldn't imagine her in the capacity of a hard-nose attorney.

Well, he'll be in for a rude awaking if he comes after Drake or Samantha. No one goes after her loved ones—not even a murderer.

CHAPTER 24

"The detective was quite interested in the argument between Marcus and you." Roni's heart beat triple time. She hated to bring up the subject with Drake already feeling the weight of what took place.

"The argument was mentioned by Hazel, and though he didn't want to say anything, by Charles also. The police will look at you strongly as a suspect."

"That's nonsense." He paced to the window and stood with his back to her, his fingers rubbing his neck. "Everyone knows I wouldn't lift a hand to my father or to anyone." He tilted his head skyward, his shoulders bowed with the weight of all that was taking place.

"Yes. But the police don't know you personally. As a matter of routine, the first place the authorities look for a suspect is at family members and close acquaintances before they investigate elsewhere. And since he died in this house and there are no signs of a break in ..." She shrugged, doing her best to calm her racing heart.

"Drake, look at me, please. This isn't the time to be angry or upset. This is the time for strategy."

He turned giving her his full attention.

"I don't believe for a second you are guilty or that you are even capable of such an act. However, the way Detective Jeffers was acting when he left, it won't surprise me if they call you in for questioning."

"He can't believe I had anything to do with dad's death."

"Right now, he's looking at all of us closely." She took a breath doing her best to still her emotions. "You need to be extremely careful what you say if they do call you in. Don't give them anything other than direct answers. Yes or no when at all possible, adding nothing—much like you did today. If they call you in and I'm not around, make sure you invoke your right to have an attorney present. Call me immediately. Don't answer questions until I'm with you. They have to honor your request."

"Do you really think it will come down to that?"

"I honestly don't know." Her gut feeling was *yes*. "But we must be prepared in case. If you are called in for questioning, as your lawyer, I will be by your side the whole time. I will do my best to steer them away from the argument, but I'm sure they won't be deterred since that's the only thing they have."

Roni took a deep breath, not wanting to say what had to come next. "As your attorney, they can't ask me questions about you or anything you might say to me. They also can't make me testify against you in court. Attorney-client privilege."

"Roni." He watched her closely. "You don't believe I killed Dad, do you?"

She touched his arm, wanting to infuse the truth of her answer. "No, Drake. You are not capable of such an act."

Roni motioned for him to sit down. "Please, so I won't have to crane my neck looking up at you."

When he did, she took the chair opposite of him. "Now, I need to know what you and your father argued about. And we have no time for hedging. I have to know everything down to the smallest detail."

He shook his head without looking at her.

"Drake, listen to me. This is not the time to be stubborn. In order for me to help you, I have to know what the argument was about. Otherwise, I don't know how to deal with what looks like a motive for murder to the authorities."

He shook his head again. When he glanced up, Roni saw the raw pain in his eyes, yet she had no words to ease the hurt.

"If, as you suspect, the police charge me, I will tell you everything. But until then …" Again he shook his head and stood without looking at her.

Roni got up and moved next to him, then touched his back. "I can't possibly know how to defend you without knowing what took place. What is so horrific that you can't tell me?"

Roni could see her efforts were futile. "I'm your friend and your lawyer. You tie my hands, Drake. I hope you know your stubbornness may cost you your freedom."

He shrugged away from her touch, the insult wounding deeply.

"Drop it Roni. If it comes down to them charging me, I'll tell you but not before. So don't pressure me, because it's not going to happen." He moved away, heading for the door. "I need to get dressed to go to the office. If you're going with me, I suggest you do the same."

Riveted with shock over Drake's rude behavior, Roni watched him storm from the room. She knew it wasn't in his nature to be cruel. Yet it didn't lessen the blow to her heart.

CHAPTER 25

For the first time Drake could remember, he'd hit an all-time low. With the nasty business of discovering first his father's underhanded dealings, then his murder, and now the possibility of becoming the number one suspect, everything seemed to be crashing down around him. Still, it was no excuse for him to take his frustration out on Roni.

His behavior was despicable. As if he didn't have enough troubles, he had to complicate matters more by allowing his frustration and temper to alienate Roni.

He owed her an apology, which he'd give first thing, that is, if she would speak to him. Drake knew saying *I'm sorry* wouldn't make up for his disgusting behavior. She'd probably tell him to go jump in the lake.

He couldn't blame her. If need be, he'd beg on bended knee, then go jump in the lake.

The door opened and a cautious looking Roni walked into the library. His gut twisted knowing he was the cause of her uncertainty.

She looked beautiful. Come to think of it, beautiful couldn't begin to describe her. She was the essence of loveliness. Today, the blue of her eyes seemed bluer and her hair shimmered like gold, drawing Drake like a magnet. He would like nothing better than to gather her in his arms, breath in her essence, and beg for her forgiveness for all the wrongs done. Somehow, he knew he didn't dare act on his feelings—apologize, yes. Hold her, no. She wouldn't welcome his touch.

Beneath her eyes were faint traces of dark half-moons she hadn't been able to hide with makeup. Shame filled him with the knowledge she not only had to deal with his father's death, she was dealing with his own rude behavior.

"Shall I make lunch since Charles and Hazel were dismissed for the day?" She appeared reticent and withdrawn.

"If you'll agree, I have a better idea."

"What do you have in mind?"

"First off, I need to tell you I am a jerk. And I'm so sorry about how I acted earlier." He walked around the desk separating them, leaned on the edge, then reached for her hands holding them gently.

"I have no excuse, except I'm an idiot. However, I beg you to forgive me. Please accept my apology for how I acted and spoke to you."

Roni glanced down. "It's not necessary. We're all under a great amount of stress. But if you need my forgiveness you have it." She locked her gaze with his, a tentative smile in place. "Apology accepted."

He pulled her into a hug, doing his best to make it friendly, but couldn't help but notice how sweet she smelled and how right she felt in his arms.

"Thank you, Roni. Your forgiveness means more to me than you will ever know. I'll do my best to reign in my temper from now on."

Her chuckle made him pull back and give her a suspicious look.

"Not sure you'll be able to reign in your temper, but I'll remind you if you forget."

"Gee, thanks, just what I needed, your vote of confidence." He gave her a hangdog look then smiled.

"Lunch … Since it's already late and we need to go to the office, how does the Marina Restaurant sound?"

"You want to leave now?"

"As soon as you're ready. We'll have a nice quiet late lunch-early dinner. We won't talk about what might or might not happen, though it will be on both our minds. And then after we have eaten, we can talk about dad and how much we will both miss him. We'll celebrate the good times. How does that sound?" He could see she was on the verge of tears.

"I'd like that. It'll do us both good to get out of the house."

"I agree. We need to be at the office at three for the all-hands meeting. We'll get there in plenty of time."

"I'll grab my things and meet you in the entry."

Drake's gaze followed her when she left. If only he had told Roni how he felt about her on Saturday. Speaking now was out of the question. He'd have to wait until his father's murderer was caught.

He prayed she wouldn't go back to Dallas. If she did leave, he wouldn't like it, but he'd accept the decision as best for her.

His thoughts turned to Peters Corp. He'd been trained for this day—to take over the company—just not like this.

The thing gnawing at his gut the worse wasn't the company, the work, or the chain of command, but his last words to his father. Hot, angry words filled with derisive accusations replayed in his mind and doing a good job of tearing him up inside.

Would he ever be able to forgive himself? *Not likely.*

CHAPTER 26

Except for the unspoken cloud hanging over them, lunch with Drake turned out to be all Roni had hoped and more. The lake, food, and even the service were exceptional. And the coconut cream pie Drake insisted she order was the best ever. Maybe the reason the pie tasted so good, they shared the huge slice.

The hour helped Roni to relax some and get her second wind. She was certain an onslaught of anxious moments would be coming sooner than later, at least until the murderer was caught.

The probability of the police looking at Drake as a suspect had Roni refusing to take the tack *wait and see*. She would put into motion plans to hopefully keep Drake out of jail. Taking a look at the corporate contracts gone bad or labor disputes would be her first priority. She'd search for the out-of-the-ordinary transactions, concentrate on troubled areas, and then maybe she'd someone other than Drake responsible for Marcus's death.

"What has you in deep thought?" Drake pulled into the company parking space reserved for him before turning off the engine.

"Nothing worth mentioning."

"You don't look this zoned out unless something *is* worth mentioning. Want to bounce it off me?"

"Not really."

"Well, if you do, remember we make a pretty good team."

"I know we do. And if I'm ever in need of help, you'll be the first I ask."

"It looks like I'll be asking for your help, if what you say is true, that I'm a suspect." He gave her crooked grin with an apprehensive look. "Would you mind accompanying me when I speak to the employees?"

Worried over Drake's emotional state, since she'd never witnessed his vulnerability before, she answered, "I'll be right beside you. I hope you know I'll do whatever I can."

"Yes, and I'm grateful."

Drake got out of the car. When he opened Roni's door, he waited for her to get out and then matched his stride to hers.

Roni slid her arm though Drake's with a need for human touch as much for him as for her. Her loss of Marcus didn't compare with Drake's. To lose your father, and then to be hit with the information someone killed him, and now you were under suspicion, would make it difficult to cope.

They walked inside the building and found the news of Marcus' death was already known. The guard on duty greeted Drake with condolences. Others they passed expressed the same sentiment.

When they entered Marcus' office, Geoff was there looking a bit bewildered, his hair ruffled as though he'd forgot to comb it, a sad, disturbed look on his face.

"The all-hands meeting is set for three as you requested." Geoff fidgeted with his collar, craning his neck. "Drake, I'm sorry about Marcus. We'll all miss him. If there's anything I can do just let me know."

"Thanks, Geoff." Drake glanced at his watch. "Roni and I have a few things to go over. We'll see you at the meeting."

Drake headed toward his father's desk, stopped, and then turned around. "Geoff thanks for everything."

"Don't mention it. He was like a father to me." Geoff hesitated for a moment, as if waiting for further instructions, took one final look around, then left. "I'll see you in a few minutes."

Maybe like her, Geoff felt the overwhelming presence of Marcus in the room. Drake had kept his own office. His father's was untouched for those times when Marcus would pop in to check on things, as he liked to put it. She heaved a sign. *No more.*

After Drake opened the safe, Roni found a bag, and feeling a bit like an intruder into Marcus' private affairs, she shoved all the paperwork into the sack, cleaning out the safe of all documents, and then put the bag back into the safe, closed and locked the door.

"I've collected everything but thought it best to keep it locked up until we are ready to head home. I will go over the documents there."

A noise at the door drew their attention.

Nick Holdum stepped into the room, his eyes narrowed in suspicion, fists balled, looking like a fight waiting to happen.

"What's this I heard about Marcus?"

Drake with equal anger, advanced on Holdum.

Roni caught hold of Drake's arm, doing her best to stop him from doing something he'd regret later. Under her breath she said, "Please, let me handle this. It will do no good for you to knock him out cold."

Drake took an angry breath, holding a stance equal to Nick's.

"Mr. Holdum, please have a seat." Roni motioned to one of the side chairs, gave Drake a signal to also sit down. He did. For a second or two Roni thought he might not. "How did you come by this information?"

"Well did he or did he not die? Or is this a ruse thinking I'd go home. If it is, you've figured wrong. I'm here and don't plan on leaving anytime soon."

Roni couldn't believe he would speak so outrageously. "I'm sorry to say you heard correctly. Mr. Peters passed away late last night. We are all still in shock, mourning his death."

"Why wasn't I called? I bet you were hoping I wouldn't find out the old man had kicked the bucket."

"Why you-u-u—" Drake rose from his chair.

Roni stood, her look pleading with Drake. "Please, this will settle nothing."

Drake eyed Holdum like he was a specimen he would love to dissect piece by piece.

"Mr. Holdum, it would be best for all concerned if you left the premises. There's nothing here for you."

Nick stared at Roni as if she were joking. "Yes, I can well imagine you would like nothing better than to get rid of me." A derisive smile rode his lips.

"Let me explain something to both of you. I'm not leaving town, at least not until I have checked with an attorney about my rights. As a son, I should be entitled to a portion of the estate. He owes me big time. I intend to collect."

"Leave now, before I call a guard to throw you out." Drake's harsh words were forced through gritted teeth as he pointed at the door. "And don't come back."

"I'll leave bro." Holdum, with a smug look in his eyes, stood but didn't leave. "But you haven't seen the last of me. I intend to make my presence known. And I won't be careful who knows I'm Marcus Peters' son." He strolled to the door then stopped to stare at Roni.

"How's the DNA test coming, counselor? Received proof yet?" His grin was self-assured and meant to needle Drake.

It worked like a charm. By Drake's barely controlled breathing Roni knew his fuse was about to blow.

"I should hear something before the end of the week. I'll call when I do."

"I expect you will." Holdum raised a brow. "By the way, Veronica, I did some checking into your background." The glint in his eyes told her he enjoyed playing games.

"Glad to hear it. You never can be too careful when dealing with people you *don't* know." He had probably looked into the law firm and her credentials, which was fine with her. She had nothing to hide. If he asked around, he would know he wasn't dealing with a silly woman who would be easily duped or manipulated.

"Your track record is impressive. But I did have a question." His devious glance swung at Drake and then back to her. "Why would you be in bed with the Peters' Corp and someone like dear ol' daddy?"

Drake's hiss had Roni moving closer to him, hoping to step between the two men if need be.

"But then you are a lawyer and business is business. Hopefully they haven't talked you into making any investments." Holdum's smile was anything but genuine.

Something was up. Roni felt it in her bones. Holdum had a hidden agenda, but what? Was it to irritate Drake and provoke him into losing his temper? Or was there something more sinister behind his words? With Drake, he was close to accomplishing his goal.

"Thanks for your concern, but my investments are my business."

"Well … you'd best take heed. It seems the Peters' have a way of duping people out of their life's savings and then getting away scot-free." He sent Drake a loathing, meaningful look. "Have you told Veronica about her parent's investment? Or was it something she'll have to find out on her own?"

Drake's face hardened yet he said nothing.

Holdum's laughter, nasty and harsh, chilled Roni to the bone as the room fell silent.

Roni, completely baffled to Holdum's reference, wouldn't give him the satisfaction of shock or question. She figured when he left, she'd ask Drake if he knew what Holdum was talking about.

"Well, since I seemed to have hit a sore spot with my brother, I think I'll take my leave." He walked out the door. "You have my number, Veronica," he shot over his shoulder. "I'll be waiting to hear from you. Maybe we could have dinner sometime soon." His laughter floated down the hall.

Drake moved to the desk, angrily punched a number on the telephone. "Make sure the man you directed to my father's office leaves the premises. And in the future, *do not* allow him to get any farther than the front desk. Do I make myself clear?" The veins in his neck bulged. He slammed the receiver down, but didn't turn to look at Roni.

Her stomach tightened. A chill coiled at the base of her spine. The terrible feeling of impending disaster hung in the room. It brought back the memory of when she was told her parents were dead. As back then, today something was terribly wrong, and it had nothing to do with Holdum, but everything to do with her.

CHAPTER 27

Drake didn't have time to deal with Holdum's innuendos. Not now. Not ever. But there'd be no getting around the elephant in the room.

In addition to coping with his father's death, he had to clean up the mess he'd left behind. And there was no way to avoid what would come next. How could so many things go so wrong at one time? And how did Holdum learn about what his father had buried years ago?

He didn't have to look to know Roni's eyes were drilling holes into his back ... he felt them. She wanted and deserved an explanation. However, Holdum's underlying accusations weren't so simple to answer and would take more time than what he at this moment.

"Drake, do you want to explain what Nick was hinting at?"

He wanted to alleviate her concerns, but it wasn't that simple. And at the moment, he needed her help. He knew it was selfish on his part, but he needed her sharp mind focused and willing to help field the questions they would receive from the meeting. But more importantly, he knew telling her could sever their relationship.

Drake turned and saw what he hadn't witnessed since the first day he met Roni—distrust. He should have knocked Holdum out cold before he gave Roni reason to doubt him.

"Right now I need you to focus on this meeting. Holdum seems to have the knack for stirring up trouble at the wrong time. And this isn't the time to divert our thoughts to his accusations. Are you with me?"

Roni stared at him, her eyes cold and sharp. He could tell she wasn't happy with the dissolution of the bomb Nick dropped on them. But being the professional she was, she nodded.

"What do you need from me?" She moved to her briefcase, pulled out her iPad, switching it on.

A ton of weight on his shoulders hadn't lifted exactly, but had at least shifted, giving him breathing room. He would deal with the problem when he had more time and effort to put toward all of the questions he knew Roni would ask. She deserved to know what his father failed to tell her years ago. And the unpleasant job was left to him.

An unspoken truce took place as they worked. Since Drake had been acting for his father for the last six months, Roni believed it would work best to show a solid front. And though they were in mourning over the loss of Marcus, it would be business as usual. Drake would continue to mirror his past months' performance and his father's former leadership with innovative management.

"No mention should be made as to the ongoing investigation of murder." Roni looked up from her notes to Drake. "If the question arises, just say, *at this time I have no comment*. Then add, as soon as you know something tangible it'll be known to them as well.

"For the most part, that should stop the questions at the meeting, but won't do a thing about conjectures or speculations circulating. You'll have to deal with those on a one-on-one, need-to-know basis."

"I agree." Drake marveled at her calm demeanor and how she could switch from curious to all business. He glanced at the clock on the wall behind his father's desk. "We should go. They're probably anxious to hear what's going to take place."

"Just reassure them as much as possible Peters' Corporation is solvent and capable of continuing in the manner it has for the past thirty years. I believe all they want to hear from you is they still have their jobs, the doors will remain open, and Peters Corp will continue status quo."

"I keep saying this, Roni, but thank you for being here and giving me your support." He hoped she would recognize the sincerity and truth of his words. "And though I still can't accept what has happened, you being here has made all this little more bearable."

Roni stacked the papers in front of her before giving him a long hard stare.

"Drake, I'm sorry for what you're going through, but know this, I'll always be here for you. Though death is enviable, no one is ready to deal with a parent's loss. However, to learn the loss is by foul play is inconceivable. You are more than capable of running this meeting today, with or without me."

"That may be true, but you being by my side will give me the confidence I need."

She closed the cover to her iPad and placed it in the crook of her arm.

"I will stand by and deflect anything you can't answer."

His heart squeezed painfully under her penetrating stare.

"However, know this. You and I *will* talk when we get home tonight. Holdum has received information from someone about my parents and yours. Whether lies to stir up trouble between us or truth to cause dissention, I'm not sure. Yet, your expression told me there's more to his words than mere unfounded accusations."

CHAPTER 28

Roni was proud of how the meeting went and how Drake deflected questions. He held up remarkably well as he gave everyone enough information to satisfy their curiosity. He let them know their jobs were not in jeopardy and the corporation or stores weren't in danger of closing.

She only stepped in to answer a couple of questions regarding the legalities—Marcus to Drake—which she explained was already in place before Marcus died.

Samantha stood on the other side of her brother, along with Geoff. Surprisingly, she held up well in spite of the wear and tear on her emotions.

Before leaving, Sam hugged Roni and whispered in her ear she needed to speak to her about something personal and private. Her words left Roni with a burning curiosity with no time to ask. Samantha was probably worried about her brother and the days ahead. She'd just have to wait and see

The strain of the death and investigation, Holdum's explosive reaction to Marcus' death, and then lastly the company meeting, all of it had given Roni one bruiser of a headache. Neither she nor Drake spoke as they grabbed the sack of documents from the safe, then headed for the ranch. She wasn't sure she had the stamina to go another round with anyone.

Drake, quiet, jaw tight, hadn't said a word. Though curious as to Nick's reference this afternoon, Roni decided to leave the explanation until later. She hoped Drake and she would be in a better mood and that he would able to answer her questions. She closed her eyes, willing the headache to go away.

Her eyes popped open when they pulled into the garage and Drake turned off the engine. The short nap had lessened her headache to a small degree.

Drake leaned his head back against the headrest, letting out a huge, heavy sigh.

Roni wasn't sure if she should wait to open the car door until he was ready to leave, or give him time alone with his private thoughts?

He turned. Tired, haunted eyes stared at her. The weight of the world seemed to press down around his shoulders, shutting him off from her reach. A vise tightened around her heart. How much more could he take before breaking?

"Drake—"

He shook his head. "Let me take a shower and get into something a little more comfortable. I'll meet you in the kitchen." His ragged, tired smile tore at her heart. "We'll raid the fridge and see what we can come up with, then we'll talk over food. How about it?"

"Something to eat sounds good, but we needn't talk tonight. It can wait until morning. I think we both could use a rest."

He grabbed her hand starring deep into her eyes. "Have I told you that you are one amazing woman? I couldn't have made it through this day without you. You gave me the confidence necessary and the strategy to make it work. We make an unbeatable team."

He squeezed her fingers, his look serious. "Please don't change. And promise me regardless what you hear or find out, you won't desert me. I won't make it if you leave me to fend for myself. I can't express how much I need you."

"Drake, you know I'm here for you. Please, what's wrong?"

"Later … I'll explain everything when we meet in the kitchen."

He was out of the car and coming around to her door before she could ask more.

Roni couldn't imagine Drake needing anyone, let alone her. She had never seen him vulnerable and needy before. His father's death was having an overwhelming effect on him. When they met to talk, she'd give him reassurance she was here for as long as he needed her.

Roni took a shower to be rid of the sludge of the day, hoping to clear her head of all the questions running amuck through her mind. And prayerfully, she'd get rid of her headache.

To some degree refreshed, Roni hurriedly dressed, hoping Drake wasn't waiting on her. She decided to pull her wet hair back in a clip and let it dry later before going to bed. A pounding on her bedroom door had her running across to answer.

Charles stood outside in the hall wringing his hands. He looked like he'd aged ten years.

"Oh, Ms. Roni, come quick. The police hauled Mr. Drake off. He said to come get you. Please hurry." Charles practically ran down the hall.

Roni caught up with him and maneuvered the stairs as quickly as she could. By the time she reached the door, the police car was pulling out of the circle heading down the long stretch of driveway to the road.

"Charles, what exactly did the police say to Drake?"

He wagged his head. "I couldn't hear them. Something about Mr. Marcus' death. I'm sorry, I'm not any help to you. It happened so quick-like."

She patted the older man's shoulder. "Don't worry. I'll get my things and drive into town. I'll see what's going on. Drake and I will be back later."

God, let it be so.

"Oh, Ms Roni, thank you. I didn't know what to do. How could they think Mr. Drake would have anything to do with his father's death? He loved Mr. Peters."

"I know he did. We'll get this straightened out. Don't worry."

Roni ran up the stairs, gathered what she needed, and then headed to the garage.

Seeing Drake's car, she barely held back the anguish she felt over his arrest. His words came back to her ... *please don't leave me regardless what you hear. I won't make it if you do.*

What if they charge him? Would she be able to get him out on bail or prove his innocence? Others have been convicted and put away with circumstantial evidence. The same could happen to Drake.

Roni's car swerved crazily out of the drive onto the blacktop road as she tromped the accelerator. She wanted to catch up with the police or at least be there before they questioned him. Hopefully, he would remember to ask for his lawyer. She pressed the connection to her cellphone on the wheel, waited for the familiar response, and then called out, *Samantha—home.* She drummed her thumbs on the steering wheel, her impatience low and her speedometer rising.

"Pick up, Sam, pick up the phone."

"Hey, Roni, what's up?"

"The police have just taken Drake to the station for questioning."

"Drake? What for?"

"I'm assuming it has something to do with your father's murder."

"First Daddy. Now Drake. When will it stop?"

Roni could hear Sam's hysteria rising on the other end.

"Sam! I need you to hold it together and listen to me." She took a deep breath, her mind racing. On the other end she heard Sam sniffle and then blow her nose.

"You know how news travels in this town. Drake being brought into the station is bound to get out. You may be plagued by reporters wanting the latest scoop. So listen, and listen carefully."

"I'm listening."

"If anyone, regardless who they say they are, calls or comes around asking questions, tell them *no comment*. Give them my telephone number. I don't want you or Geoff to speculate or discuss anything in front of the kids or with anyone about your father's death outside the private confines of your home—do you understand?"

"Yes, but …"

"Sam, listen." Roni whipped around a car, and then pulled back in the lane. "Anything you, Geoff, or anyone else might say, no matter how small or trivial, can, and will no doubt, be taken out of context to be used by the prosecutor if Drake is charged. It could also help to prove up a case against him."

"Charged? You don't think they suspect Drake, do you."

"No, I'm not saying Drake is a suspect, but whether right or wrong, one can never know where an investigation may head."

"Roni, you know he wouldn't hurt anyone—especially Daddy." Sam began sniffling again.

"I believe it's a simple case of wanting to question Drake more about the evening before Marcus's death, nothing more. But regardless, you will need to do what I say, and tell Geoff to do the same. And keep in mind, if worse happens your brother's life may depend upon on your silence."

"I understand. I'll meet you at the police station."

"No! Your coming would be the worst thing you could do. Stay home and do as I asked, please Sam … for your brother's sake."

"Okay, I'll stay home. But you call me the minute you know something."

"I will." She took a much needed fortifying breath. The picture of Drake in a room being interrogated caused her stomach to clinch and her speed to increase. "I've got to let you go. I need to make a couple more calls before I get to the station. I'll get back in touch when I know more. Love you, bye."

She hated hanging up so abruptly, but it couldn't be helped.

Roni made a call to Ed Purser detailing the witch hunt the police were on. Ed told her he'd start the ball rolling just in case, and then get back with her once he found a criminal lawyer who could be available at a moment's notice.

Next, she made a call to her investigator, Frank Thornton.

"Hi Frank?"

"Yes, ma'am. What can I do for you? I'm not quite done with the Holdum guy yet. But I can bring you up to speed on what I do have."

"Thanks, but not at this moment, I'll get it from you later. I've called because I have something far more critical for you to do."

"All right. Do you want me to turn Holdum over to my man, Walsh? He isn't busy at the moment, and he's a good investigator."

Taking a curve too fast, the car's tires went off onto the gravel. She received a jolt of adrenalin at her near miss as pebbles pinged the undercarriage and spit into the air. She managed to steer her CX5 back onto the road only to have it fishtailing down the middle of the striped line.

Roni's body shook as she gripped the steering wheel tighter and backed off the accelerator to a less dangerous speed. She wouldn't be of any help to Drake if her car landed in a ditch or she hit an oncoming car.

"Hey little lady, if that sound is what I think it is, you'd best slow down to live to see another day."

Frank's short laugh and admonition had her smiling, yet still feeling shaky.

"My thoughts exactly." With the sun hanging low and in her eye, she lowered the visor, thankful the country road had been deserted, or the outcome could have been drastically different.

She explained to Frank what took place and what she needed him to do.

He whistled through his teeth. "Hate to hear that, but I'll get right on it."

"There's a Holiday Express on Highway 31 east of town. Call me when you get here. You can come out to the ranch tomorrow and we'll talk."

"Will do. Get back with you later."

Roni entered the edge of town, slowing her speed considerably, not wanting a ticket. Turning on Murchinson Street, she pulled into a parking space in front of the jail, stopped the motor, then lowered her head on top of her hands still gripping the steering wheel. Her body trembled with repressed anger and fear. Anger, that they would suspect Drake in the first place. Fear, they might hold Drake on unfounded information. If they charged Drake for Marcus' murder, what then?

She prayed he was here for questioning only, and they weren't viewing him as a suspect. In her heart she feared the worse—*he wasn't coming home tonight.*

Athens, like any small Texas town, devoured local news like someone who hadn't eaten for days. And the report of Drake Peters, now CEO of the largest company in Athens, being hauled in for questioning for the murder of his father, would blast through the community like a forest fire run amuck.

The injustice of it all, the reputations of Drake and the Peters Corp would be at a never-before-heard-of low. If they were fortunate, the news media wouldn't make something out of nothing to muddy their good names, but highly unlikely.

She just hoped and prayed Drake had enough presence of mind not to answer any questions. Any misdirected word could have him facing a judge and jury.

CHAPTER 29

Roni maneuvered the small S turn in the road, the one where earlier she almost landed her in the ditch. Her headlights sliced the darkness shrouding their countryside. Without a car in sight, it was as if the world chose not to exist, and Drake and she were the only two people alive.

Three hours of relentless interrogation at the precinct had taken its toll on both Drake and Roni. Questions asked and answered, then asked and answered again with the same result. Roni objected over and over to their line of questioning, often instructing Drake not to answer. Still they persisted in their relentless pursuit.

Thankfully, he had been unflappable. In the heat of their brutal attacks, Drake held his tongue and temper. She could see it tore him up inside. During the whole ordeal of accusations being slung as the responsible party for his father's death, he never reacted.

As her tires ate up the distance to the Triple Cross, Roni took a quick glance at Drake. His long legs were stretched out in front of him as far as her little car would allow. Head back, eyes closed, fatigue etched deep in his brow, she had the overwhelming desire to brush away the hurt. Instead she gripped the steering wheel tighter.

How could she love Drake so deeply and he not know?

"What's the matter?"

Startled, she jerked the wheel. Her hand moved to the base of her throat. "You scared me. I thought you were asleep."

"I'm tire enough. But I'm too keyed up. Trying to rest with my mind going a million miles a minute is difficult."

He breathed in, deep and ragged. "It seems like I've been saying this on a regular basis lately, but thank you, Roni. I appreciate you being there for me with your legalese and expertise." He gave a short, gruff laugh. "I would still be answering questions or locked up if you hadn't been there."

"Just doing my job."

"Your job, *hmm*. Well, if you need a recommendation, I can testify to the fact you do your job well. You're one tough lady. I'd hate to be on the opposing side, facing you in court."

She inwardly glowed in the warmth of his praise.

"What do you think? Are they going to continue to look at me as a suspect?"

"Yes." She had to tell the truth, but she didn't need to elaborate. If she'd been the detective asking the questions, she would have nailed his hide to the wall.

"I thought so. How do we go from here to prove my innocence?"

"I've already started the ball rolling. Frank Thornton, the P.I. hired for Holdum, should be here in Athens by now. He'll snoop around, try to find out who, how, and why, and hopefully come up with our suspect, aka, the murderer."

"What can he do the police haven't already done?"

Roni turned her right blinker on, pulled her foot off the accelerator to slow down as the gate to the Triple Cross opened. "Not sure. But he comes with an excellent track record of solving cases. Hopefully, he'll work his charm on this one and find something the police overlooked."

Her high beams illuminated the tall Italian cypresses lining the sides of the concrete drive to the house. Ahead, the yard lights blazed brightly, no doubt Charles' doing, hoping for the masters' return.

How odd to think of Drake as master of the Triple Cross.

Driving around to the side, Roni parked her car, turn off the key, and then didn't move. She was too tired to drag her body out of the seat, and too weary to bring up what needed to be said.

"I'm sorry, but I have to say this before we go inside."

His brow raised in question. He didn't move, just watched her devoid of emotion.

"Unless the murderer is caught and caught soon, the police will no doubt come after you again, may even come with a warrant for your arrest. Their line of questioning tonight, all their probing, makes me believe they are looking at you heavily as a suspect for the murder. And, they may not look any further."

Drake sat silently, gazing off into space.

"I've already called Ed Purser to find an attorney in case they charge you."

He looked at her. "You won't be my lawyer? Why?"

"Yes, I am your lawyer, but you also need a criminal attorney who knows what they're doing. I've never worked on criminal cases. My expertise is corporate law, so I would do you little good. However, if it gets to the point you need defense, I will be second chair to the attorney Purser finds."

"I see. Do you think they will arrest me?" He watched her intently.

"I can't be for certain, but I'm working toward any possibility." She hated to see Drake so downbeat. "And as I mentioned earlier, Frank Thornton will be working on the other end to prove your innocence.

"However, you and I are going to have to talk. I'm not saying tonight, but in the morning, after breakfast. We'll go for a drive out on the ranch, away from any possibility of being overheard. I need an explanation what caused the rift between you and Marcus."

A long silence prevailed. Drake released an exhausted breath, nodding. "Tomorrow after breakfast. But right now, I need to wash off the filth of the precinct and try to get some rest." The tired smile he offered waned quickly. He moved out of the car shutting off any further conversation.

Silently, Roni followed Drake into the house. And as earlier, they parted heading for their separate bedrooms.

The moment her door shut, she tugged the clip from her hair, rand her fingers rapidly over her scalp, massaging as the slightly damp strands jiggled up and down then fell around her shoulders. Her mind reeled with the events of earlier. If a miracle didn't take place, a whole lot worse than what Drake experienced tonight would be coming down the pike.

Everything hinged on proving his innocence.

Who and why were the questions.

Marcus had been well-liked, respected, and didn't have enemies, at least none Roni knew about. That left only family. She couldn't believe any of them would kill Marcus, even with money as a reason. They all knew he was living on borrowed time with the inoperable cancer.

No, there had to be something she had overlooked, some hidden agenda to cause someone sneak into the house and murder Marcus. Maybe while Drake and she were eating dinner. The alarm wouldn't have been set. But who? That was something she had to find out. Drake's life was at stake.

CHAPTER 30

Two calls before one cup of coffee. So much for starting my day slow and easy.

Roni scribbled notes on a legal pad from her telephone conversations with Frank Thornton and Ed Purser. Gathering her cellphone and iPad, she headed out the door of her room to find some breakfast and hopefully, Drake.

When she reached the mid-landing her heart gave a jolt. The object of her thoughts stood at the base of the stairs looking up at her grinning. She couldn't help but reciprocate. Drake's smile was contagious, and she could always rely on him to stir her emotions.

Dressed in cargo shorts, t-shirt, no socks, and old tennis shoes, Drake looked relaxed and ready to meet the day.

"Well sleepyhead, I was about to come and get you. I'm glad to see you're dressed casual. Are you ready to go for a ride?"

She continued down the stairs, stopping in front of him. "Ride?" Then it dawned on her what Drake referred to—last night's mention of leaving the house to talk.

Her shoulders slumped. "Yes, but I need a cup of coffee and at least a piece of toast before I'm fit to go anywhere."

"Your coffee is waiting in the Jeep cup holder. Breakfast is in a heat pack in the back seat. If you can wait for about another ten minutes, you'll be fed and ready to meet the day. You can sip coffee on the run, can't you?"

His cheerful mood had her smiling. "I believe I can do that. Lead the way, master."

"Good. I thought it would be nice to at least start our day on a pleasant note, regardless how it ends."

Roni wished this whole unpleasant affair was over and done with, but knew the wish was a pipedream. "It sounds like you have everything under control. Where are we headed?"

He opened the front door. "You'll see."

Once inside the Jeep, Roni sipped at her coffee and felt the caffeine seep all the way down to her toes, warming her insides. She wondered what caused Drake to think of breakfast on the go. Whatever had given him the idea, she was grateful. This was more like a play day, not a day for facts and who did what—which would come later.

The top of the Jeep had been removed, and the cool air swirled around them as they drove down the caliche road. Normally, a white plume of dust from the tires would trail behind, but due to the predawn storm, the dust was practically nonexistent.

Roni breathed in the sweet smell of new mown hay as they passed huge rolls of golden bales waiting to be stored. On the other side, a herd of longhorns and Herefords grazed peacefully in the pasture without note of the Jeep's passing.

The day after her parents were buried, Roni was dropped off at the Triple Cross Ranch due to an agreement her parents and the Peters had drawn up years before, giving Elle and Marcus guardianship of her. When the lawyer for her folks' estate told Roni where she would be living, she begged and pleaded not to go. Her complaints about living in the middle of nowhere fell on deaf ears.

She vowed in her heart to hate the place and run away the first chance she got. One look at the Triple Cross and she was more certain than ever she wouldn't live there for long.

She knew the quiet of the wide open spaces would drive her nuts. However, with the help of Samantha, the peaceful atmosphere of the countryside began to sooth her hurting and wounded soul. Before she realized what had taken place, the Triple Cross became home.

Now she couldn't seem to get her fill of the ranch. Her guess, it all boiled down to maturity, perspective, and being with those she loved.

At the top of a rise, Drake stopped the Jeep and let it idle. He leaned his forearms on the steering wheel gazing out over the land below, and much the same of what they had already passed. However, sitting high above the land she could see for miles. To the right and at the base of the hill was a huge pond surrounded by oaks. When they were younger, Drake, Samantha, and she would come here during the summer for picnics and swimming, even with the threat of cottonmouths in the water.

"You never know what you'll miss until the threat of it all being taken from you is there waiting to happen." He waved at the land in general.

Roni knew to what he referred.

"This place holds fond memories, memories a person can't buy." Drake didn't move, just gazed at the scene of rolling hills and meadows with trees older than the both of them combined.

Roni wished she could make everything right but knew her wish wasn't reality. Things could get a whole lot worse before they got better.

Drake shoved the gearshift into first, and then tromped on the accelerated. The Jeep responded with gravel spitting up into the air. They fishtailed slightly as they careened over the hill and off the road, bouncing and make a path to the pond.

Roni gripped the strap to keep from being thrown out of the seat, laughing. She didn't wonder at Drake's mood. She felt much the same way. The things a person holds dear can be snatched out of their grip without so much as a say so, never to be seen again. Hadn't it happened with her parents, even Elle and Marcus, and now maybe Drake? Like Drake, she didn't want to think about the consequences if the murderer wasn't found, or how their lives would be forever altered.

The vehicle slid to a stop. Drake hopped out of the Jeep before Roni could unfasten her seatbelt. By the time she'd stepped down, Drake was coming from around the back of the car, carrying the food container.

"If you will, grab that blanket in the back and throw it under the tree over there." He gestured in the direction of the huge oak with twisting limbs a child would delight in climbing. It was the same spot they always picked when the three of them came to the pond as teens.

She grabbed her cup of coffee and then the blanket from the backseat before following Drake. She handed her cup to him, and then began shaking out the folded blanket, throwing it over the ground. The food carrier came next along with Drake and her coffee.

Roni unzipped the bag, pulling out plates, napkins, and a virtual feast from the insulated bag, sitting everything on the quilt. The anticipation of breakfast burritos that were wrapped in foil, salsa, fruit, and cinnamon rolls, made her stomach clinch. Until now she hadn't realized just how hungry she was until she saw the food.

"I think Hazel went a little overboard. There's enough food here to feed five or six people."

Drake grabbed the salsa, unscrewed the lid, and then picked up one of the stuffed breakfast burritos. "Speak for yourself. I'm hungry. If you remember, we didn't have dinner last night."

Last night's events filled Roni's mind. She shoved aside the thoughts to enjoy the pleasant outdoor breakfast with Drake before he got down to the more serious business of supplying answers.

"Well, with all this food, I think we'll be able to make up for last night and then some."

Drake held out her plate with a burrito. "Don't know about you but I know I will."

"How did that happen?" She pointed to the three long, ugly scratches on Drake's left arm.

"Monday, just before you came. Dad got up from the chair and almost fell. I reached to steady him, he grabbed my arm, but his knees buckled. His nails bit into my flesh as he tried to gain his balance." He touched his arm. "I was just glad I was there to keep him from falling." Sorrow crossed his face then disappeared.

"We better dig in before these things get too cold to enjoy.

He unwrapped his tin foiled tortilla rolls, spooned salsa over one end of the burrito, then took a huge bite before chewing slowly. He pointed his burrito at her. "You better eat up before I eat them all."

To settle her racing heart and keep her mind off of Drake, she opened the foil on her burrito and followed suit, but not before wishing their relationship could be more.

The moment she sunk her teeth into the flour tortilla, the flavors of scrambled eggs, sausage, cheese, and peppers burst inside her mouth. The food settled the gnawing in her stomach and made her feel human again.

A peaceful quiet settled around them as Drake devoured his food and Roni ate slowly, enjoying her impromptu breakfast outdoors with him. She loved being in Drake's company even when they were quiet, like now.

"Roni, if things were different would you have considered dating me? And I don't mean as a friend but us dating to see where it would lead?"

Her startled gaze swung from the pond back to Drake. "What?"

She'd heard him, but how to answer him was the crux of the matter. Her fingers fiddle with the edge of her plate. Her appetite vanished like the bird taking flight across the water into an oak and disappearing.

"You heard me. If all of this wasn't hanging over my head, could you think of me as more than a friend—and I don't mean a brother either?" His serious gaze never left her face.

"Drake, in no time at all, you will be free of suspicion and your old self again. When everything is back to normal, you will see things differently. I'm here for you. I'm not planning on going anywhere."

He took her plate and set it down then took hold of both of her hands turning them over. He looked at her palms as though looking for something.

"My thinking isn't hazy, and none of what's taken place has motivated me to speak. My father's death certainly has me worried. I want the killer caught, but I know I'm innocent.

"However, where you are concerned, I want more. I would like ..." He shook his head, gave her an odd look, then released her.

"Never mind. The timing's not right. I can't, not until the murderer is found and my name is cleared." Silent and unmoving, Drake stared off across the pond.

Roni didn't know what to say. Was he about to tell her he loved her? Surely not. Drake Peters would never look at her as a love interest. Never, in the entire seventeen years of knowing each other, had he ever acted or even hinted about becoming more than friends. Though she felt more for him, theirs was a mutual love between friends, nothing more. He was probably afraid she'd leave him stranded.

When he turned to look at her, his countenance had changed. His resolve appeared to be altered—more determined. She wondered if the uncertainty of all that had taken place had affected him more than she realized.

"We've come here for the sole purpose of me telling you what took place before Dad was killed." He made a fist, released it, then flexed his fingers several times before resting them in the hollow of his crossed legs.

Roni wanted to know, but she would have rather had a few more minutes of being here with Drake. She pulled her lawyerly instincts together and grabbed her iPad, ready to take notes of anything important that might help in his defense.

"When you hear what I have to say, I hope you won't judge my father, or by default, me. But I'm afraid the knowledge of what took place years ago will irrevocably change your opinion of us." He shrugged, offering up a humorless smile.

Drake's demeanor, even his words were unsettling. Roni was uncertain if she wanted to know what took place. And why would she judge Marcus, or for the matter Drake, over something from the past?

Her breakfast sat like a rock on her anxious stomach. A cloud overhead momentarily darkened the sun, causing a shiver to skitter up her spine and her scalp to tingle.

Surely, what Drake has to say wouldn't be so horrible.

He pulled a long blade of grass, resting his elbows on his knees, running the blade between his finger and thumb, causing a squeaking sound. He glanced up at her with deep, troubled eyes.

"You may have been too young to realize your father and mine were partners in a business venture."

Her brow wrinkled in thought, she challenged her memory but came up dry. "When was this?"

"A year or so before your parents were killed in the car accident and you came to live with us." He ran the blade through his fingers again, the squeaking, high-pitch sound rattle her nerves. Then he tore the blade into tiny pieces, throwing it to the wind.

She watched the fragments float down and disappear in with the other blades of grass.

"What kind of venture?" Something at the back of her mind niggled, yet she couldn't quite grasp the details.

"Oil wells." Drake stopped and inhaled deeply before continuing. "The venture was in oil. My father had invested in drilling equipment and crews. He had several successful wells paying great dividends. The potential in expanding looked good, and he sought more investors for more wells."

"Did my father invest in his wells? Is that what you're trying to say?"

"Yes."

The word hung between them, sounding dull, yet promising something she didn't want to know, yet had to hear. It triggered memories, not exactly unpleasant but not happy either.

Now it was coming back to her. She vaguely recalled an argument her parents had late one evening after she'd gone to bed about an investment. The only reason she remembered, they were yelling, which they never did, and then her mother started crying.

Was this what Drake referred to? Fear absorbed Roni, twisting its way to her heart, squeezing, cutting off her breath. She didn't want to hear what Drake had to say. Yet, she needed to know the full story, especially if it remotely dealt with Marcus' death or Drake's innocence. But how it did connect she couldn't fathom.

At first, Roni thought he wasn't going to say anything more. Then he glanced at her. She saw the pain and remorse.

"Dad convinced your father the oil wells were a sure thing, even showed him the reports of all the prior wells and their profits, making rich men richer. He told your father he couldn't lose.

"There were three pieces of land judged to be good drills. Each considered had great potential for a huge return on the money. He assured your father if he invested he would reap enormous dividends." Drake looked out over the lake avoiding her gaze.

She could tell what he had to say pained him.

In her line of work, she had sat across the table from far too many people weighed down with guilt not to recognize this was what Drake carried. She prayed the information wouldn't alter her opinion of Marcus, a man who had raised her like one of his own.

"Drake, please, all of that was in the past. If my parents lost money they invested with Marcus, and this is what you quarreled about, I forgive your father. My dad was a grown man and at an age to be able to make his own decisions, his own mistakes. Just because the investment was with Marcus doesn't mean I love him less or view my father as a fool."

"Roni, you haven't heard the whole. Let me finish and then if you are still of the same persuasion …" He held his hand up as if to say *then so be it.*

He swallowed and looked down, guilt eating at him.

She wanted to brush the worry away. Instead, she didn't move, but waited for him to continue.

"As I mentioned, my father convinced your dad it was a sure thing. He told him if he didn't jump right in, it would be his loss. Your father drew out his life's savings, mortgaged the house, everything he owned, and gave the money to Dad to invest in the wells."

Breath snagged in Roni's throat. She wanted to scream *stop*, but couldn't.

"All three wells your father invested in failed, came up dry holes. The day my father called to explain the investment was gone, down to the last penny, is the same day your father and mine parted friends. A week and half later you came to live with us."

Her mind whirled as she struggled to comprehend what her parents' death had to do with the fight between Marcus and Drake. Comprehension dawned.

"I'm sorry." Drake reached for her.

Roni waved him off, scrambling to her feet. She moved to the trunk of the tree and face forward, leaned in, bracing her forearms against the rough bark. She ignored the ridges cutting into her skin as her head hung between her arms. Black dots appeared in the dirt at her feet.

Panic attacks were something Roni had heard about, but had never witnessed. She never believed they could happen to her.

She gasped, as her chest tightened and squeezed painfully refusing to accept the air trying to fill her lungs. Her heart raced uncontrollably, as in the violent spasms of a heart attack. Her limbs trembled and tingled not wanting to support her body as her head buzzed, ready to explode. Numb from head to toe, she searched her mind, doing her best to control the panic that held her body in the throes of this assault.

All she believed to be true, all she had learned to love … a sham, a cover up. Her ideals torn by the wind of deceit, disintegrated and scattered to the four corners of the earth as the storm ragged inside her. The realization the seventeen years had been a pretense to cover guilt and nothing more had her reeling.

"Roni, please."

She felt his hand on her back. "Don't touch me," she hissed and jerked away from his hand. She turned to lean against the tree, her head back, eyes closed. Her world had been torn apart, leaving her with contempt ... contempt for Marcus.

Could her parents' death be connected to the bad investments Marcus told her father about? She remembered reading and hearing accounts of other people who had lost their life's saving and ended up killing themselves. Surely, this wasn't what happened to her folks. No, she couldn't believe they would leave her on her own, knowing she would go to the very man who had ruined their lives.

"When did you find out?" Her voice sounded weak, pitiful.

"Saturday night before bed. Dad gave me paperwork the week before the party asking me to handle anything that needed attention. Whether foreordain or a slip on his part, I don't know. However, in the paperwork I found a business agreement and a complaint from your dad on the investments he had made. I got the rest of the details from my father."

"He took me in out of guilt." The words tore from her, leaving her raw inside without a shred of self-worth.

What she mistook as love was Marcus' guilt in spades. He probably never wanted her at their house. She was a constant reminder of what he had done.

"I don't believe so. Since you were an only child with no living relatives, my folks raised you, gave you the same advantage we, Sam and I, received."

Roni shoved away from the tree. "Oh, he certainly did do that! He couldn't be faulted for taking in a girl he helped to make an orphan. What a saint. May his crown be filled with shards of glass, not worth the paper my dad's agreement was written upon."

She regretted the words the moment they left her mouth, but not enough to stop the flow of anger. "Now, I can't even accuse Marcus to his face for the unalterable harm he did to my family. Someone took that privilege out of my hands."

"Roni, I—"

She shook her head and held out her hand to stop him, then bent to pick up several flat stones from the ground. Jiggling the rocks together, she walked down to the pond, her steps pounding out her anger.

She palmed the first rock, threw it as hard as she could. The stone skipped once and then plopped beneath the surface, mirroring the rock-bottom plunge of her heart. Yet, it did nothing to elevate her frustration.

How could she have been so duped in regard to Marcus? Her parents' lives were cut short by what? Her father? Stupidity? Fate? She may never know. How would she learn the truth of what really happened? Everyone who knew the truth was dead.

She heard Drake come up behind her. He stood a few feet away not saying a word, probably wondering if her temper had cooled any. It hadn't. But it would eventually. Although, she wasn't sure she would ever believe a Peters again, or trust one.

She dropped the remaining rocks at her feet, then turned to leave.

"Roni, I'm truly sorry. If I could change the past I would. What I revealed about your parents was why I was so infuriated with my father. I begged him to tell you, to do his best to explain, make it right." He took a breath. "That's what we argued about."

She didn't acknowledge Drake. She wished she could escape the world she thought she knew, but hadn't. Was the love she experienced from Marcus and Elle a sham?

"He was afraid you would blame him for your parents' death and hate him. I told him he owed it to you to tell you the truth regardless the outcome. He refused." He touched her arm, this time she didn't shrug it off.

"For what it's worth, I believe he was truly remorseful. He didn't speak for fear he'd lose you." Drake looked away. "And now I'm afraid that's what I've done ... lost you."

She wasn't sure what Drake meant. However, words that would have stirred her earlier only hardened her resolve. He was saying them to soften the blow so she wouldn't leave.

Drake moved around in front of Roni, making her look at him. "Please, Roni, don't take it out on Samantha or ... me."

"Does Sam know about this?" *Did they all pity me?*

"No, I didn't plan on telling her. But if you want me to, I will." His eyes were dark with compassion. "I know you don't owe us anything, but I'm asking ... please, don't leave. I—we don't want to lose you. You're part of our family."

Her anger raged over the duplicity. The laughter she released came out harsh and ugly.

"Family? Was I ever part of your family?" She saw Drake wince, but the anguish inside took over her tongue. "Marcus took me in simply to appease his conscience." She took a long hard look at Drake. Though she loved him deeply, she now knew nothing could come of it. The question of her parents' death would always stand between them.

Roni walked back to the blanket and began shoving the breakfast things back into the carrier. "If you don't have any more revelations to spring on me, I would like to go back to the house. There are several things I need to do."

"Roni, please. I need you and I believe you need me." He touched her arm.

She moved away, offering him a hollow laugh. "Don't worry. I won't leave you in a lurch. I'll stay until you're proven innocent. I am quite aware you could never kill your father over a trifling thing as him being one of the key causes of my parents' death."

Drake looked as if she'd slapped him.

She didn't care. She rolled the blanket into a ball, then threw it on the back seat. Her anger wasn't even slightly appeased by her childish action. She wanted to strike out, hurt those who had hurt her. But Marcus was no longer here.

After putting the carrier in the back, Drake got into the vehicle. He gave her a miserable look then started the engine.

The ride to the house was silent. Neither of the occupants said a word. And though Drake glanced at her several times, Roni refused to acknowledge him.

After seventeen years of believing one thing and finding out another, Roni knew she would have to work through her anger and grief all over again. And she would. However, at the moment, she wanted to hold on to the hurt, nurse it a little longer. If for no other reason … for her parents. They deserved her righteous indignation directed at Marcus.

CHAPTER 31

The quiet was deafening as they drove back to the house. Roni, though still angry, felt horrible for taking her fury out on Drake. He wasn't responsible. Her anger with him was by default. Still, she wasn't ready to discuss the matter or let go of the hurt.

He stopped the car in front of the house and turned to her. "Roni, I'm sorry. What can I do to make it right?"

Drake's words nipped at her conscience but she ignored it. "I don't want to discuss it now. Maybe later."

She scrambled out of the car, grabbed her things, heading straight for her room. Time and space was what she needed most. Maybe then she could deal with the aftermath of the revelation.

Uppermost in her mind was her parents' death. Had it really been an accident or death of intent? If planned … she didn't want to entertain the possibilities.

She shuddered at the thought her father might have taken his life and her mother's. But something happened to end their lives. What? And who was responsible—her dad unable to face life knowing he'd lost everything? Was Marcus, for persuading her father to invest?

To discover what took place seventeen years ago would be impossible.

What hurt her most, she wondered if Elle and Marcus took her in out of shame or duty? Either reason caused pain. All she thought to be true was a lie. She had been a charity case after all. The girl in ninth grade taunted and had received a black eye for speaking the truth.

Roni shoved the avalanche of information and questions to the back of her mind. She would come back to it later. Right now, there were more pressing matters. Keeping Drake out of jail was top priority. The other could wait since it had already waited seventeen years.

She contacted Mr. Thompson about Marcus' will and set up an appointment with him later in the day. Drake and Samantha would have to rearrange their schedule if need be to fit the meeting into theirs. With Nick Holdum breathing down their necks, it was of the utmost importance to know about the designation of assets and how they would deal with him. After today there'd be no mystery.

When Roni hung up from Mr. Thompson, she punched in Frank Thornton's number.

"Hi Frank. Sorry I didn't get in touch with you sooner, but I've been stomping out major fires. Did you find the motel and get a good night's sleep."

"Sure did. Thanks for setting me up. I've been out snooping around town this morning. Rumor has it our boy, Drake, is top man for suspect. Seems all leads point to him. The write up in the newspaper of him being brought in for questioning didn't help."

Her heart sank. "I haven't seen the paper yet."

"The reporter didn't speculate much, which surprised me. Probably didn't want to make an enemy out of the biggest company in Athens."

"No doubt. Have you learned anything else?" Roni pulled out the desk chair and sat down, kneading the knot in her stomach. If she didn't have an ulcer by the time this was over, it wouldn't be the fault of the truckload of worries dumped into her lap.

"Not much yet. I don't put a lot of stock in what the rumor-mills have to say—sometimes their reliable, most times their not. I'll do more checking. If I can find a contact inside the precinct, I'll be able to know a little more what's fact and what's fiction."

"You can do that—find a precinct contact?"

"Most times." He released a deep throated chuckle. "If Athens has a woman dispatcher, or woman officer, or maybe a female in internal affairs, I'll get the information we need. Just a matter of time."

Not having met Frank in person, she thought he must be quite the charmer if the women were so forthcoming with information.

"Don't tell me how or who. I don't want to know. I may have to testify on your behalf." She laughed. "The less I know about your contacts, the better for us both."

"You're a woman after my own heart. You think like I do." There was a slight pause as if he were checking something.

"On our other order of business—Holdum—I heard from my man Walsh. He couldn't find any dirt on the mother. Seems she and Holdum were pillars of the community. Faith Holdum was loved by all. The company where she was employed gave her high praise. Said, she was a hardworking woman who put her son through college with an added night job so he could finish without debt."

"If the woman could raise her son and not ask Marcus for help, she couldn't be all bad. It couldn't have been easy being a single mother." Roni felt a little better about the Holdums.

Did Marcus make this woman promises he didn't keep?

As in her father's case, after so many years, she might never learn the truth of what happened between Faith and Marcus.

Scribbling down some notes, Roni asked, "What is Holdum's profession, or does he have one?"

"CPA, at least up until he quit his job two weeks ago. His reason for quitting? A personal matter directly related to his mother's death."

"*Hmm.* Looking up Marcus, no doubt." Roni hoped he didn't have an ulterior motive. However, it sounded more like he was seeking that pot of gold at the end of the rainbow. "Did Walsh ferret out how and when Marcus and Faith Holdum met?"

"It appears Marcus Peters visited New York City on business for a few weeks in 1980."

Roni knew Drake was born in July 1980. What would have possessed Marcus to commit such an act against his wife? Elle was either pregnant or had already given birth to Drake. It didn't make sense. Yet, the Marcus she knew no longer made sense. Maybe he was deceptive by nature.

"During that trip, Peters met Faith at the office where she was a secretary and then again at a business party. According to her oldest and dearest friend, Peters and Faith had a couple of one night stands before Peters left town. He probably wasn't aware of the mess he'd left behind—and as they say—the rest is history."

Frank was silent for a moment. "The woman was thoughtful enough to give her son a derivative of Marcus' name. Nicholas Mark Holdum."

"Holdum's DNA also checks out. I received the report this morning." Roni rubbed her forehead. A killer of a headache had her squinting, her thumbs messaging her temple. "I'll let Drake and Samantha we know Holdum is their brother."

"Yeah, if for no other reason, it seems Holdum left town an angry man. His mother's friend said he told her he was going to make Peters pay."

"Thanks for the report." Roni looked out the window at the black clouds gathering from the south. "Do you believe Holdum could have been angry enough to kill Marcus?"

"Could be. People have killed for less. According to Walsh, Holdum holds Marcus responsible for everything. In my estimation, his thinking is kind of squirrely. If Marcus knew about Holdum, totally ignored his responsibilities, it could be enough to throw the man over the deep end to murder him. I'll have my guy check further while he's in New York. And I'll keep an eye on him while he's here."

Before this morning, Roni would have said with surety, Marcus wouldn't shirk his responsibilities, but now, she wasn't so sure. He didn't shirk her, but neither had he been honest about his dealings.

"I'll continue to snoop around town. I'd also like to visit the crime scene, see if I can ferret out anything additional the police might have overlooked."

"I'll be here until two thirty going over Marcus' legal concerns. When would you like to come?"

"How 'bout noon. I'll bring sandwiches from McAlister's."

"Forget McAlister's. Lunch will be waiting when you get here. You and I can go over strategy while we eat and figure out what our next move should be."

"That's a deal. See you then."

Ending the call, Roni moved to the window and gazed out over the grounds. She rolled her tight shoulders several times, trying to loosen the stiffness. The impending storm obscured the sun. The day's beautiful beginning a mere memory.

The wind whipped branches into a wild frenzy, snatching leaves, hurling them into the unknown. Like the leaves, her world had been ripped from her hands and hurled into uncertainty. Truth shrouded in doubt. Questions of who and why. Everything changed, appearances deceiving.

All this time, she would have sworn Marcus and Elle loved her. Now she doubted their show of affection as sincere. To learn it was all a sham, a pretense to hide Marcus' horrendous deeds, made her physically ill. She doubled over, grabbed her stomach and slid down the wall onto the floor. Her face buried in her knees, sobs shook her body.

Holding nothing back, she cried over her frustration, hurt, even the loss of her parents. Hate welled up, beat her soul like the rain and hail beating against her windows. She felt cheated. Marcus would never know her wrath or answer her questions. Her disillusionment ran deep, anger unquenchable until her tears were spent.

The thought to pack and leave, never to look back at the Triple Cross Ranch and all it stood for, crossed her mind. However, her sense of responsibility wouldn't allow her to leave Drake while he was under suspicion. In spite of his father's duplicity, he wasn't to blame, and she still loved him.

Like everything else she thought true, maybe her parents' accidental death was deliberate. Maybe Marcus had been behind their death, afraid the scam he'd played on her father would be revealed, making him loose credibility?

That's insane.

The wreck had to have been an accident. Yet how would she know for sure? The uncertainty of what happened would lurk in the back of her mind. She needed answers. Yet, to clear up the questions after all these years would be next to impossible. But she had to try.

Better to search for the truth than to believe Marcus was behind their deaths, or even worse, her father had committed suicide and taken her mother with him, leaving his enemy to raise his child. Too farfetched. She couldn't believe for a minute her father would do something so horrible.

Enough of this pity party.

Roni splashed cold water on her face hoping to clear her head of all the horrible thoughts revolving in her mind. It wasn't like her to convict without evidence. Marcus had been good to her. He didn't deserve her indictment on his character, or her indignation. Neither did Drake. She'd continue as before until proof to the contrary.

After repairing her makeup, she called Ed Purser. He gave her the number of his friend, the criminal defense lawyer, and said he was ready and willing to help.

In the process of dialing the number of Ed's friend, her phone rang.

"Hello?"

"Roni, this is Nick. And we need to talk." His voice sounded agitated.

"I don't have time today, but I will have time this evening or tomorrow morning." She didn't need this to be added to what she already carried on her plate.

"How about tonight?"

No need stalling. As much as she didn't want to, she said, "All right. What time and where?"

"Six-thirty. In Athens. I just discovered Tex-Mex and find I have a real affinity for the stuff." He laughed. "How about meeting me at The Jalapeño Tree. Do you know where it is?"

Roni wanted to refuse, but decided it would get her out of the house. And she could let Nick know his fate as far as the estate was concerned.

"Yes. I've been there many times. And six-thirty will work for me. I'll see you there."

After several calls, she noticed she had little time to tell Hazel they were having a guest for lunch and to prepare for Frank Thornton's arrival.

Almost down the stairs, she saw Drake coming out of the library.

"Roni?" He seemed surprised to see her.

It pained her to see him looking so drawn. She would take time to make her apologies after lunch.

"I was coming to look for you. Frank Thornton is here to see you. Said you were expecting him."

"Oh, thanks. He's the PI I hired. I was just on my way to tell Hazel we'd have one more for lunch. Frank's joining us."

Drake looked at her oddly. "What's he doing in Athens?"

"Don't you remember? I asked him to come. We need another pair of eyes to search for the facts and Marcus' killer. He's came to look at the room and search around the house and grounds."

"That's right." He motioned her on to the library. "You go on in. I'll let Hazel know about lunch."

"Thanks, but when you're through, would you join us, please." Roni didn't wait for his answer but moved on down the stairs and to the library.

"Frank." She moved toward a tall man, with dark hair in a buzz cut. He turned from the wall of books and family photos to look at her.

Knowing Frank was a retired CIA agent, Roni was a little surprised. He looked to be in his late thirties, early forties. She expected someone much older, but he looked competent and well-suited for the job. And he wasn't bad looking, actually. The man, nicely built, had warm chocolate eyes, eyes that could size up a room and its occupants in seconds, no doubt.

By the time she crossed to where he stood, he had cataloged, labeled, and filed his summary of her in the back of his mind, which humored her.

"So nice to finally meet you." She offered her hand.

He enveloped hers in both of his large hands, a wickedly, appealing grin spreading across his face. She had been right earlier, this man was a charmer. She'd have to watch her step with him.

"Same here, Counselor. You're voice doesn't do you justice. You're a good deal prettier than I imagined. I'll bet the men you come up against in court underestimate your abilities the moment you walk into the room. Am I right?" He winked at her.

"Some do." She smiled, motioning for him to sit down. "And thank you … I think."

"You can take it to the bank. Coming from me, that's a compliment." Frank waited until she was seated then sat across from her, face serious. "I came a little earlier than planned. I wanted to deliver some news before I started looking around."

Roni knew Frank could be quite appealing with his lean, rock-solid body and dark good looks. Yet something about his face told her he'd faced a deep sorrow at some time in his life.

He crossed his leg over his knee, and grabbed his ankle. "I met our mutual friend in town, Nick Holdum." His gaze shifted behind her and then back to her. "He's spreading the word around town he's Marcus Peters' son."

Roni heard a hiss coming from the doorway.

She turned and motioned. "Drake, come join us. Frank, you've already met Drake Peters."

"Yes. And it seems you failed to tell him I was coming." He chuckled. "He seemed a little shocked to see a man at his door asking for you."

Drake moved to the sofa, sat down looking a little peeved.

"Sorry. Time got away from me. Too many calls. Too many fires to stomp out." She figured Drake's gruff demeanor was due to what he'd heard about Nick. "As you know, Drake is the one you're working to prove is innocent."

"Figured as much." Frank, watched Drake closely, smiled as though he held a secret. "As I was saying, Holdum is spreading the word he is Marcus' son."

"Yet to be proven." Drake's surly reply didn't go unnoticed.

This wasn't the venue she'd wanted to disclose her information, but Roni knew she'd needed to set him straight before it went any further.

"Drake, I haven't had the chance to tell you until now, I received the DNA report this morning and Nick Holdum is Marcus' son." She glanced at Frank before continuing. "In addition, Frank called me earlier and said all of Holdum's information checks out in New York. So, it's a done deal."

CHAPTER 32

Drake loathed that his father had been so careless with his personal matters that he left behind this mess for him to clean up. He'd always respected his dad, looked up to him, and many times tried to emulate him. To find he lived a double life shot holes in all his beliefs.

Did his father know about Holdum? Had he supported him? Or had he done as Holdum said—left the mother to deal with raising *his* son without any support from him?

From the beginning, he'd fought hard against the possibility Holdum was his brother but deep down he knew the man was kin, whether by his dad or one of his uncles. And now proof confirmed what he tried to deny the first day Holdum ... *his name is Nick* ... Nick showed up at the ranch.

"How old is Nick?" His fingers ached from his hard gripe on the end of the armrests. Drake forced himself to relax. He knew Nick wasn't the source of his anger. If anyone should be on the receiving end of his ire, it should be his father.

"In late 1980."

The compassion in Roni's voice caused his insides to churn. He was either an infant when his father had his affair, or his mother was in the last months of pregnancy. What type of man could do such a thing? Had he ever really known his father? Worse yet, was his mother aware? He hoped not.

He tried to reason and not throw blame around until he had full knowledge of all the facts. With all parties to blame being deceased, it didn't seem likely he'd find the truth.

"What have you learned from town?" Roni directed the question to Frank Thornton.

"Not much. As I mentioned, I ran into our boy, Holdum." Frank chuckled. "Believe it or not, he's staying at the same motel. We had breakfast together." He wrinkled his nose. "Well, not together, but at the same time. I eavesdropped. He seems a friendly sort and likeable enough."

Frank shifted in his chair, stretching his legs out in front of him. "Breakfast is where I heard him telling the day manager he was Marcus Peters' son. Even told about being barred from seeing him." Frank's gaze shifted to Drake. "I assume that was you?"

"Yes. Until I had proof, I wasn't about to let him come near my father. But it seems I didn't have worried on that score."

Frank shrugged. "Understandable. I would have done the same." His gaze returned to Roni.

Drake didn't like how this guy watched Roni—way too personal—hungry like. He'd set him straight if need be.

"I should learn more this afternoon when I get back to town."

"Is there a reason for your visit this afternoon, other than looking around?" Drake didn't miss the annoyed look Roni threw him, nor the glint in Frank's eyes.

"That about sums it up. I'll need a list of people who have a key to the house and know the alarm code."

Roni moved to the desk, pulled out a note pad and pen, giving both to Drake. "I'll let Drake give you the information. You mentioned over the phone the authorities were looking heavily at Drake as their suspect. What, if anything, can we do to keep him out of jail?"

"Probably nothing. As you know, we're in a waiting game."

"I understand." She cleared her throat, ill at ease. "Nick called me this morning."

"What did he want?" Drake didn't like Holdum calling Roni even though she'd given him her number as their attorney.

"Said he wanted to speak to me. I feel sure it's about the estate, but I'll know more once I meet with him."

"I'm going with you." Drake wasn't about to let her meet Nick alone.

"That won't be necessary." Her voice emphatic.

"I'm going." He could be just as stubborn as Roni. This time he would be. He would go whether she liked it or no.

"Until we know more about Holdum and why he's here, I think Drake is right on this one. He should accompany you."

Drake could tell Frank's comment didn't set well with Roni.

"It'll give me a chance to meet Nick and apologize for my reception of him on Saturday and yesterday. He needs to know, even if I don't agree with what took place between dad and his mother, it doesn't negate the fact he's family."

"You're right." She looked resigned. "Having you along might not be a bad idea."

"When?" Drake was glad she'd accepted without a fight.

She looked at him oddly.

"Dinner, what time?"

"Oh. Six-thirty. The Jalapeño Tree." She gave them both a quirky smile. "It seems our Mr. Holdum has an affinity for Tex-Mex. Can't get enough of the stuff. One bite and he was hooked."

Drake muttered under his breath. "Let's hope that's the only thing he has an affinity for."

Frank chuckled, giving Drake an all-knowing look. "You being there, I'm sure, will set him straight on many points."

"You can be certain of that." Drake nodded, not smiling.

Roni was plainly puzzled. "Am I missing something?"

"No, little darlin'." Frank chuckled directing his gaze at Drake. "Our man, Drake here, will be there tonight to make sure Holdum feels welcomed into the family, but without fringe benefits where you are concerned."

Charles stepped into the room and announced lunch was ready.

Any further explanations fell by the wayside as they stood to follow Charles. Drake figured he'd give the man a bonus for interrupting what could have been a prickly situation.

Frank, all smiles and charming, took Roni's arm and ushered her out of the room.

Drake saw red and forgot the charitable thoughts he'd had toward the man earlier. Now, instead of just Nick, it looked like he'd have to set Frank straight on a few things too.

Thornton better think twice about playing games where Roni was concerned, or the man would answer to him.

CHAPTER 33

Roni felt uncomfortable riding with Drake to Mr. Thompson's office. But he acted normal and as though she hadn't lost her temper this morning. If he had disregarded her behavior of earlier and of not speaking to him until Frank arrived, maybe she should do the same.

Her conscience pricked, prodding her to do what she knew to be right, making it impossible to ignore her earlier actions.

She swallowed, then said, "Drake, I apologize for my behavior this morning. I shouldn't have taken my temper out on you. It's wasn't your fault."

He gave her a quick glance, a mixture of remorse and relief evident.

"No apology necessary. I understand completely. If I could, I would have left it unsaid, but you had to know."

"Yes, I did. Thanks. I'll try my best to look at the whole picture objectively."

Drake laughed. "If I'd been given that kind of information, I'm afraid my objectivity would have flown out the window, and I might have thrown you out along with the news."

Roni touched his arm and felt the warmth of his skin. "No you wouldn't. You're not like that."

"Some might say differently."

"And they'd be wrong. I will admit what you unloaded on me was a lot to take in. However, at the moment, we have weightier matters before us, namely you, and keeping one step ahead of the investigation."

He gave her crooked smile. "Yeah, I don't look good in prison stripes."

She laughed. "I'm working hard to keep you out of them."

"Thanks, Counselor. I can use all the help I can get."

Roni wasn't sure if she should tell him her other decision, but decided it was best to be above board with him.

"About this morning subject, I've decided once Frank has completed his work proving your innocence, I'm going to hire him to look into my parents' death. I need to know if they died by accident or ... you know." She shrugged. "I hope you understand."

"If I were in your shoes, I'd want to know."

The memories etched on her mind came to the forefront. "All I was ever told, my parents died in a car crash. If there is a remote possibility of finding out what took place, I have to try. And I believe, if anyone can find the answers, Frank can."

The passing scenery flash by but none of it registered with her.

"Roni, you don't need my permission. But if that's what you're asking, you have it. I will back you one hundred percent. And if there's anything I can do, let me know."

She felt his large hand cover hers giving her reassurance ... pleasure. When she looked up, his unreadable gaze searched her face. He returned his attention to the road and released her.

"In fact, I want to pay Frank's fee."

She was moved by his offer. "I can't allow that. The fee is mine alone."

Drake didn't put up an argument for which she was grateful. She hated bringing up the next topic, but regardless, like the last, it had to be broached.

"Will you grant me a favor?"

"Anything within my power."

"Regardless what Nick Holdum says tonight, please don't overreact. I'd rather not play referee over enchiladas and tacos. And he is your brother. I hope you will try to find some common ground."

"In other words, you'd rather not have to dodge flying chips and hot sauce?" A sheepish grin appeared.

"Yes."

"I think I can manage to behave." He drove around the town square, found a parking place in front of Thompson's law office. "You do know if Sam finds out we are meeting Nick, she won't be left behind."

"Yes, but I don't plan on telling her until afterward. I hope she doesn't find out, at least, not until it's over and we know why Nick wants to meet. You showing up will be a big enough surprise. Add Sam to the mix, he'll think we're ganging up on him."

"I agree. Shall we?"

He walked around to assist her out of the car, and then placed his hand on the small of her back. She loved how his touch made her feel—as though she belonged to him.

She'd seen the Thompson's building many times before, but never gone in. Inside and out, the office bore the stamp of a bygone era. Though nicely done, the only upgrade over the years, paint and carpet.

They were led to the conference room with an oval mahogany conference table with chairs, a console table sat against one wall, and bookshelves stuffed with law book lined another. A glass and oak showcase was beneath a huge painting of large robust man.

Roni moved closer to view the picture. The engraved gold plate bore the name JR Thompson. The artist had depicted JR with a wickedly handsome smile and a sparkle in his eyes, as if he held the answer to the world's secrets, but would extract a price for their solution. His jovial expression made her smile.

In his late sixties with a gray-haired fringe, he was dressed in a pen-striped suit, the coat open to reveal a buttoned vest. A watch chain stretched from one vest pocket across his rotund belly to the next where a bullet dangled from the button hole acting as a watch fob. His elbows rested on the arms of the chair, and from his right, beefy fingers he held a huge cigar.

Inside the display case were several smaller pictures of JR, along with a sheriff's badge, gun, holster, and a rope that bore the tag, *The Hanging Rope.*

"That's Mr. Thompson's grandfather."

Drake's minty breath fanned her cheeks, startling her some since she hadn't heard him approach. His closeness jumbled her nerves. She wished she could lean into him and allow him to take away the hurts, but knew the thought was foolish.

"JR started the law firm back in the early 1900s, and commissioned this building to be built for his law practice. My father met JR once when he was a boy. Said he was quite a character and could put the fear of God into you with one look. But he always carried peppermints to give to the kids, so he couldn't have been all that bad." Drake pointed at the gun in the case. "He walked around town with the gun strapped to his hip until the day he died. Some say he wanted to be buried with the gun, but his son wouldn't hear of it."

"Did he ever shoot anyone?"

He grinned. "Don't know, but I bet Mr. Thompson could answer your question."

"No, thanks." She shivered, visualizing a JR look-alike walking into the room with a six shooter on his hip, laying his pistol on the table before pulling out the will. Her mental vision of him made her laugh.

The door opened and the assistant ushered in Samantha. She looked a little harried as she slung her purse on the table. "I wasn't sure I'd get here in time."

Drake led Roni over. Sam gave her a hug, and then gave one to her brother. They took their seats with Drake in the middle.

"At the last moment Elle didn't want to go down for her nap. A good thing Geoff came home as I was leaving. I left him to deal with her even though he said he had an appointment. Once he gets her down, Linda will watch her and the other kids when they come in from school."

The door opened again and in walked a man, medium built, in his mid-sixties but looked nothing like the JR of the painting—too subdued and pale, and not nearly as robust.

"Good afternoon. I'm Jeb Thompson." He set a file on the table.

Roni liked him. His smile was genuine, country friendly, not your stuffy, big-city lawyer type. He had a shiny, bald pate with a salt and pepper fringe much like JR's, only cut shorter. Instead of JR's rotund belly, Jeb looked as though he had tried to keep his weight down, maybe even exercised some to keep fit.

When he turned to Roni, she noticed he hadn't lost the JR bad-boy attorney look entirely. JR's wickedly attractive sparkle was there in his faded gray eyes when he smiled.

"Shall we get down to business?" Jeb had taken the seat across from the three of them. He opened his file and flipped over a few pages.

"Your father came to me about a year ago. He wanted to draw up a new will, which I did to his specification. Now, if you'd like, I can read all this mumbo-jumbo legalese, or I can get to meat of what you want to hear, the distributions, am I correct?" He directed his question to Drake and Samantha.

"Yes, and if there are any special provisions."

Roni knew what Drake was referring to but didn't come right and ask.

"Since it seems we are in agreement, I'll get to the meat of the document." Mr. Thompson slid his finger down one of the pages then looked up at them

"To begin with, your father's will is pretty straight forward. But ... about three months ago, Marcus asked me to draw up a codicil, which, I did to his specification. He expressly asked that I read specific portions of the codicil, which I will now."

He turned his attention to Roni then looked at the document.

Apprehension filled her.

"I, Marcus Drake Peters, of sound mind, do hereby add this codicil to my original will to reflect the following changes and additions: after the bequests mentioned below are taken out of the estate, the remaining portion of my estate shall be divided equally among my son Marcus Drake Peters, Jr., my daughter Samantha Elle Peters Hansen, and my God-daughter, Veronica Luann Reeves"

Roni sucked in a harsh breath. She didn't want Marcus' blood money, because, to her, his bequest sounded more like contrition without asking. He owed her nothing but an explanation, and there wasn't any amount large enough to pay for the life of her parents.

Samantha looked around Drake, beaming with joy. "I'm so glad Daddy thought to include you as one of us."

Roni couldn't tell what Drake thought about the bequest. He sat stiff, unmoving. His eyes never left the attorney.

The lawyer's unemotional gaze turned to Drake and then to Sam before reading again.

"It has recently been brought to my attention I may have another son. Therefore, to any of my other living issue, I leave one million dollars and nothing more. If this person comes forth and proves he is my child by DNA and other documentation, one million dollars is the extent of what he will receive from my estate, and my sincere apology that I never knew he existed until now. However, if he contests my will, then this bequest to his benefit is null and void, and he shall receive the total sum of one dollar.

A small tick in Drake's jaw was the only tale-tell sign that he was remotely affected by Marcus' acknowledgment of Nick.

So Marcus hadn't abandoned Nick or his mother after all.

But something she might never know, was his gift to her out of guilt for what he'd done to her father? Until she knew for certain what involvement Marcus had with her parent's death she wanted no part of the inheritance. Mr. Thompson couldn't force her to take the gift, even with a six-shooter. The thought gave her a laugh she held inside.

She sat quietly, barely holding her emotions together. Her fingernails pierced her palms. Marcus' gift punched holes in her well-fortified armor of reasoning, making it difficult, if not downright impossible, to decipher between fact and fiction leaving her uncertain what to believe.

"Ms. Reeves?"

Drake touched Roni's arm pulling her back to the present. She realized everyone was looking at her and waiting on her response. "I'm sorry, what did you say."

Mr. Thompson held out an envelope. "Mr. Peters asked me to give you this letter in hopes it will answer some of the questions you may have."

With an unsteady hand, Roni reached for the envelope, and then shoved it in her purse.

The attorney finished with the business of the distribution of Marcus's estate. As it stood, Drake would have full control of the corporation; however, Samantha and she would have voting or veto rights. The Triple Cross Ranch went to Drake except for five acres to be set aside as a permanent place for Samantha and her family in case they wished to return to the ranch and build a house to live. However, the piece of land couldn't be sold off but would remain as property of the Triple Cross Ranch for the sole use and purpose of Samantha and her descendants.

Roni thought it odd that Marcus would think Samantha and Geoff may at some time want to move back to the ranch, especially with their large home on the edge of town. But maybe this was his way of protecting her, just in case something happened to Geoff, and Sam would want to be near her brother. He was no doubt hedging against a future eventually or need later in life.

CHAPTER 34

By the time Drake and Roni left the attorney's office and headed for the car, she was too tiffed to discuss her feelings with Drake or meet Nick for dinner. Roni knew, in good conscience, she couldn't accept Marcus' gift.

At the moment, all she wanted to do ... get back to her room, shut the door, and not come out until she was good and ready—which might be never.

Get over it! You sound like a child.

She slid into the passenger's seat, buckled up, then leaned back, closing her eyes, hoping Drake would take the hint.

The car jostled when Drake slid into the driver's seat.

She didn't open her eyes, but her copout made her feel like a heel for giving Drake the cold shoulder.

The thought struck her. Would Drake resent Nick for receiving an inheritance? Or worse, would he resent her?

Wow! Something to look forward to ... a tension filled dinner with warring opponents and me in the middle. The evening doesn't promise to be dull.

To bail out on Nick at this late notice wouldn't be possible. Instead she was resigned to an evening of ...

No use borrowing trouble that might not happen. And she did have some good news for Nick.

What type of man would Nick prove to be? Would he feel he deserved more? Maybe throw the inheritance in their face, or drag them through a long drawn out battle for a larger portion?

"I'm sorry."

Instantly alert, Roni opened her eyes. She had a good idea what Drake referred to. But he started the conversation, let him broach the subject. "For what?"

"My dad's attempt to right wrongs." Weariness was etched deep in his brow and in the fine lines at the edge of his eyes.

At sixty-five miles per hour, Drake turned the wheel back and forth maneuvering his car through the S curve before straightening out.

"I just wish Dad would have come clean with you, instead having to learn about the mess from me. You needed to hear his side of the story. But he was hoping you would never have to find out."

"Don't worry about it." She leaned her head back, closing her eyes, putting an end to the topic. But her mind wouldn't let her.

If only she could walk away from everything—the money, the murder, even Drake. But she couldn't. She was committed ... especially to Drake.

"Roni, I know you may not believe this, but I regret what took place."

Apparently, Drake wasn't willing to let it go. She didn't open her eyes this time. "Please, Drake, there's no use hashing over what can't be fixed. What's done is done. It's not your fault"

"But I wish things were different. I don't want this to come between us."

She really didn't want to have this conversation here ... now. But Drake seemed to be of a differing opinion. Roni looked at him.

"We both know what your dad was doing by giving me one-third of the estate—buying my forgiveness. The last time I checked, forgiveness couldn't be bought. It has to be given freely or it's not worth the words spoken." She paused, and then figured she might as well go for the whole pie, not just a piece. "Tell me, Drake. What do you want from me?"

Roni sat up straight, looking out the front window. Her anger was growing faster than the painted stripes on the road disappearing as they passed.

"Would you pull over, please."

She motioned to what was left of an abandoned blacktop drive up ahead. The weeds had all but reclaimed the entrance, choking out any semblance of a road leading to the crumbling deserted Riddler farm. Still the blacktop struggled to hold on to what had once been necessary and viable.

Was that what she was doing? Holding on to a semblance of normalcy for fear of becoming unrecognizable, losing everything, belonging nowhere, to no one? *How did she reach this point?*

Drake applied the brakes, giving her a quick glance as the car slowed, then pulled off the road. When they came to a stop, he shoved the gear in first, turned off the engine, then angled his body to face her.

"I didn't really want to do this now, but the matter of your father's gift needs to be settled between us."

Looking contrite, the responsibility of Marcus' sin was sitting squarely on his shoulders, and the blame was etched deep into his brow. What Drake failed to recognize, his father was the only one who could offer the solution, but even that was a moot issue now.

"Tell me what to do. I'll do whatever you ask."

Roni wished she could push all Marcus had done aside and go on as nothing had ever happened. But she couldn't. She knew the past would raise its ugly head at some time in the future to bite her on the backside. The problem needed to be dealt with to move on.

When Drake opened the door to that chapter in her life, uncertainty took root deep and became a part of her. She couldn't forget about the past and move on until she overturned every stone to learn the truth, regardless how ugly.

"First off, I don't want the money your father left me."

"Roni, please—"

She waved him silent. "Hear me out. You and I both know why your father left me that inheritance. Blood money."

Drake winched as if she'd slapped him.

"I can't believe he intended the money that way. Dad loved you. He wanted to take care of you."

Her stomach clinched. It always did when she had a distasteful discussion. However, this debacle with Marcus had taught her a valuable lesson. Things of importance should never be shoved under the rug to be dealt with later. And this was one of those things that needed to in the open.

"I don't mean to sound cruel or ungrateful, but you and I will probably never see eye-to-eye on the matter of your father. When Marcus had a chance to redeem himself, he took the coward's way out. He should have had the decency to tell me, help me understand. But no matter."

She paused long enough to calm down some. "As I mentioned earlier, once the person who was responsible for Marcus' death is found, Frank will research my parents' accident. I won't be satisfied until Frank has either unearthed the truth, or he tells me there isn't any evidence other than originally thought—they died in a car wreck … no one's fault."

She swallowed, hoping Drake wouldn't take what she had to say next personally. "Regardless, the outcome, I don't want the money. You can place it in the bank, give it to charity, or divide it between Samantha and you. I don't care. Marcus owed me nothing to begin with except an explanation, and which he didn't seem fit to give, so I don't want his money."

Incapable of keeping her emotions in check, Roni saw Drake though blurry eyes. She turned to the passenger window unable to hide her tears.

Pain sliced through her, severing her ideals, shredding her dreams into nothing. She saw her world for what it was— lofty sand castles buffeted and washed away by the sea.

How could she have lived in a lie for so long and not known? Piece by piece, all the respect and love she held for Marcus had been ripped away, leaving behind emptiness. She had loved him like her own father. Yet had his exploitation led to her parents death?

"Why, Drake? Why would Marcus take me in? Petty? Guilt? What?"

"He loved you."

"You say that, but what proof do you have?"

"I don't have any, but I know in my heart both Mom and Dad loved you. I pray for both our sakes Frank will find the truth and put your mind to rest." His voice held a wealth of conviction.

Drake's seatbelt clinked against the wall of the car. Roni felt her belt unsnap and then a tug on her arm.

"Come here, please." He opened his arms, leaned toward her, and then pulled her to him.

His touch brought all of her raw emotions to the surface as her tears soaked his shirt. Shame filled her, but she couldn't hold back the torrent of her misery. To be blissfully ignorant would have been better than learning about her dad's business dealings with Marcus.

"I wish I had the answers, but I don't." Drake ran his hand soothingly up and down her back, gently coaxing the hurt away. "If I could, I'd take away your pain.

His fingers brushed the loose stands of hair from her face. He consoled her much like a parent would a child. His tender touch began to heal and mend as no words could.

She gave herself over to Drake's gentle care, soaking up all he offered. Locked in Drake's arms, Roni allowed his soothing words, his offered solace to ease the pain to her raw and bleeding heart.

Far too long she'd been on her own. No one had ever been there to hold her or care. What Drake offered was the closest thing to love she had received in such a long time. She willingly took what he gave.

The more she cried, the more she needed him. He was her lifeline as she groped for the light in the surrounding darkness. All her concerns failed to exist.

Roni didn't know how long she had cried in Drake's arms. Spent, she took a deep, shuddering breath, then shame rush in.

Drake must have felt the change in her. He pulled back a little, locking his gaze with hers. Cupping her face, he used his thumbs to wipe away the remnants of tears.

"Forget the money. Find your answers. But, please, Roni don't leave." His eyes turned a darker shade of green and he acted hesitant. "I know this isn't the best of time to speak, but I need to say this. I don't want to lose you. If you leave or exclude me from your life it will tear me up inside."

"I'm not going anywhere." What she left unsaid … she could never leave him.

He moved in close.

She held her breath.

The butterfly touch of his lips moved slowly from her brow to one cheek then to the other, scrambling her emotions further, sending erratic sensations racing through every inch of her body.

His touch removed the turmoil of seconds before, replacing the chaotic feelings with emotions of a different kind, the kind she was afraid to examine too closely.

Warning bells went off inside her head—*Don't be foolish, he's offering reassurance as a friend, nothing more.*

She did her best to accept her own advice, even tried to calm her breathing. However, the heady smell of Drake's cologne added to the dreamlike quality of the moment, spiked her emotions off the chart.

He angled his head toward hers. She closed her eyes as his lips covered hers.

His undemanding kiss caused her warning of earlier to disintegrate. Confusion took over. There wasn't a marked difference between his friendship for her and her love for him—they felt one and the same. If this wasn't love ... *no* she wouldn't even hope.

Drake broke the kiss, resting his forehead against hers. Their breathing was uneven and jagged. She kept telling herself, theirs was a mutual need, yet her heart wouldn't listen.

"I can't tell you how long I've wanted to do that."

He leaned back, then flashed her one of his drop-dead smiles, turning her insides out and her pulse racing faster than before.

"And it was so much better than I imagined."

"Drake, I ..." He meant to kiss her?

No, she misunderstood. The kiss was meant to ease her hurt, dry her tears. To hope was foolish. "I'm sorry."

"Sorry? Well, I'm not. I enjoyed it." After giving her a bold smile, he straightened in his seat and started the ignition.

She felt heat fill her cheeks, yet missed the warmth of his touch.

Glancing at her again, he wore a huge grin as he clicked his seatbelt in place. "Buckle up, sweetheart, we're headin' home."

He popped the clutch sending gravel flying into the air as he whistled an off-beat tune.

Speechless, she fastened her seatbelt and turned her face to the side window. Her fingers gently ran across her lips, reliving the feel his. She would remember Drake's kiss for a lifetime.

The scenery passed by unnoted. Her heart wanted to believe his affection was more than mutual need, but her head overruled.

"Roni."

When she didn't acknowledge him, he slowed the car.

"Look at me."

She didn't want to face him fearing she would see remorse or something worse—pity. She did as he asked.

His smile was still in place. "That kiss has been waiting to happen since you went off to college. I won't apologize for my actions. If and when the opportunity arises, I'll do it again."

His rascally smile had her blood racing and returning his smile. If Drake was playing a game with her emotions, she wouldn't survive.

CHAPTER 35

Roni's mind cautioned not to put much stock into what just happened. The whole episode was of mutual need, nothing more. Her flyaway heart wouldn't listen. Instead, she experience each moment, each touch, each look. And though his wasn't a declaration, she hashed over each word Drake spoke to her while she dressed to meet Nick.

Her gaze landed on her purse. *The letter.* She didn't have much time before they would leave to meet Nick for dinner, but she needed to know what Marcus had to say to her.

She dug the envelope out, kicked off her shoes, before scooting back against the bed headboard. Slipping a trembling finger beneath the seal, the flap opened, and she pulled out his letter.

Dear Roni,

You are my daughter, not of blood, but by choice. And because I love you, I want to make sure you have many options in life without financial worry. This is the sole purpose of my gift to you.

However, I do have a confession to make. You will probably think I am taking the coward's way out, and you'd be right. I have failed to explain what took place years ago before you came to live with us. My excuse, I didn't want to witness your disappointment in me or lose your affection.

Before your parents passed away, on my recommendation, your father invested heavily in several oil wells that were later found to be dry holes, losing all he owned. When I told John his investment was lost, we never spoke again. Several days later, I received word your parents had died in a car accident and that you were coming to live with us. I am truly sorry about the loss of your parents, but I thank God everyday that you became part of our family.

The inheritance is yours, not to repay your father's loss, but to show I love you as much as I love Drake and Samantha.

I hope one day you will be able to look back and remember me fondly.

With all my love and admiration for what you are and what you are capable of being.

Marcus

Roni's thoughts bounced all over the place.

Logically, she couldn't blame Marcus for her father's bad investment decisions. To be absolutely fair, her father was a grown man. No one twisted his arm to invest everything he owned on a speculation. His was folly of the worst kind.

What worried her most, the thought her father may have deliberately taken his and her mother's life. Did he? She may never know the answer.

She tried to remember. Was her father acting strange when he dropped her off at school that day? No. If anything she remembered him smiling. He teased her about how pretty and grown up she looked, and how she was the picture of her mother. He even mentioned for dinner they'd go out for pizza. His words didn't sound like a man bent on suicide. But then what did she know?

Roni folded the letter not sure what to believe. Better to allow Frank to have a stab at figuring out the whole mess before throwing blame.

For sanity's sake, she would remember her parents and the Peters as caring and loving family, unless proven otherwise. And then, her only course of action was to forgive.

CHAPTER 36

Drake knew he was acting more like an overactive school boy who, for the first time in his life, realized there was more to girls than hitting and chasing them around the playground. He smiled over the image.

Roni hadn't pushed him away or seemed put off by his kiss, which gave him hope.

He yanked off his shirt, and then threw it into the clothes hamper. How could he have been so foolish to wait to speak to her? He should have done it years ago.

The first time she came home from college, he knew he loved her, but he was afraid to speak up. Now, with all the trouble looming, he'd have to wait until he was out from under suspicion. He wouldn't saddle her with his proposal while the possibility of a jail sentence still hung over his head.

Tonight ...

His blood began to boil at the thought of dinner with Nick. His anger had nothing to do with accepting Nick into the family or making amends for previous behavior, but his fury had everything to do with Roni.

Drake knew his half-brother was attracted to her. He saw it in his eyes on Saturday and again yesterday.

He also knew it was a given ... Nick would flirt with Roni. And hopefully, Drake would hold back from slamming his fist into Nick's face.

It would be tough. But he was determined to keep his word. After all, he'd promised Roni.

My new brother better not go too far. She's mine—if she'll have me.

Drake kicked off his shoes, leaving them where they landed. He stepped out of his trousers, balled them up, throwing them so hard the clothes hamper toppled over.

The more he thought about sitting by while Nick flirted with his woman—*well not exactly his woman yet*—had his blood boiling.

He jerked one leg at a time into his jeans, snatched a shirt from the closet, all the while knowing this meeting tonight might turn out to be a disaster.

Twelve years he'd waited. Twelve long years—hopefully not twelve years too late. He was no closer to his goal of asking Roni to marry him than he was to learn who killed his father.

Why had he thought she needed time to spread her wings and become established as a lawyer before he asked? *Shoot!* Hindsight wouldn't help him in this matter.

He shoved his arm through his shirt sleeve rather roughly, buttoned the buttons before poking his shirt tail inside his jeans.

Love was a tricky business. And though he'd dated some, it didn't mean he was an expert in the business of love. Now he may have allowed his better judgment to get in the way of winning what he cherished most. If he'd taken the time to explain how she had become a vital part of him—the good half that made him whole—he wouldn't be worrying about losing her now.

Shoving his belt through his jean loops, he buckled it with more force than necessary.

He fully understood why God gave Eve to Adam. Like Adam, Drake would be incomplete without Roni.

With one final brush through his hair, he turned from the mirror satisfied with how he looked, but not happy with the upcoming dinner. He would have rather spent a quiet evening at home with Roni. However, the meeting was necessary for everyone's wellbeing, even if it did mean he'd have to hold on tight to his temper.

Strange to think of Nick as a brother, yet Nick was his own flesh and blood, *thanks to his father.* Nick wasn't to blame anymore than Drake for their predicament. He figured he'd never know the true reasons for his dad's affair. None of it made sense. But then, how does one make sense of infidelity?

He rushed out the room anxious to see Roni. When he reached the landing, he found her waiting in the foyer looking exceptionally gorgeous. The blue of her blouse brought out the color in her eyes and hair.

Regardless how many times he saw her, each time it amazed him how the room would light up when she walked in.

You've got it bad, old boy.

"Sorry I kept you waiting." The woman didn't know it, but she could twist his insides into knots and make him go wild with one look. Right now, he had all he could do to keep from gathering her in his arms and kissing her senseless, but something in her eyes stopped him. Did the dinner meeting have her apprehensive or was it him?

"What's going on? Something bothering you?"

"Nothing. Just thinking." She avoided his gaze.

"I'm a good listener." He moved up close and stood in front of her.

This time she turned her beautiful, but anxious blue eyes on him. He barely stopped himself from reaching for her.

"I know you are. You've listened to me grouse over my problems too many times to count."

Her sweet smile reminded him of the first time he saw her, cautious, guarded—only now she was much older and more beautiful.

"But since you've asked, I'm worried about this dinner with Nick."

She pulled her bottom lip through her teeth making him wish he could draw her close and kiss the worry away.

"If you're worried about me, don't be. I gave my promise I'd be on my best behavior, and the promise still stands."

"I know you did and thanks, but ..." Three little kissable worry lines appeared between her brows. "He seems to have a knack for pushing your buttons."

"Especially where you're concerned," He mumbled beneath his breath before grinning and then adding, "I won't let him affect me, you'll see. In fact, I plan on welcoming him into the family. He's my half-brother, regardless how he got here."

Roni chuckled shaking her head. "I can hardly wait to see how receptive he will be when you state it so eloquently."

Drake laughed and then chucked her under the chin, turning serious. "Listen, Roni, regardless what he says or does, even if it becomes a challenge for me, I promise I'll keep a lid on it. In fact, I'll do my best to be cordial and accepting of my newly found brother. Like you, I know we are in this predicament together even if it's undeniably not of our choosing."

Roni placed her small, cold hand on his arm, sending a sparks of desire through him.

"Thank you. I know how hard this is for you, especially with everything else you have to deal with."

He jammed his fingers into the back pockets of his jeans to keep from pulling her into his arms and kissing her until they were both breathless.

"And who knows, you may learn to like your new brother. Shall we go?"

"I'm not sure about the liking," he growled, "but *yeah*, we can go."

He held open the door for her. The breeze lifted and carried the sweet scent of her perfume. His senses went on *Roni alert*. Once again, he wished they were dining alone, out by the pond, waiting for the sun to set. One day ... *please God, let it be soon.*

Once in the car, Drake eased out of the drive and onto the road, wishing they were heading in the opposite direction.

He wondered if he would ever be able to like Nick, or would his brother always be a thorn in his side? He hoped he wouldn't be, especially where Roni was concerned. If Nick even looked crosswise in her direction, he'd let him know straight out she was off limits, or at least he hoped she was.

"Drake, I hate to bring this up again, but ..." Roni glanced out of the front window chewing on her bottom lip again. "What if Nick is unreasonable?"

"In what way?" Drake had a pretty fair idea of what she referred to.

"Well, what if he thinks he should have more than your father left him." She rushed on. "By law he's not entitled to more than what was in the will, but Nick could cause a long, drawn out court battle over his rights as a neglected child, which would undoubtedly be thrown out of court, showing your father's generosity."

Whew! He was way off base with what he thought she'd say. But this wasn't much better. Considering Nick might be greedy didn't set well with him either.

"However, if Nick found a hungry lawyer, it might be expensive to fight and could tie the estate up for a long period of time." Roni seemed justified by her concerns.

"Look, I don't want to have a legal battle with him, but if it comes to one, then I'll do what I need to do to keep the estate and corporation protected."

Roni nodded, continuing to worrying her lip.

"And if you don't stop biting your lip, you'll soon have a hole in it."

She smiled at him, letting out a pent up breath. "I guess I'm borrowing trouble, as your dad so often reminded me *not* to do."

"I don't think we have anything to worry about. But if worse comes to worse, we'll work together to see what we can do to get Nick to change his mind."

"Thanks. Hopefully, he'll be happy with what he received."

"But if not, with your expertise in law and my talent in friendly negotiations, we'll win him over."

"*Yeah.*" Roni laughed outright. "I can just see your *friendly negotiations* ... a fist in the face."

Drake tried for affronted, but failed miserably. "When have you ever seen me put my fist in someone's face ... not that I haven't wanted to a time or two. I'll have you know, I live by the *Golden Rule.*"

"Do unto them before they do it to you?"

Her laughter echoed around him, holding him captive, He wished the time was right to ask for her hand.

"Ah, come on now. You're pinning a bum rap on me." He loved the sound of her laughter and was pleased she was able to tease him once again. Thankfully, they had moved past the hostilities of this morning.

Had it only been this morning? It seemed like he'd lived with Roni's displeasure for a decade. He didn't like it when she was hurt or upset, especially with him.

"Seriously, will you be able to talk civilly with Nick or will I need to wear my referee hat?"

Drake knew his brother hadn't warranted his temper Saturday or Tuesday, even though Nick's cocky attitude had pushed Drake past him limits. Truth be told, he probably egged the guy on by his own surly temper. But what a shocker to find he had a brother. It took some getting used to—even now.

"No, I'll be on my best behavior … Scouts honor." He saluted, face mockingly-serious.

"Goofball, you were never a Scout."

He shrugged. "It sounded good. I had to give it a try."

Roni shook her head. "Honestly, Drake. Just promise you won't provoke him."

He gave her a fake wounded look. "I'll have you know I haven't fought with anyone since grade school—and I had a good reason. The guy was picking on Sam."

When he heard her exasperated huff he added, "Okay, I promise I will not say or do anything to push him over the edge. In fact, I promise to be the epitome of good behavior. Does that suit you?"

"Yes, thanks." She let out a sigh, so telling of how tightly wound she had become. "I'm about up to here." Her hand made an imaginary slice under her neck. "With everything coming all at once, it's piling in on me—your father's murder, reliving my parents' death, Nick, and trying to keep you out of jail. There doesn't seem to be a reprieve in sight. At the moment, one more shovel load might tip the scales, if you know what I mean."

He grabbed her hand, gave it a slight squeeze, then placed a gentle kiss on her fingertips. He continued to hold her delicate fingers, relishing the feel of her.

"Roni, I'm sorry you have been placed in the middle of all this and doing a good job holding it all together. I hope you know I have complete confidence in you and your abilities. And I want you to know how much I admire you." He wanted to add *love you* but couldn't—not yet.

"You're a bright, intelligent, and gifted woman. And I have complete faith in you. I wouldn't want anyone but you in my corner."

"Thanks, Drake. Your words mean a lot to me."

The Jalapeño Tree came into view and Drake released her hand to down shift. He turned into the parking lot and found a reasonably close parking spot across from the entry.

After he helped Roni from the car, he asked, "Shall I ask for a table on the patio?"

"Knowing how loud it is inside, outside might be best. At least the weather is cooperating."

Drake placed his hand on the small of her back, feeling the warmth of her skin radiating through her top. Her scent, her nearness caused his male hormones to explode. *If only ...*

"Well, it seems I will not only have the company of the lovely Veronica but of *my* big brother Drake."

Drake hadn't planned on Nick's words needling him, but they did. Could be he wasn't used to having anyone other than Samantha call him big brother, or maybe because he had been left to deal with the fallout of his father's indiscretion. But most likely, it was because his younger brother had the intentions of making a play for his woman.

"I thought it would be a good chance to become better acquainted, since we *are* brothers."

"*Oh-ho.* The man has finally accepted defeat." He winked at Roni.

Drake remembered his promise and unclenched his fist as he forced a smile and pulled Roni a little closer to his side. Nick's smug attitude galled him, but he put aside his anger and tried for friendly. He hoped his brother would oblige.

"Not defeat, exactly. More like a truce since nothing will come from us being at odds. I'm willing to make a new beginning, if you are." He held out his hand.

At first, Nick looked at his hand as if it were a snake. After a slight hesitation, Nick raised his brow. He grabbed Drake's hand, squeezing a little harder than necessary, which Drake ignored—*barely.*

"Never gave much stock in new beginnings, but I'm willing to give it a try. It might be entertaining to see what develops. Does this mean I'll be privileged enough to meet my sister too?"

"Yes. Samantha wants to make your acquaintance."

"Good. Can't wait to meet Sam."

Drake ignored Nick's use of Samantha's nick name. Then Nick turned his gaze on Roni. He gave her a *come-on* smile. He barely contained his need to forcibly knock Nick's lights out.

"Hey good-looking, you sure look beautiful tonight." Nick gave Roni a slow once-over.

"Thank you."

Drake mentally kicked himself for not telling Roni earlier how gorgeous she looked. Now his brother had beat him to the punch.

Hopefully, this wasn't the beginning to one horrible evening. Otherwise, he'd be hard put to keep his promise.

CHAPTER 37

The moment Nick took her hand, Roni felt tension in Drake. For whatever reason, Nick was goading him and using her to do it. But Drake didn't take the bait, and she was so glad he had kept his promise.

Though not an easy feat, she extricated her hand from Nick's grip and said, "Shall we." She motioned toward the entrance, hoping they would take the hint.

When both men rushed to open the door, Nick beat Drake. Then she felt Drake's strong hand at the small of her back. Unlike earlier when his touch sent her senses off the chart, it didn't happen this time. Instead she felt sandwiched between two testosterone driven hostiles. With the heighten state of doom, she wondered how she would keep the men from coming to physical blows.

The hostess led them outside to the patio and seated them away from the other guests, which she figured was Drake's doing, since he'd spoken with the young woman upon entering the restaurant. When Nick held out her chair, she thanked him but didn't look up to see how Drake was fairing with his brother's over attentiveness toward her.

Roni waited until their orders were placed before asking, "Did you have a reason for this meeting?"

He shrugged as he placed his napkin on his lap. "I wanted to make sure you had all the information you needed, or if there was something else I could supply? Now, it seems to be of no consequence."

Drake placed his hand over Roni's resting on the table. He gave her fingers a gentle squeeze raising his brow, as if to say *may I?*

She gave a slight nod.

Instead of releasing his hold, his warm fingers curled around grasping her palm.

The pounding of her heart was partially due to fear Drake might say something to turn the next few minutes into a free-for-all, but greatly due to his continued touch.

She figured he was showing Nick she was off limits which caused her to seethe a little inside thinking he might be using her as pawn in the game both men were playing. His actions had her nerves on edge.

What next … a sparring match or a duel at twenty paces?

"Roni received the DNA results this morning and, yes, you are my brother. And though under difficult circumstances, let me, along with Roni and Samantha, welcome you to the family."

Was he including her as a sister or staking his claim? It had to be a male thing, turf war, or whatever they call it. The exhilaration of his touch moments before plummeted with a heavy thud in the pit of her stomach.

She hoped her face didn't show her disappointment. When she tried to extricate her hand, Drake wouldn't let her. Rather than make a scene, Roni relaxed and didn't fight him.

When she looked up and met Drake's gaze, her breath was nearly snatched from her throat. He didn't have the look of a brother or someone proving a point, more like someone who admired and loved her beyond reason.

"Well, thank you, I think." Nick looked at both of them strangely. "And just what does it mean and where do we go from here?"

"As to what it means, Roni can fill you in on what my father left you in his will. However, let me add, if you are thinking about moving here permanently, if you'll tell me what you do for a living, I'll do my best to find you a position in Peters Corp. Or if you'd rather not work for us, I'll do whatever I can to ease your search by way of introductions into whatever company you choose. There aren't many large companies in Athens. There are a few more in Tyler. However, Peters Corp does have connections in Dallas and other large cities, and I still offer my help."

Roni was astonished and proud of Drake for showing the generous side of his nature. She admired him for taking a sticky situation and turning it into something positive. However, she admired him most for stepping up and showing Nick genuine concern for his plight by offering his help.

Nick emitted a whistle through his teeth and then cocked his head to one side giving Drake a speculative look of suspicion. "Now, why would you be so generous? Is there something you're not telling me?"

Drake gave a short laugh, shaking his head. "No, I'm not hiding a thing. As to my character and my word, ask Roni, I believe she will vouch for me." His smile was warm and gave her goosebumps.

"I know we aren't responsible for what our parents did. But I'm willing to do my best to treat you fairly, even if from the beginning we got off on the wrong foot."

"*Humph.*" Nick leaned back giving Drake a narrowed-eyed gaze. "Just like that—" He snapped his fingers. "—and we're bosom buddies, or in our case … brothers. Now why do I find it hard to believe? There's got to be more to the story." His face turned into a suspicious sneer.

Drake shook his head. "I have no hidden motive." He lifted his free hand, palm up, then rested his forearm on the table edge, aligning his fork with his knife.

"If you were born into the Peters family you would have had the same advantages we had. So let's just say, I'm trying to make up for our not so auspicious beginning. I hope you will accept my gesture as intended, a peace offering."

Nick leaned forward, placing both elbows on the table, starring down at his hands, then looked up at Drake.

"Okay. If it's truly as you put it, I'll give some thought to your offer and let you know." He nailed Roni with his gaze. "And the will? What did my dear ol' daddy leave me?"

Drake's fingers constricted slightly. Roni didn't want to look at Drake, but prayed for understanding.

She couldn't quite figure Nick. He showed no surprise or reaction when she told him what Marcus had left him. He didn't even ask what the others received, just watched her as she explained how he would need to go about collecting the money.

Nick turned to stare at Drake. "Accountant."

At first, she was a little confused, and so was Drake.

"Have you done anything else besides accounting?"

Nick was a complex man. He hid his feelings well. Nothing seemed to faze him unless they mentioned Marcus.

"Managed a team at my last company."

Drake released Roni's hand, pulled out his wallet and withdrew a card. "Do you have a pen?" He directed his question to her.

She dug into her purse and handed him one.

"You can get in touch with me at this number." He turned the card over, writing on the back. "The number and name of the attorney you need to get in touch with for the inheritance, is here also. The other number is my cell phone."

He passed the card across the table. "Once you have decided whether you will be staying or going back to New York, give me call. As I mentioned earlier, I know we got off on the wrong foot, and I apologize. However, I would like for you to keep in touch. Samantha and I want to know you. You are family now."

Roni hadn't seen this coming at all. There had been no reason for worry after all. Drake apparently had planned all along to make amends with his brother, for which she was delighted in his behavior.

The waitress came to the table with a tray of steaming fajitas and other Mexican dishes. Conversation stayed on the general side as they ate.

Nick told a little about his life in New York.

Drake told about the ranch and some of the businesses of Peters Corp.

Roni let down her guard and enjoyed the food and her companions.

The men were alike, yet dissimilar. Some of their mannerisms were so identical, Roni marveled at how they could be raised in different households, separate parts of the country, and yet do things so much alike.

Nick, in his own right, was a handsome man, but in Roni's opinion, not nearly as striking as his big brother. Drake held a distinction Nick couldn't quite match—then again it could be loving Drake made the difference.

When they were finished with their food, Drake offered to have Nick out to the house for dinner the next night to meet Samantha and her family, to which he agreed.

"Will you be there too?" Nick directed the question to Roni.

She noticed Drake bristle, yet he didn't say anything.

"Yes. I'll be in town for at least another week. While I'm here, I stay at the ranch."

Nick's gaze traveled from Roni to Drake. "Are you two an item?"

Shocked, heat filled her cheeks. Without looking at either of the men, Roni laughed, then decided to make things clear to Nick. "Drake and I—"

"Yes." Drake leveled his gaze on Nick. "Roni is taken, if that's what you're asking."

Nick shrugged. His eyes narrowed in amusement while a smile played at the corners of his mouth. "No harm in asking. Just making sure, otherwise …" He shrugged.

Stunned by Drake's blatant lie, Roni decided not to call him out in front of his brother. The ride home would be a different story. She'd give him a piece of her mind for telling such a whopper.

Was he trying to protect her from Nick? If so, he could stop. She didn't need protection from any man. She could take care of herself and make her own choices of who to date and who not to date. And Nick didn't appeal to her.

As each man continued to size up the other, Roni simmered, wishing she could kick both of them in the shins and tell them to quit discussing her as if she wasn't sitting right there between them. For fear of saying too much, she smiled sweetly and stood, ready to leave.

Both men followed suit. She heard them talking cordially as she led the way out of the restaurant. However, when they stepped outside, she did her best to act pleasant while offering a forced smile and a goodbye to Nick.

He sauntered off to his car. When he was out of sight, Roni stomped over to Drake's car to open her door before Drake could. She was steamed that he took it upon himself to make Nick think they were an item. Why would he do that?

She wasn't at all interested in Nick, but how could Drake know? He shouldn't presume he could pick and choose her men.

"Well, fancy seeing you here, counselor." Frank Thornton stepped out from behind a black muddy truck with oversized wheels that could have been chrome but were to dirty to tell. It looked as if the owner had been out muddin' it all day.

"How did dinner go with the brother?"

"It went well. What are you doing here?" She shoved her agitation with Drake to the back of her mind.

"Checking out a few leads and thought I'd have some supper while I was at it."

"Were you in the restaurant?" Roni hadn't noticed him, but then again she hadn't been looking for Frank either. She felt Drake's presence behind her, then his hand on her waist. Though still upset with him, his touch did a number on her.

"Thornton, good to see you again."

"Peters." He nodded before smiling down at Roni. "In answer to your question, yes, I was inside having dinner. I decided I'd eat and be out of sight before you were through. Didn't want little brother to put us together." He leaned his hip against Drake's car fender, his gaze on Roni. "Y'all looked mighty friendly, at least up until the last, and then you, little lady, got your feathers ruffled. Something I should know?"

Drake's low rumble of laughter aggravated Roni. Yet the warmth of his body and the touch of his hand heated her blood in ways she didn't want to feel, at least not this minute. She hated that one touch could stir her desire for him.

He slipped his arm around her waist. A slight tug brought her up against to his side. "I think Roni was upset over something I said."

The scent of his cologne enveloped her. His nearness made it tough for her to stay mad at him.

For Pete's sake, she didn't have the fortitude of an armadillo.

Frank raised his brow in question. "Something private or something I should know?"

Roni was about to throttle Drake for chuckling. A change of submit was in order. "Why were you following Nick?"

"Nick … I see." Frank nodded as though he already knew what must have taken place. "*Well*, Counselor, I figured it wouldn't hurt to tail him to see what our boy was up to. If he'd made any friends, and if so, who? The usual. I never know where a tail may lead."

He turned his focus on Drake. "Did you know Nick called the ranch the night your father was killed?"

"No. What time?"

Roni could hear suspicion in Drake's voice, making hers go up a notch or two also.

"Around nine o'clock." His penetrating gaze never left Drake's face. "Would your father have let him in the house?"

"He could have. But Nick wouldn't know how to reset the alarm when he left. Dad wouldn't have given him the code—at least I don't believe he would."

"*Hmm*." Frank cocked a brow.

Surely Nick wouldn't have killed Marcus. What purpose would it serve? Unless he was angry enough to kill him for the years of neglect.

Frank shook his head. "No matter, I'll get to the bottom of it before it's all said and done. Always did like a good puzzle. And I have a couple of other suspects who are looking pretty good at the moment too."

"Anyone we know?" Drake's arm tightened around her waist.

"I'd rather not say until I've checked them out further. Don't want to go off halfcocked. I need to make sure their alibi is rock solid during the time of your father's murder."

"Do you think you'll be able to prove Drake's innocence?" Roni hoped he could.

"I feel fairly certain." Frank's face was a mask of hidden thoughts. "Just need to check out their alibis. But I won't know until I've researched everything in detail."

He glanced at the entrance to The Jalapeno Tree and then back at Roni. "I'd best be leaving. I'll give you a call tomorrow with a full report."

"Thanks, Frank."

He waved, then just as quickly disappearing behind the truck.

Roni wondered why the abrupt departure. Could be he didn't want to be seen with them, which stood to reason if he was trying to keep a low profile and gain information.

She turned to look back at the restaurant and was surprised to find Geoff coming out the door with Cheryl Smith, the administrative assistant from Peters Corp. They appeared far too chummy. His arm was around her waist and his head close to hers, talking as they walked. If she didn't know better she would think them lovers. Cheryl's shrilly laughter was drawing attention. All of it smacked of impropriety.

"Drake, there's Geoff and Cheryl. Where's Samantha?"

He angled a stormy look in their direction. "I don't know, but I intend to find out." He turned around and headed for them. "I'll be right back."

"I'm going with you." Roni had to run to catch up with Drake.

Geoff was opening the car door for Cheryl, when they walked up.

"What's going on? Where's Samantha?" Drake's pointed look took in both Cheryl and Geoff.

Stunned by the intrusion, Geoff recovered quickly with a nonchalant posture and friendly smile. "Drake, good to see you. Roni." He nodded at her and clapped Drake on the back. "What do you mean *what's going* on?" He appeared puzzled.

Cheryl stood there smiling with her bosom spilling out of her top, her gaze swallowing Drake whole.

His stern features and narrowed eyes had Roni stepping up next to him, hoping to prevent an altercation. But it didn't stop her from fuming over how Geoff seemed to be up to no good.

"What are you doing here? And where is your wife?" Drake's words were intent in their meaning.

"Sam's at home. Everything's so upside-down, you know, with Marcus's death and all ..." The words slipped glibly off Geoff's tongue while he lifted his hand as if to say *you know the rest.*

He smiled at the assistant. "Today is Cheryl's birthday. I knew you were too busy to take her out, but I thought someone should do the honors from the head office since she's such a loyal employee. I treated her to dinner. Sam's aware."

Geoff glanced at them, his smile too slick for Roni's liking.

"If I'd known you and Roni were going out, I would have said something and we could have all celebrated with Cheryl."

"Oh, that would have been grand fun." Cheryl directed her breathy reply and suggestive gaze at Drake. "Maybe another time. I looove to celebrate." Her words came out like a purr as she batted her fake lashes.

Flirting seemed to come too easy to her, especially where Drake was concerned. Did she do it in the office too?

Cheryl turned, slid onto the driver's seat sideways, her long legs still on the ground, her short skirt riding up to the top of her thighs, which didn't leave much to the imagination.

"The food was exceptional tonight. The only thing that would have made it better, if you had joined us."

Drake gave a tight smile, his gaze darting between the two dinner partners.

Roni couldn't remember Cheryl dressing so provocatively before, or her being such an outrageous flirt. But Roni hadn't been around the office in quite some time. Things and people often change.

Geoff turned to Cheryl. "We'll see you at work tomorrow. I should be getting home to my lovely wife. Happy Birthday again, Cheryl."

"Thank you. I so enjoyed dinner." Cheryl swung around in the seat, pulling her long, thin legs inside.

Drake shut the door rather forcefully.

"Well, I best be getting home to the family. See you tomorrow, Drake." Geoff dipped his head toward Roni. "Good to see you again. I'm sure you and Sam will be spending some time together while you're here. See you later." He turned and walked off.

Drake's gaze followed his brother-in-law. He led Roni to the restaurant sidewalk and then gave her the keys. "Here. Wait for me in the car. I'll be right back."

He rushed out into the parking lot and flagged Geoff down, then walked to the driver's side, bending down eye-level with his brother-in-law.

Roni couldn't hear what was said, but by the look on Geoff's face and his gestures, he wasn't happy with the conversation.

Drake stood back as Geoff peeled out of the parking lot like a petulant child, leaving behind the smell of burnt rubber.

When he saw Roni was still waiting where he'd left her, he motioned for her to join him. His face mirrored his irritation and she could feel his barely restrained anger as he interlocked their hands.

"What's going on?" She looked up at him. "Something you'd like to tell me about?"

"Suffice it to say, Geoff's been warned about Cheryl before. He should have known better than to take her out to dinner without his wife or others being present—birthday or no birthday."

"*Hmm.*" Roni didn't like where this was headed. Did Sam really know about the dinner? "He isn't having an affair with Cheryl, is he?"

A tick appeared in Drake's jaw. "He better not. If he is, I'll beat him to a pulp for cheating on my sister. And unlike my father who I didn't lay a finger on, you just might be defending me for murdering Geoff, which I would do with great pleasure, if he and Cheryl are having an affair."

She squeezed his arm. "Don't even jest about it. I'd be the first to say he deserves a beating and worst, but promise me you won't do anything foolish."

Sad, tired lines appeared at the edge of Drake's eyes. They had reached the car and he opened the door for Roni and assisted her into the seat.

He crossed his heart, a quirky grin in place. "Since you've already shot down my Boy Scout honor, a cross-my-heart will have to do. Now buckle up." He motioned at the seatbelt, shut the door, and then walked around to the driver's side.

She laughed, her heart tightening with love for Drake. He was a good, compassionate man, which made her love him all the more. Even if she was supposed to be angry with him, she couldn't be now.

With his worry over Samantha and Geoff, she wasn't about to raise the question of what Drake was trying to accomplish by warning off his brother Nick earlier at the table.

In the car, Drake turned to Roni. "I would take great pleasure in ramming my fist into Geoff's face, but I won't touch the guy. Unless I find out he is having an affair. If he is, I'll ask you to find the best divorce lawyer money can buy. And believe me, he'll wish he'd never cheated on Sam when the lawyer and I get through with him."

He let loose a humorless laugh. "If he is cheating on her, I intend to kick his sorry backside all over town."

"Do you really think they're having an affair?" Roni's heart twisted with pain as she prayed it wasn't so. Deep inside, she feared the worse and ached at the thought of the devastation her friend would face if Geoff was being unfaithful.

"Don't know. But I intend to find out."

He backed the car out of the parking space and headed for the street. "A few months back, I caught them at the office being far too chummy. If I could, I would have fired her back then. At the time, I didn't have grounds to do so outside of suspicion. I cautioned Geoff then to keep his distance. Apparently he didn't heed my warning. Well, he better this time."

Drake turned from the parking lot onto the street a little faster than warranted, making the wheels squeal. He gave Roni a sheepish grin, shaking his head. "Sorry, I'm a little up tight. I shouldn't take it out on the car or you. Shall we talk about something more pleasant?"

CHAPTER 38

Roni usually enjoyed the ride to the ranch. But as the headlights from Drake's car cut through the dark countryside, her turbulent thoughts were as black as the sky. Drake was far too quiet. He hadn't brought up Geoff or Cheryl, which caused her more anxiety.

Her head reeled with the possibility of Geoff's infidelity. How could she keep such a secret from her best friend and not let it show?

Roni leaned her head back against the headrest, closed her eyes, praying all of the disastrous things that seemed to be escalating and spiraling out of control would magically disappear. But the likelihood of it happening … *nil to none*.

What would she say to Samantha if Geoff were indeed cheating on her? No words could take away the depth of suffering brought about by his infidelity. The act alone would sever bonds of unity and trust that might never mend. She knew the reminder of his deed would always be in the back of Samantha's mind.

In her line of work, Roni had seen affairs destroy families and lives. A partner's betrayal had to be far worse than a loss by death. Death came with no fault. Adultery came with betrayal and rejection. And though both were hard to accept, with adultery, blame and feelings of worthlessness were often the aggrieved partner's plight. Roni had seen it happen far too often than not.

"I meant what I said back at the restaurant."

Startled out of her deep thoughts, Roni looked at Drake. "About what, Geoff?"

"No. Well, I did mean what I said about Geoff. And I will find out if he's having an affair behind Sam's back. And if he is ... I'll beat him to a pulp for hurting my sister and the kids." Drake shook his head and cleared his throat. "Why would he do something like that?"

"There are many reasons why a man cheats on his wife, but none of them are defendable or justified. Once a person makes up their mind to cheat, they generally don't turn back."

Drake responded with a derisive grunt.

Glancing out of the window, she worried her bottom lip over the problem. Samantha and Geoff hung heavy in the silence between them.

"Earlier at the restaurant, I meant what I said to Nick."

She turned her attention on him. When she didn't respond, he gave her a quick glance then looked back at the road

"You know, when you got all bent out of shape with me telling Nick you were taken."

"Yes. I remember. I also remember seeing a spark of jealousy in your eyes." She knew it was a guy thing—possessiveness, trying to defend his turf to what he perceived was his.

"Don't worry about it. Sam's problems supersede your error in judgment with Nick. I understand why you did it. It's a male thing—one-up-man." Her laugh sounded hollow. Her heart ached.

"Not where you're concerned. Jealousy, yes. But more like hopeful thinking on my part. I want it to be true."

Roni's stomach twisted. She feared Drake was only saying this because Nick might make his move on her if he didn't. He couldn't know she wasn't interested in his brother. "Look, Drake, I—"

"Please, hear me out. I know this isn't the best of times to speak to you. But before I lose my courage, I need to let you know how I have felt for a long time." He cleared his throat.

Roni nervously plucked at the arm rest as the road blurred in her vision. Her heart beat double time.

Don't let this be a game to him, please.

The glow of the dashboard caused the shadows to emphasize Drake's strong Nordic features, features endearing to Roni. From her first glimpse, she had never stopped loving Drake. She hoped and prayed one day he'd come to love her, but not because of a sibling jealousy. Fear struck a blow that Drake was mistaking possessiveness for love.

"I'm not sure how you feel about me ... us. Do you think ..." He hesitated as if searching for the right words, and then swallowed as if they were stuck in his throat. His intent gaze was focused straight in front of him.

Reeling from all the warring emotion, she didn't want to listen to what he had to say for fear he was only speaking up because he had competition. It couldn't be love, not after so many years.

"Roni, I've known for some time how I've felt about you, but I wasn't sure you could or would consider me as anything more than a friend." He took another quick glance in her direction.

"That's pretty low, Drake." Roni wouldn't play this game. "You're saying these things because you think it will keep me out of Nick's reach."

"Well there is that." He chuckled, raising his one brow and tilting his head, and then got serious again. "Not really." He pulled in a shaky breath. "Tonight, Nick made me realize I could lose you, if not to him then to someone else, if I don't speak up. I'm not willing to take that chance any longer. So I'm speaking now."

The gates to the ranch were opening when the car slowed to make the turn into the drive. The tall cedars flanked the road on each side like dark sentries guarding the driveway. If only they could guard and protect her heart from Drake. *Oh how I wish ....*

He couldn't be serious. Nick's attraction to her is what prompted him tonight. If she believed him and he wasn't sincere, she'd be destroyed. She would have to cut all ties to Samantha and the kids, something she wouldn't let happen.

The house came into view. Drake didn't continue. Roni figured he'd changed his mind. He pulled up and stopped, then turned to her.

"I hesitate to mention this with dad's murder hanging over my head. But if you're willing to wait until I'm free of suspicion for a proper proposal, I want to marry you, Roni."

What could she say? He couldn't be serious.

Roni's heart stopped then kicked in racing as silence hung between them. From the first day she saw him—a lost, lonely teen and he a handsome, sophisticated university man—she loved him and it had never changed, only grown stronger.

His eyes anxious, he watched her. "For some time, I have known how I felt about you. I never thought the timing was right, so I didn't speak up."

She couldn't be hearing him correctly.

"Roni, we've always been good friends, but my feelings for you run much deeper. I can't think of anyone I would rather spend my life with than you. What I feel inside is so much more."

Speechless, she had waited for years to hear him say these words. Now, he was doing just that, but was Nick the instigator. Could she trust Drake to really know his own heart?

"Drake just because Nick finds me attractive and you're afraid you'll lose me to him, it's not a good enough reason."

"No!"

His outraged reply shocked her.

"Nick has nothing to do with us." His seatbelt slapped back against the wall of the car and he was out the door and walking around to her side before she knew what was happening.

Had she angered him? She hoped not, yet she needed to protect her heart.

Drake's brows were scrunched together and his face thunderous.

Roni's heart sank. She'd gone too far with the mention of Nick. But so be it. She couldn't survive in this tug-of-war if Drake was only competing with his brother.

He helped her out of the car, held her hand as he silently walked beside her. When they reached the porch, he gently pulled her toward the glider. "Sit with me for a few minutes, please." He motioned for her to sit down, then sat beside her.

One shove of his foot sent the rocker in motion.

The thrill of him next to her, touching her, not as a friend but as a lover, sent her sensations soaring. If only his words were true.

When he gazed into her eyes, she knew without a doubt Drake was serious, but did he love her. He hadn't said the words.

"From the first summer you came home from UT, you were so excited about campus life, it was then I realized I loved you. Later when you told everyone you wanted to become a lawyer, I knew I'd have to wait." He slid his fingers through hers, intertwining them. He glanced out into the darkness where the security lights didn't reach and the shadows turned from gray to black.

"I've waited, Roni. Waited for you to graduate. Waited for you to become a lawyer. Waited for you to establish yourself with the law firm. And now I find I don't want to wait any longer. And yes, Nick made me realize if I don't speak up now, I'll lose you. If not to Nick, then to someone else.

"When you moved away, then found things to keep you in Dallas instead of coming home, I thought I'd lost you for good. I cursed myself for not speaking up when I could have." He scowled at the memory as his fingers tightened around hers, then he looked at her with a silly grin.

"I made a vow at Dad's birthday party I would take you out that night and let you know how I felt. I had planned on asking you then. But ..." He shrugged. "Nick happened. After that, everything seemed to blow up in my face, and then go downhill from there."

They sat in silence slowly swinging. Roni's heart raced at the knowledge Drake loved her.

"Roni, can you think of me ... No, I'm going about this all wrong." His foot stopped the swing. He turned and looked deep into her eyes. "I love you. Do you think you could ever come to love me?"

Her breath snagged in her throat as she witnessed the warmth of his love and sincerity. Slowly, the warmth began spreading through her, reaching the dark places of doubt and filling her with hope.

She wanted to shout *yes, I love you!* But she didn't. Taking a breath, she wasn't sure if she could say the words that had been locked away for so long.

"I know I was foolish for waiting, but I wanted you to be happy. And you wanted a career. There never seemed to be the right time to speak." His gaze delved deep into her soul. "Roni, you're scaring me. Is there no hope for us?"

She shook her head, a smile tugged at her lips. His countenance dropped. He looked away releasing his gripe, but she held on.

"I can't believe you have wanted me all this time."

He gaze searched her face, hope in his eyes.

"Drake." Roni touched his cheek, felt the stubble tickle her fingers. It felt so right and something she'd longed to do for years.

"For me, it started the day I first saw you. I've hoped and prayed you would love me. And now to find you have all along ..." She felt ecstatic. "From the first day you walked into my life, I have loved you. My heart has never wavered once where you were concerned."

He raised her hand, kissed the top of her fingers. His eyes darkened with emotion.

"Why have we wasted so much time? If I would have asked you way back when, we could have been married right now, even had a few kids ... *or not.*" He laughed. "But we would have definitely had each other to fill our lonely days and nights."

He let out a shaky breath. "I've wanted to speak to you for so long." He moved toward her. "Come here, love. We've wasted enough time."

His arm slid around her waist bringing her closer as his finger tipped her chin upward. "I love you, Roni, and I will until I die."

Their lips met.

Roni gave herself over to his kiss, his love, as their hearts beat wildly together as one.

Gone were the worries of tomorrow. Gone was the evil that had surrounded them from the past. They would make new memories together. Somehow, someway, they would make it possible.

As he deepened the kiss, the contentment of being truly loved by Drake was hard to grasp. The joy she'd long prayed for, she found in his arms. His love was far better than her dreams had ever been.

Drake pulled his head back, his breath as labored as hers. "I love you, Veronica Luann Reeves. And my love for you will never change."

He gave her another kiss, this one shorter, but just as breathtaking. When he pulled back this time he reached for her cheek and tenderly pulled her head down to rest on his shoulder.

She felt secure in the crook of his arm, their hearts beating as one.

Drake gave a shove of his foot, causing the glider to gently sway back and forth as he breathed in a deep shuddering breath. The quiet of the night surrounded them.

Peaking through the clouds and hanging low on the horizon, the moon cast off a yellow glow on the earth. In the distance, the call of a night owl brought about a feeling of peace. Yet Roni knew someone was out there hiding, waiting to harm those she held most dear.

Tonight, she wouldn't let the evil one ruin this moment she had long waited for. Years ago, she'd learned to relish each wonderful experience that came her way. The contentment she felt in Drake's arm she would savor for a lifetime.

She hugged the memories to her heart, reliving Drake's kiss and the declaration of his love. How long had she prayed for him to say the words. For both of them to have held back all these years was such a waste. How foolish to have squandered those lost, precious moments.

Drake stopped the swing and turned toward her. "Roni, until everything is resolved, I'm not asking for your promise. But once I'm out from under suspicion, I want you to be my wife."

She ran her hand along his cheek, then rested her fingers at the base of his chin. "Drake, I don't care if they think you are guilty, I know you aren't. I care about you. And we don't have to wait. I'll stand beside you regardless."

He grabbed her hand, moved it to his lips, kissing her palm. His eyes, filled with devotion, looked deeply into hers speaking the promise of love. The sensation she could lose herself in him scared her a little, yet she wanted so much more. She knew the full commitment of their love would come in time.

"I love you, and yet those words don't begin to describe how I feel about you." He breathed in deeply, releasing it slowly. "One more kiss, love, before we go inside."

Roni lifted her lips to meet his. Again, the passion of his kiss nearly consumed her but was too brief for her liking.

Drake stood, held out his hand. "If we don't go inside, I won't be able to let you go. And the next step in our relationship isn't something I'm willing to take until we are married."

CHAPTER 39

A note from Drake was on the breakfast table waiting for Roni. He explained he had to leave for the office early, but would see her later tonight before dinner with Nick and the family. The note was signed, *with all my heart and soul, Love, Drake.*

She folded the sheet of paper, running her fingers over the note lovingly. This was proof last night hadn't been a dream. Drake hadn't changed his mind. And she was loved by a most amazing man. Amidst all the trouble, love managed to manifest itself. *How odd?*

Roni wished she could shout her happiness to the world. But with all the problems still brewing and Marcus yet to be buried, the news was best left unsaid.

The cellphone rang. She picked it up and saw it was Sam. Her heart jerked to a stop then began to beat heavy in her chest. In all her happiness, she hadn't once thought about Samantha and her problem—*if there was a problem.* She wouldn't say anything about Geoff to her friend until she had proof. Last night could be as Geoff said, a birthday dinner.

Her gut told her it was a lie.

She managed to answer upbeat. "Hi Sam, what's up?"

"Drake called and said Nick Holdum is coming to dinner tonight. I would like to have something new to wear. How about meeting me for lunch and then let's go shopping? We haven't had a chance to really talk since ..." The unspoken sadness hung between them.

"I'd love to. Where do you want to meet and what time?" Roni tapped the edge of Drake's note on the table. Her stomach already too upset to eat breakfast.

"How 'bout the Sweet Pea Bistro on the square? We can eat, then you can leave your car and ride with me. Around eleven, or is that too early?"

"No. Eleven works for me. Just as long as we get back in time to dress for dinner."

"See you then. Love you."

"Love you too, Sam. Bye."

No sooner had she set her phone down, it rang again—*Frank*.

"I hope you have some time to spare, counselor. I need to come out and discuss a few matters privately with you that I didn't want to mention last night in front of Drake."

Roni's stomach tightened then revolted. Had he found some evidence implicating Drake? "Can you come now? I have another appointment and I need to leave the house by ten-forty. Will it give you enough time?"

"Sure. I'll be there in a few minutes."

She laid her phone down, her mind reeling with all types of scenarios of why Frank couldn't speak in front of Drake. It had to be bad news if ...

"There you are, Ms. Roni. What would you like for breakfast?"

Hazel's cheery smile and offer of food had Roni wishing she hadn't come down this morning. Her stomach clinched at the thought of eating. Yet she knew Hazel would worry if she didn't eat something, and would probably report it to Drake.

"I'll have a cup of tea and a piece toast, very little butter. I'm meeting Samantha in a little bit, and I'll be eating with her."

"I'll have it right out."

When Hazel delivered the tea and toast, Roni took it to the library to wait for Frank. She picked at the bread and sipped at her tea, all the while worried what Frank had found, praying it didn't involve Drake.

She heard Frank drive up and met him at the front door before leading him into the library.

"Have a seat." She motioned to one of the wingback chairs by the window and chose the other one for herself. "Would you like some coffee or tea?"

"No, I'm good." Frank sat down and pulled out a small notepad from his shirt pocket, flipped through the pages, before he looked up at her.

"The reason I left so quickly last night ... Geoff Hansen. I saw him coming out of the restaurant and didn't want him to see us together."

He squinted.

Roni could tell he was choosing his words carefully.

"He and Cheryl Smith, if you were wondering ... wonder no more. They're having an affair and have been for some time now, according to the clerk at the hotel." He shook his head. "At least six months. I was told they're regulars."

Roni felt horrible for her friend. "Where? At your motel?"

"Yeah." He nodded.

Roni couldn't believe Geoff would be so stupid. But then she didn't think he would run around on Samantha either. So much for thinking he was a good example of a husband and father.

Since she'd moved to Dallas, she hadn't been around Samantha and Geoff as much. That, and her preoccupation with Drake anytime she did come home, was probably why she hadn't picked up on their discord.

"The man should have better sense than to meet anywhere in this small town, but then ..." Frank shrugged, giving her an ironic smile. "I hate to admit it, since I come from the same species, but men are plain stupid when it comes to affairs. They're only thinking with one thing—and I don't believe I need to tell you what. They never give a thought to all the people their stupidity is affecting."

How can I meet Sam knowing this about her husband? "Are you certain?"

"Yes, ma'am. I saw him with my own eyes coming out of one of the rooms down from me yesterday afternoon. When he left, I waited at the end of the hall. Ten minutes later, out came the woman, a smile on her face, swinging her hips." He chuckled. "Believe it or not, she even had the moxie to flirt with me when she passed by."

"How disgusting."

Roni felt a horrible headache coming on. Sweeping her hair back off her face, she wanted to cry, shout, even throw something, but knew a tantrum wouldn't solve anything.

So sickened by Geoff and his betrayal, the thought of strangling him with her bare hands was most satisfying. She understood now why Drake would like to kick his sorry backside all over town. The man deserved that and a whole lot worse for what he was doing to Samantha and the kids.

"Frank, I hate to ask you, but do you think you can get pictures of them together, hopefully, in a compromising situation?"

"I figured you might want some, but I thought I'd present the problem to you first."

"Oooh, I do … and the more the better." Her rage was so over the top her stomach felt like acid had been poured down her throat. "And, Frank, keep this confidential."

"Yes, ma'am. I should have those pictures by tomorrow afternoon if our man stays true to form."

"Is there anything else to report?"

Frank studied Roni. She saw he was about to tell her something she wasn't going to like any better than she had about Geoff, which scared her beyond reason. In her heart, she knew it dealt with Drake.

"My source at the police department said the DA is getting ready to ask the Judge to file a warrant for Drake's arrest. They want to book him for first degree murder."

Roni thought she was prepared, but nothing had equipped her for this news. Drake's imminent arrest scared her beyond reason.

How would Drake face the charge of murder for his own father when Marcus wasn't even buried yet?

"Are you certain?"

Somber, Frank nodded. "I have it on good authority the arrest could come as early as tomorrow morning, Monday the latest."

"Do you know what evidence they have?" Roni picked at the cording on the edge of the armrest. Her mind raced with probabilities. What could she do to keep Drake out of jail, or out of reach of the police?

"My informant couldn't tell me what exactly, but she said it had to do with DNA found on the body."

"DNA? What kind? Blood … skin tissue?" Roni's heart raced. Drake's arm had scratches, could that be the source? "Where exactly did they find it on Marcus?"

"My source couldn't say. Except, what they did find seemed to link Drake. It's only a matter of time before he will be brought in for questioning and, more than likely, behind bars."

Frank raised his brows. "They also received an anonymous tip. There was talk of Marcus ousting his son from the company. Have you heard anything about that?"

"No, and I don't believe it for a minute. Marcus relied heavily on Drake, especially once he was diagnosed with cancer." But could she be so sure, especially since Marcus seemed to be a master of disguises? No, he wouldn't do that.

Frank looked at his watch. "Well, that's all I have to report." He stood. "I should be getting back to town."

"One more thing before you go." She stood, uncertain what to say. "I know I'm asking a lot of you and your people, but I need you to look into my parent's death."

"I wasn't aware they had died. Sorry. My condolences."

Roni shook her head. "No, it wasn't recent, but thanks. They died in the car crash seventeen years ago."

"I see. That's a while back. What are you looking for exactly?" He made a note in his little book.

Roni walked over to the desk, pulled out a folder from the drawer, then gave it to Frank.

"Everything I know about what happened back then, most of it coming from my father's attorney, is in there."

Frank scanned through the pages rather quickly.

"I know it isn't much, and after so many years it may be useless. However, if you can find anything at all to clear my mind as to why and how the accident happened, I would appreciate it. I will pay you your regular fee and expenses, of course."

Frank closed the folder and stared at Roni through half-hooded eyes. "You do know, with it being so many years since their death, my research could lead to nothing."

"Yes, but unless I have you look, my mind won't be at ease."

"I'll put my man right on it. We'll see what he uncovers. But don't set your hopes too high. Most, if not all, of the evidence might be gone by now." Frank slapped the folder against his leg. "But we'll check it out. One never knows."

"That's all I'm asking. If you come up dry, then I'll let it rest and figure it wasn't to be."

"Fair enough."

Roni walked Frank to the front door and stepped out onto the porch.

He glanced around the ranch. "This spread is quite a place. I assume it's rather large."

"Yes. Farther than your eye can see from where we stand. In my opinion, the ranch is one of the prettiest around. It was homesteaded years ago by one of Drake's great-greats. The tale handed down, he was a little crazy." Roni smiled, remembering the story as her gaze took in the ranch.

"How so?" Frank used the folder to shield his eyes as he looked out past the rod iron fence keeping the cattle from coming up to the house.

"The land was homesteaded by Thor Peters, fresh from Sweden, back in the 1800s. Tale has it he lost one of his ears from a Comanche raid defending his house and lands. Which back then the house was nothing more than a shanty. From that day on, Thor was known as One Ear by the Indians and ruthless and little crazy by his neighbors.

"Some say it was Quanah Parker who cut his ear off, but that's just rumor." She shrugged.

"Thor lived here about ten years before he sent off for a Swedish bride. When she arrived, they say she cried for months, begging to go home. But when Thor wouldn't relent, she soon fell in love with the big ox of a Swede and gave him ten children before it was all said and done."

Frank laughed, shaking his head. "That's quite a tale."

"Yes, and I'm not sure how much of Thor Peters' tale is true or how much is fiction." Roni's smile faded. "It's kind of like what's taking place right now with Drake, and also my folk's death. I need to know, Frank, on both accounts, what's truth ... what's fiction."

CHAPTER 40

Roni parked down the street from the Sweet Pea and Samantha's Tahoe. If Samantha wouldn't have been full of questions, Roni would have called and cancelled their lunch. Now, she was in the predicament of hiding the fact Sam's husband was a no good cheat and womanizer.

She sent up a prayer she wouldn't accidently let the information or how she felt about Geoff slip.

You are a good attorney who knows how to hide your feelings. Go in there and do it for Sam.

Plastering a smile in place, Roni entered the small bistro and saw Samantha waving her over to their table.

"I ordered you strawberry tea." Sam gave her a tight hug. "It's been ages since you and I have had a girl's day out. I've missed you terribly, Roni. And now with Dad ..." The mutual grief they shared didn't need to be expressed.

"I know." Roni sat down at the table. "Same here. I miss you, the kids, the quiet life—well, it hasn't exactly been quiet since I've come back, but you know what I mean."

"Yeah." Sam's smile didn't reach her eyes.

A woman came up to take their orders. When she left, Samantha looked around, and then leaned in closer to Roni. "I need to talk with you about something. But it's got to be kept just between you and me."

Roni's heart jerked to a stop then beat erratically. She had a good idea what Sam was going to say.

She gave another look around the little bistro. "You must promise me you won't say a thing to Drake. I don't want him knowing. I'm afraid he'd go ballistic."

Seeing Sam's beautiful green eyes filled with so much grief, Roni had an overwhelming desire to do bodily harm to Geoff. Roni masked her loathing.

"You know I won't say anything to Drake if you ask me not to."

"I don't know how to say this." Samantha's gaze darted around the room, then down, her arms resting on the table. One thumbnail nervously flicked the other. "I believe Geoff is having an affair."

Self-doubt evident, Sam's shoulders slumped and began to shake. Tears spilled over her lashes. She swiped at her face. "I don't know who it is. And I don't know what to do." The last came out a whisper and a wealth of hurt.

Samantha, the epitome of self-confidence and composure, crumbled before Roni's eyes. Never had she seen her friend so distraught. She knew there was nothing she could do or say to lessen Sam's pain.

All she felt for Geoff ... *contempt*.

Roni soothingly rubbed Sam's back doing her best to console her friend. She couldn't tell Sam what she knew until Frank had proof. "I'm so sorry, Sam. Are you sure?"

Unable to look at Roni, Samantha glanced down as she twisted her wedding ring around her finger.

"In the daytime I'm unable to reach him by telephone, even when I text him. Geoff is secretive about where he goes. He arrives home late at night—sometimes midnight or after. Says he's snowed under at work, but I know that's not the case. And he drinks now, which he never did before."

When Samantha glanced up, Roni noticed how haggard and worn she looked. Why hadn't she noticed it before now?

"Lately, all Geoff does is criticize me—what I'm wearing, how fat I am, how my straggly red hair is ugly. He used to tell me how much he loved the color of my hair, how my hair drew me to him. Now all he can do is find fault about me period." Samantha swiped at her cheek.

"Roni, it hurt terribly when Dad died, but Geoff's infidelity is tearing me apart little by little. Soon there won't be anything left of me. What did I do wrong?"

She wished she could wring Geoff's neck. The pain in Samantha's eyes was almost too much to bear.

"You did nothing wrong. Listen to me, Samantha. It's not you. It's him."

She shook her head, unwilling to blame Geoff. "Maybe if I'd been more attentive. Paid less attention to the kids, more to what Geoff ..." She trailed off, shaking her head. "It must be me."

"Stop it, Sam." She squeezed her hand to gain her friend's attention. "Listen to me. It has nothing to do with you, but everything to do with Geoff. It wouldn't have mattered how you looked or acted, or what size you were, or the color of your hair. Not even how little or how much attention you showed him.

"Men, and even women, don't have to have an excuse to be unfaithful. Once they've made up their mind to have an affair, no amount of talk will discourage them from their path.

"He's the one who is looking elsewhere. Whether he went looking, or the woman fell in his lap—he alone is responsible. You couldn't have changed the outcome regardless what you did or how hard you tried."

Sam sniffled before giving Roni a miserable, watery smile. "Thanks for being such a good friend."

"I'm not saying it as a friend. It's the truth. In my profession, I've seen it happen too often, and the outcome is always the same.

"When a man has a roving eye, he'll soon act upon what he perceives as better, more appealing, when in fact, it's not. His libido gets in the way, and he can't see what he's going after is all smoke and mirrors. Most times, the one they have the affair with is far worse than the one left at home."

The waitress walked up with their plates.

Samantha averted her face.

Roni smiled sweetly at the woman. "I'm so sorry, but I've just discovered we can't stay and eat. If you wouldn't mind, could you please place our lunches in containers, and give us two to-go cups also."

"Certainly. Would you like to add a dessert?"

"They do look wonderful, but no thank you."

They both fell silent with their own private thoughts as they waited on their lunches to be packed.

"Drake told me you hired a PI to check out Nick's credentials." Sam fiddled with her drink straw, stirring her tea haphazardly.

"Yes. Frank Thornton. He's in town. I asked him to search for leads in your father's death. I felt we needed extra eyes on the case."

"Good. I hope he finds whoever ..." Hurt filled her eyes. "Do you think he ah ... Frank, would he have time to do some checking for me? Maybe follow Geoff, see if my suspicions are founded?" Sam's cautious voice held the lack of confidence she normally exuded.

Roni wished she dare tell her friend Geoff was a no good, low down, cheating dirtbag who was probably at this very moment in bed with the other woman. She would also like to say Frank was already in the process of gathering proof. But she couldn't. At least not until they had all the conclusive evidence they needed to sway the judge in their favor, if it came down to that.

"If you take this step, and if Frank gives you evidence your worst fears are true, what do you plan to do?"

"I have to know." Sam picked up the fork and drew lines in the tablecloth that disappeared as quickly as they were drawn.

Roni wished Sam's problems would evaporate as rapidly.

"I can't live with a man who would lie to my face while cheating behind my back. I couldn't trust him again." A small spark of fire ignited in Samantha's eyes.

"If Frank finds he is cheating on me, then it will mean Geoff has broken every vow he pledged to me on our wedding day. He will have trampled our vows of faithfulness and trust beneath his feet."

Again tears brimmed at the edge of Sam's lashes, but Roni recognized the steel in her voice this time.

"I won't tolerate his infidelity. I deserve better. So do my children. They also deserve a father who loves their mother, and who will give them security, not instability. I won't live in ignorance or with his surly temper."

"I understand. If you're sure this is what you want, I'll have Frank look into the matter."

"I'm sure." Samantha glanced up with determination in her eyes. "Now, let's think on something more pleasant. Since I unloaded on you, I believe it's only fair you tell me what's new with you?"

Roni would have loved to tell her friend about Drake's declaration. She knew Sam would be ecstatic. Yet it didn't feel right to be so happy when her friend's life was being torn to shreds.

"Not much. Work, work, and more work. I'm enjoying my few days of freedom from the office, even under these sad circumstances. This brings about another sad note.

"I heard they may be releasing your father's body by Monday. If they do, we will need to make arrangements with the funeral home."

"It all seems so surreal, as if Daddy was just away on one of his business trips. Maybe once we have his funeral and he's buried next to mama, it'll all set in.

"This mess with Geoff has me all up in the air. Everything seems to be tumbling down all at once. At times, I feel like I'm losing my mind. The two things keeping me sane are my children and God. Without them, I'd be lost."

Roni nodded. "I understand."

They continued to talk about other small things in general, skirting the main issue prominent in their minds—Geoff.

Roni paid the check, grabbed the bags while Sam grabbed the two teas, then they left the little restaurant.

Across the street from the bistro, Roni recognized Detective Jeffers coming out of the county courthouse. "Sam, cool off the car, I'll be right back. I see someone I want to speak to for a moment."

"Want me to come with you?"

"No, it'll only take me a minute or two. It's a legal matter." She placed the bag of food and her purse on the car seat.

Roni j-walked across the street, angling toward her quarry, hoping she could get a straight answer whether an arrest was imminent.

"Detective Jeffers, may I have a word with you?"

He turned toward her. "Ms. Reeves, you know I could give you a ticket for crossing the street at an undesignated crosswalk."

His crooked smile and quip made Roni grin.

"Sorry about that, but I hope you won't. I was afraid I'd miss speaking to you if I went the conventional route. And I did look both ways." She grinned.

"What can I do for you?" He glanced to where Samantha was in the Tahoe then back at Roni. His eyes missed nothing.

"I heard a rumor you are about to make an arrest for the murder of Marcus Peters. Is that true?"

Detective Jeffers tilted his head to one side, giving her a narrowed gaze. "Now where would you hear such a rumor?"

"You know, a small town and all, talk's bound to get out when something as big as an arrest is in the wind." Roni wanted an affirmative or denial.

"You shouldn't be listening to rumors. In my experience, rumors most often steer you in the wrong direct. And, if I told you one way or the other, just what would you do with the information?"

She smiled sweetly. "It would depend on who you were going to arrest."

"While I can neither deny nor confirm what you heard *around town.*" He gave a short chuckled. "What I can tell you, the investigation is ongoing. We hope to make an arrest as soon as we have enough conclusive evidence. But until then ..." He shrugged.

His intent gaze strayed across the street again to the Tahoe, nodding in its direction. "Is that Drake Peter's sister? Mrs. Hansen?"

"Yes. We were just in the Sweet Pea." Roni was a little surprised he recognized Samantha.

"Well, I won't detain you any longer then." He gave a quick dip of his head. "Have a nice day, Ms. Reeves."

"You too." Roni struck off toward Sam's car.

"Oh, Ms. Reeves."

She turned, puzzled. "Yes?"

His keen attention was directed at her. "You might think about crossing at the light. Much safer and, I might add, ticket free."

"My thoughts exactly." She gave him a quasi-salute.

Detective Jeffers' chuckle had Roni shaking her head and waving goodbye. She would have liked nothing better than to j-walk to Sam's car for the sheer pleasure of seeing if he would truly give her a ticket. All that stopped her ... she didn't want to pay the fine if the man was serious.

Roni was a little miffed how Jeffers had completely skirted the issue and hadn't eased her mind one bit about Drake's arrest.

Now she had a double worry—Samantha and Drake.

CHAPTER 41

When Nick arrived at the ranch, Roni noticed he was distant and a little on edge. She figured he wasn't sure what to expect from Drake or from the others. More than likely, his first reception weighed heavy on his mind.

She could well relate to his feeling of unease since she experienced the same the first day she arrived at the Triple Cross. Not knowing what to expect and having just come from her parents' graveside, every mile that brought her nearer to her new home was a cause for concern. However, when she was met by an enthusiastic girl her own age, Samantha, and after receiving a friendly welcome from Elle and Marcus Peters, though it took a while, she eventually began to think of the Triple Cross as her home.

Like her first day at the ranch, everyone gave Nick a true friendly Texas welcome, something he hadn't received the first time he walked through the door.

Roni saw the change in him. He joined the conversation and became less distant.

At dinner and through dessert, Drake and Samantha regaled him with stories of growing up in Athens, old family history—One Ear and other savory family tales. They also explained how Roni came to be part of the family.

Samantha's ability to cover up her hurt over Geoff amazed Roni. Beautiful and bubbly, Sam joined the conversation with enthusiasm. One would never know she'd spilt her guts to Roni earlier this afternoon. And her treatment of Geoff, quite normal, as if he wasn't the cheating, lying womanizer skunk she knew him to be.

Roni found it next to impossible to even look at Geoff without revulsion.

When Samantha asked Nick about his family in New York, his eyes narrowed and he became reserved again. But after the initial rough patch, Nick seemed to work past his anger and amused them with his childhood memories.

He turned a little somber when he mentioned his mother's death. "Before she died, mom told me who my father was and that he lived in Athens, Texas." He swallowed.

Before Nick lowered his gaze, Roni noticed a flicker of dislike.

Nick unclenched his jaw. "After her burial, I did some research. As a result, I came here to find out more about Marcus Peters and his family. And then I met the charming Ms. Veronica Reeves, and my brother, Drake, who welcomed me with open arms." Nick's gaze went around the table, with a raised brow and a wickedly handsome smile in place.

Laughter filled the room as Drake's color deepened. Again Roni was astonished at Nick's remarkable resemblance to Drake.

"I apologize for my bad, first impression." Drake laid his hand over Roni's.

The warmth of his touch was soon clouded when she wondered if his show of affection was for Nick's benefit or hers. If Nick's, she understood, yet the action chafed a little.

Drake's show of ownership wasn't missed by Nick as he nodded. "Apology accepted. I believe I owe you one also."

"How so?" Drake's brow wrinkled in question.

"The other day at the office … the day Marcus died."

"Ah, yes."

"I was doing my best to needle you, to cause trouble between you and Roni. I thought you were trying to get rid of me, trying to run me out of town."

"I was." Drake's laughter was cut short when Roni withdrew her hand, placing it in her lap. He stiffened slightly, then reached for his tea glass.

The others hadn't recognized her action had caused Drake pain, but she did. Roni felt horrible for acting like a juvenile and taking her spite out on him. Nick's reminder of Marcus' dealings with her parents' had soured her mood, yet Drake wasn't responsible.

"Have you decided to stick around long term?" Drake took a sip of iced tea watching Nick over the rim, his tone a little tight, but not so anyone but she would have noticed.

It was quite comical to watch both men size up the other.

"I haven't quite made up my mind about Texas yet. You mentioned something about a job in the company, are you still offering?"

"Certainly. If you—"

"Since when are we hiring?" Geoff's peevish interruption had Drake scowling.

"Since last night." He stopped Geoff from saying more by turning his attention back to Nick. "If you want to come by the office tomorrow, I'll show you around, tell you about the company. I think if we put our heads together, I'll be able come up with something best for both of us."

Nick glanced from Drake to Geoff and then back. "Hey, look, I don't want to cause problems."

Drake, his jaw rigid, straightened his plate. "There isn't a problem."

Roni figured if Geoff said anything more about not having a place for Nick, Drake would tear into him. For everyone's sake she hoped he'd take the hint and stay quiet.

"Geoff didn't understand I had already offered you a position, but he does now." Drake aligned his knife and spoon next to his empty plate, his movements slow and methodical, as he narrowed his gaze on Geoff.

Roni ran her arm through Drake's. She was proud of him for setting aside grievances for the good of all. Just one more reason she didn't want to live without him.

Drake pulled Roni's arm in snug against his side. "Where are you staying, Nick?"

"At the Holiday Inn."

Geoff looked over at Nick anxiously.

"I believe I speak for everyone." Drake's deep voice held conviction. "We'd like to have you stick around so we can get better acquainted. You're part of our family now. We'd hate to lose you when we're just getting to know you."

"Yes, I agree with Drake," Samantha chimed in. "In fact, I'd like you come to our house for dinner. It would give us a chance to get better acquainted."

Geoff mumbled something to Samantha. Her excitement crumbled, but she recovered quickly.

Roni, practically frothing at the mouth, wanted to do bodily harm to the man.

"I'd like to make a suggestion." Drake's remark to Nick, drew everyone's attention. "Why don't you move in here with me, at least until you make up your mind if you're going to stick around. If you decide to stay, I'll help you find a permanent place to live in town."

Nick seemed rather taken aback. "I couldn't do. I'm fine at the motel. I'd feel like an imposition."

"It wouldn't be imposition. We have plenty of room. You'd at least get home cooked meals." Drake smiled. "We have several bedrooms, and you wouldn't be living out of a suitcase. If you take me up on my offer, it will give us a chance to get to know each other better. It might help you make up your mind. You may find you don't like your new family, and then again, you may fall in love with us and not want to leave." He chuckled.

Nick wiped his thumb across the condensation on his tea glass. "Let me think about it. I'll give you my answer in a couple of days."

"Good enough." Drake shoved back his chair. "Shall we move into the living room where we have more space?"

Samantha's two boys, Timmy and Peter, spoke quietly to their mother, and then both said, "Excuse me, please."

The boys quick-stepped out of the dining room until they reached the hall. Their boisterous cheers and running feet could be heard until they were well out of ear shot.

Drake assisted Roni with her chair, and then took hold of her hand.

Samantha raised her brows smiling. She gave Roni a thumbs-up before lifting Ellie from the highchair.

"Me go pay, mommy." Ellie practically bounced out of her mother's arms. She grabbed Sam's cheeks, trying to gain her attention. "Me go pay, mommy. Me—"

"All right, sweetie. I'll take you to the playroom but you'll have to be good and not pester your brothers."

The little one nodded causing her whole body to jerk in Sam's arms. Elle kept up a steady stream of chatter as they left the room.

"You have some very lovely and well behaved children." Nick's gaze followed Samantha and Ellie.

Geoff pulled his phone from his pocket and began texting as he walked out of the room without responding.

His rudeness chaffed Roni. "They are super-sweet children. Samantha is a devoted mother." She purposely left out reference to Geoff. "She doesn't let the kids run wild or sass like I've seen some mother's do."

"I know what you mean. I saw a few hellions on the plane and in the airport when I flew into Dallas." He shook his head. "Not a pretty sight."

Drake motioned for Nick to go into the living room. "Have a seat." He led Roni to the loveseat then sat down beside her.

"How long have you two been dating?"

Nick's question drew Geoff out of his stupor. "They're not dating. What makes you think that?"

"You're behind times, Geoff." Drake squeezed her hand. "Roni has agreed to marry me once Dad's case is solved."

Geoff peered at them as if they were daft. "When did this happen? Does Sam know?"

"Do I know what?" Samantha swept into the room and chose the chair next to Nick. She saw everyone watching Drake and Roni. "What's going on?"

"Seems your brother and Roni are getting married. He just dropped the bomb before you walked in?" Geoff scowled.

"Fantastic." Sam rushed to Roni and Drake and gave them both a hug and then propped her hands on her hip. "I was wondering when my brother would come to his senses. And now he has. None too soon, I might add."

She squeezed Roni again. "We've got some plans to make. I'm so excited. And you didn't say a thing this afternoon." Her eyes clouded for a moment then brightened. "I can't believe my prayers have been answered. All I've got to say to you, brother … it's about time."

"I'm just glad she said yes. However, we decided to postpone getting married until Dad's case is cleared up, so don't go in hyper-mode planning our wedding. It'll be a while."

"She stays in hyper-mode." Geoff bored with the topic, pulled out his cellphone, and began texting.

Samantha turned scarlet as Nick's and Drake's narrowed gaze zeroed in on Geoff.

Roni would have loved nothing better than to have given Geoff a good swift kick on his rear for putting a damper on his wife's excitement.

"Regardless. I'll need you in hyper-mode. You and I will get together next week before I go back to Dallas. You always have such wonderful ideas. I'm counting on your help, even if we are going to wait until later."

Samantha brightened, yet the hurt stayed in her gaze. "I'll be delighted."

Geoff stood and shoved his phone in his pocket. "Get the kids. We're going home. I have work I need to do tonight."

"Can't we stay just a little longer?"

Geoff's glare had Samantha standing and Roni's blood boiling.

Sam turned to Nick. "I would love to have you come to dinner. Maybe we could make it Saturday, have a barbeque." She looked at Geoff. "How 'bout it Geoff?"

"Saturday I have a golf game. Should be gone all day."

"Great." She ignored her husband. "We will see you Saturday night then. Geoff may be a bit tired, but you and I can have a good long chat. I'll give you a call at the motel with the particulars."

Nick seemed a little perplexed, but nodded. "All right, I look forward to dinner."

"I wasn't aware you were so snowed under that you had to take work home." Drake directed his remark to Geoff, his face masked, his eyes drilling holes into the man.

"It's just a few things I couldn't finish this afternoon."

"Then more the reason for Nick coming on board. We can have him take over some of the responsibilities to free your time."

"I'm not in need of help, and it will take more of my time to train him." Geoff shot back.

"For a day or two maybe, a week at the most. Once you've trained him, your workload will lighten considerably. No need for late nights or taking work home. With Nick on board, you'll be able to devote more time to your family."

"I told you to get the kids, Sam. Do it now! I'll be waiting in the car."

Flushed, Samantha rushed out of the room near tears.

Roni stood. "Gentlemen, if you will excuse me for a moment, I'll help Samantha with the children."

She found Samantha standing outside the playroom door taking deep breaths and wiping her face.

That scum doesn't deserve her.

Roni cleared her throat drawing Sam's attention. "I thought I'd help with the children and get my hugs and kisses from them before they leave."

"Oh, Roni …" Samantha grabbed her, hugging her tightly. Neither needed to speak as Roni consoled her.

She took a deep, controlling breath, pulled back, and gave a sad smile. "I'd better get the kids to the car before he comes looking for me."

"Let him come. I'll—" She snuffed the words seeing she added to Sam's burden. "I'll help you."

Roni opened the door and was met by squeals of delight and little arms wrapping her legs.

Roni picked up the little one while Sam helped the boys gather and stash their playthings in the toy box.

Geoff was on the cellphone when they came out the door. He disconnected before they got to the car, giving them a disgruntle look for making him wait. "It's about time. I'll be up super late because of you dragging your feet."

Roni loaded Ellie into her car seat. The atmosphere so thick with tension, she wanted to tell Sam to grab the kids and spend the night, but she knew her friend wouldn't comply. Instead, she stepped back, shut the door, and then waived them off.

Was Cheryl the one he'd been calling? Had he made a date for later? If so, Roni hoped Frank would get plenty of incriminating photos, because she would use every last one of them to nail his sorry hide to the barn.

CHAPTER 42

"I spoke with Marcus the night he died."

Nick's confession wasn't a surprise, and Drake was pleased Nick brought it up without him asking. "You spoke with him Monday night? What time?"

"It was around nine. Due to the circumstances of our first meeting, I wasn't sure you were going to tell him about me. I thought someone needed to let him know I was in town."

"Since he was killed shortly after your call, why are you just now telling me? Didn't you think it might be relevant to the case?"

"Before last night you and I weren't exactly on speaking terms. Even tonight, I didn't know what to expect."

"I guess I deserved that."

"No matter. However, I figured I'd better let you know— come clean of sorts. If this means knowing I called him is a deal breaker, then ..." He shrugged. "I felt I needed to be open with you, especially if I decide to stick around."

Neither spoke while Roni walked into the living room.

"I got them off, but Geoff was in a pretty foul mood." She saw Drake's thoughtful mood, then turned to Nick. "What's going on?"

"I told Drake I spoke with Marcus Monday night."

"You did, when?"

"Around nine."

"You may have been the last person to speak to Marcus." Roni watched Nick closely.

"I realize it now. I called because I wanted to speak to him, ask why he never tried to contact me."

"What did he have to say?" Drake didn't like the sound of this. Could his father have invited Nick to the house and let him in? What if Nick was the murderer? No. Nick would have kept quiet about the phone call. He wouldn't have known the code to reset the alarm ... unless Dad told him.

"He said he learned about me from my mother. I didn't know it, but she called him a month or two before she died. She told him he had another son."

"Are you saying my father didn't know you existed until your mother told him?"

"He said he didn't. Also from what my mother said, I believe it's the truth." Nick shook his head.

"At the dinner table you told us your mother didn't tell you until just before she died." Roni rested her elbow on the arm of the loveseat. "She must have kept your birth a secret from Marcus also."

"I know how it sounds, and it shocked me too." His intense gaze was directed at both of them. "He wept. Told me how sorry he was, and if he'd known, he would have sent money for my support. Said he would have had me out to the ranch." His brow rose then settled back in place. "Maybe my mother was afraid Marcus would try to take me from her. I just don't know what to think."

"Marcus told me when my mother called with the news he made sure I was included in his will. That's the reason I wasn't shocked about the inheritance."

Drake unable to sit still, stood, walked over to the bay window. A reflection of him and the room behind him could be seen in the glass. He rubbed the back of his neck, aggravated Nick had gone against his direct order to contact his dad. But truth be told, he would have done the same thing if he were in Nick's shoes.

Releasing his pent up breath, he knew he had no right to be upset. He turned to stare at his brother, head bowed, elbows resting on his knees.

"It does sound like something Marcus would say." Roni interjected as she watched Drake, her face anxious.

"Yes, it does sound like dad. And according to Mr. Thompson, he changed his will earlier in the year to include you." Though reasoning prevailed in the matter, it didn't stop Drake from wondering if he could believe what Nick had to say.

At the very least, wouldn't his father have told them about Nick, or that he had included him in his will? Or was Dad too ashamed, as with Roni's folks, he couldn't bring himself to say anything?

Drake had never thought of his father as cowardly.

"He mentioned he wanted me to come to the house and meet you and Samantha and Roni. When I told him I had met Roni and you, and that you practically threw me out of the house, he laughed, and said, *that sounds like Drake.*

"We never set a time or date, but he said he'd call in a day or two." He turned his palm up. "But then he ..."

"Did he give you a reason why it happened ... the affair?"

"No. Other than my mother said they met at a work function, I know nothing more." Nick set unmoving then looked up. "It's getting late. I think I should be leaving. Do you still want me to come by the office tomorrow?"

"Sure. The call doesn't change anything."

"What time?"

Roni stood and made her way to Drake, slipping her arm through his. He appreciated her show of love.

"Make it nine. It'll give me plenty of time to take care of a few matters and free up my morning so I can show you around. We'll go to lunch around eleven, if you don't have other plans."

"Sounds good."

Drake looked down at Roni. "Are you free to go to lunch with us?"

"Definitely."

Roni smiled at him and his heart kicked into overdrive. There was no doubt in his mind she loved him.

When she smiled at Nick, jealousy hit him square between the eyes. Drake knew he shouldn't feel that way, but where Roni was concerned he couldn't help himself. He knew Nick had made several passes at Roni before. The idea of Roni loving him was too new and probably the reason for his spark of jealousy. But Roni did love him, and her enthusiasm wasn't for Nick, but for him.

"Roni, it has been a pleasure."

"Same here, Nick. I'm glad we had this chance to get a little better acquainted. I look forward to seeing you again tomorrow."

He moved toward the hall. "Oh, yeah, congratulations on your engagement. Apparently, big brother, you won after all." He laughed and then turned somber. "I hope I'm around to see the wedding take place."

"We hope you are too. Just another reason to move here, or at least stay a while longer." Roni tightened her hold on Drake's arm.

"Yes, I agree. It's a good reason for sticking around." Drake gave Nick a pat on the back, and then opened the front door.

Roni taking the initiative to show how she felt, made him feel good. He wasn't sure he'd ever get used to the idea Roni would one day be his.

They stood side by side on the porch, her head against his arm as they waved Nick off.

When they went back inside the house, Drake stopped her from going any farther than the foyer. He encircled her in his arms, then began to nuzzle her neck. He didn't know what it was doing to Roni, but for him, the feel of the soft skin beneath his lips was sending him into orbit.

He pulled back and looked into Roni's rosy, love-filled face, and almost lost all sense of decency. "Have I told you lately I love you?"

"Not in the last two or three hours." A sparkle filled her eyes.

"Well, Ms. Veronica Reeves, I love you beyond reason. I don't know what I would do without you."

"Well, then, you better keep me close at all times. Maybe we should get our license tomorrow and get married *ASAP.*" She wiggled her brows smiling up at him.

Drake wanted to say yes, but in his heart he couldn't saddle Roni with all the uncertainty. He knew he was innocent, but the police didn't.

He hugged her up tight, praying she would understand.

"I can't tell you how much your suggestion speaks to me." He gave her a quick kiss. "But we can't. At least, not until my name is cleared. Regardless how much the thoughts of waiting rubs me the wrong way, we'll wait."

"But Drake—"

He placed his finger on her lips. "We'll wait." He leaned his forehead on hers, drinking in her sweetness. His love for her ran so deep, even the remote possibility they might be separated tore him up inside. Yet he couldn't allow his love to pull Roni into a lifelong commitment that would bring about pain and separation—if it came down to his arrest.

He lifted her chin and sought her lips. The gentle kiss was sweet and filled with promise, leaving him reeling. He released her, turned her around to face the staircase. "Now go upstairs to your room before I forget the promise I made to myself and you."

She turned back around puzzled, still in the circle of his arms. "What promise?"

"The promise I'll wait until our wedding night to make you fully mine."

"Oh." A mischievous sparkle appeared. "That promise."

"Yes, *that promise*." He tweaked her nose then turned her back around. "Now go. I have work I need to do before I turn in."

She faced him again, giving him a beguiling smile. "I could stay and keep you company."

He laughed wholeheartedly. "Yes, and I would accomplish nothing."

"Would that be so bad?" Roni gave him a saucy grin.

"Yes, it would be, if you want to keep your reputation and our souls intact." Drake growled playfully. "I want our wedding night to be filled with firsts."

Roni's brows knit together. "Firsts?"

"Yes. The first time we say I do. The first time for us as man and wife. The first time I hold you in my arms without restraint. The first time I know you in the Biblical sense of the word." He flashed a knowing smile and watched her turn pink. "And the first time I fall to sleep holding you in my arms, to never let you go."

"Okay, you got me there." Tears appeared. "I love you more than I thought possible. You sure we can't get married tomorrow?"

Drake chuckled, then turned her around and patted her on the backside. "Get to bed you little minx. And, remember, I love you with all my heart, mind, and soul."

"How do you expect me to walk away with you saying something so romantic?" She turned, pulled his head down, and then kissed him soundly on the lips before walking to the stairs. "And you remember this. I loved you first with all my heart, mind, and soul, and it hasn't changed since I was twelve."

He stood watching Roni walk up the stairway. When she got to the first landing she turned with an odd expression.

"Drake, would Marcus have invited Nick to the house the night he was killed?"

"Hey, Good-looking, I didn't expect to see you up so early."

The room lit up the moment she saw Drake saunter into the room.

"You have turned my day into an exceptional beginning. Did you sleep well?" He lifted her chin and looked deep into her eyes.

Drake's handsome face could always make her pulse quicken, and this morning was no exception. His nearness caused her to desire more than he was willing to give, at least for now. She wished Drake wouldn't be so stubborn about getting married.

He bent and touched his lips to hers. The clean, fresh scent of just-stepped-out-of-the-shower, with a hint of cologne, surrounded her, turning her into a trembling mess of anticipation. His breath, the smell of mint, and his lips, soft and inviting, caused her to do a slow burn. One look and this man could turn her into a love-sick simpleton who would follow him anywhere.

She should have better control over her emotions. However, where Drake was concerned, she had none and she wasn't ashamed either.

He pulled back, his eyes sparkling, knowing full well how his kiss had affected her. He took his seat across from her, then picked up the newspaper paper. "Do you mind?"

"Of course not, if you'll share." She tried to act casual, knowing her emotions were still live-wired and sizzling from his kiss.

He held out the paper. "Your choice."

Knowing he liked to read the headlines first, she chose the second section.

Her gaze landed on a picture of Marcus—one taken several years ago—with a caption, *(Peters' Investigation cont'd from pg. 1)*. How could she have missed seeing the article earlier?

"Did you read this?" Drake, clearly disturbed, tipped the paper down slightly looking over the top at her.

"No. I just saw the second half." Roni pointed at the remainder of the article.

"Then let me read for you." He shook the newspaper making it stiff and straight again, hiding his face from sight.

> *The investigation is ongoing with no arrest yet in the murder of Marcus Peters, Founder and CEO of Peters Home Improvement, a nationally known chain. Peters was found suffocated Tuesday morning in his ranch east of Athens, Texas. According to one source, the Peters' murder investigation has received new evidence that should bring about an arrest in the next few days.*
>
> *Still in the spotlight is the son, Drake Peters. When asked if an arrest was imminent, Detective Jeffers, the lead investigator, had no comment other than, "... don't rely on outside sources. They are often wrong. As soon as we know something definite, you will be advised."*

Drake folded the paper, placed it on the table, and then stood staring down at Roni. "Regardless how much I want it to happen, this is why we can't get married. I love you too much to have you subjected to ridicule.

"Until I am no longer a suspect, our marriage is on hold. I know we've already told the family, but I think it best we keep our engagement quiet."

Roni rose from her chair, went around the table to stand in front of him. "Drake, you know what people say or think has never bothered me. I love you. I always have. I always will. I'll stand by you, regardless what happens. I see no reason to wait."

He touched her cheek. A look of sorrow filled his eyes. "I know you don't mind, but I do. I shouldn't have said anything to you. It would have been better not to speak until dad's murder was cleared up. But I couldn't help myself."

Drake drew Roni into his arms, his chin resting on the top of her head. "I love you more than words can say." He held her close, inhaling deeply, surrounding her with his love.

They stood locked in each other's arms while he spoke softly of wants, desires, and plans for their future. In the background hovered the threat their plans might never materialize.

When he released her, Roni's heart sank knowing if the murderer wasn't found soon, the likelihood of Drake behind bars was plausible. She didn't want to mention the DNA, but she had to.

"Frank heard a rumor they have DNA evidence linking you to the murder."

"How?"

"Could be when Marcus scratched you on the arm. Maybe some skin or blood fragments were still under his nails."

"That's a crock." His stern gaze fell on Roni. "You don't believe I killed him do you?"

"Not for a second. I've never suspected you. However, the police don't have the advantage of knowing what you are and aren't capable of doing." She wrapped her arms around him leaning her head on his chest. "We won't worry about it. They're bound to catch the person who killed Marcus."

Drake pulled her up tight. "Thanks for believing in me." He gave her a gentle kiss, and then pulled back.

"No thanks necessary."

"I need to leave. Can you meet me at the office around eleven-thirty for lunch?"

"Yes. Where are we going?"

"How does Rib Masters in Murchison sound?"

"I'll bring my bib. You know what I'm like when I eat ribs. Head to toe sauce." Her self-deprecation humor brought back the sparkle in Drake's eyes.

He tweaked her nose. "You look cute in sauce. In fact, you look beautiful in whatever you're wearing." He winked at her. "Come walk me out."

Drake put his arm around her as they walked through the house and out the front door, then gave her a kiss goodbye.

Roni stood on the porch and watched until Drake's car drove out of sight. The beautiful morning, though blighted by the news article, had her going back inside to grab a cup of coffee and a plate of buttered toast.

Choosing the glider, Roni gently swung back and forth mentally ticking off what she needed to do. She pulled out her cellphone and punched in Frank's number.

"What can I do for you little lady. Wanting to know about Casanova?"

"Who?" Roni, a little confused, realized who he referenced. "Oh, Geoff. Tell me later. Right now what I need to know is there any way you can get a copy of Marcus' cellphone calls made the week before his death? The police took his phone as evidence." Roni twirled a strand of hair around her finger, staring off toward the pasture. Something gnawed at her mind, but was just out of reach.

"I believe I can get what you want. Is there something in particular you're looking for?"

"Yes. The night of the murder, and any unusual activity that may stand out the few weeks before. Frequent calls, text messages, or what have you."

"I'll have my gal, Helen, get on it *ASAP*."

"Thanks. I really appreciate all you're doing." She took a sip of coffee, set the cup on the wicker table alongside her half-eaten toast.

"Now tell me about Operation Casanova." She chuckled. "By the way, the name fits him to a T. Were you able to get any pictures or video?"

"Sure did. He's a creature of habit. They both arrived at the motel about five minutes apart around noon yesterday. Spent over an hour in the room. I have some great video and audio footage, more than enough to hang the guy. And Casanova's either really stupid or just doesn't care, but the curtains were left open for the whole world to see, including me. Must have thought second floor rooms were safe. However, my snapshots prove differently."

"I'd love to string him up for what he's doing to Samantha and those babies."

"How many kids do they have?"

"Three—two boys and one baby girl. I never thought he'd be the kind to have an affair on Sam, but seems I've been proven wrong." She took a sip of coffee and felt the warmth spread through her, but it didn't calm her need to strangle Geoff.

"Don't beat yourself up, counselor. People change. However, as a rule, people are creatures of habits. Too often a playboy before marriage has a tendency to be one after."

"What a shame." She breathed in. "Well, get all the evidence you can. I want to nail his sorry hide to the wall."

"I like how your think, counselor. Just remind me not to get on your bad side." Frank laughed.

She smiled, then sobered. "Oh, by the way, Samantha asked me to have you do some checking on her husband. I didn't tell her I had already hired you to look into the matter. So when you write up your report make sure to have one copy for me and one for Samantha, and do the same on the pictures."

"Will do."

"Oh, yes, tomorrow, Casanova is supposed to be playing golf at the Athens Country Club. I sure would like to know if golf is what he's *really* doing."

"I understand. If our boy plays according to pattern, I'll have enough evidence to tie Casanova up into a neat little package and deliver him with a huge red bow on top. I should have more than you will ever need or want."

"Good. Send me everything. I'll give Samantha what I think she needs to present a solid case against Geoff." She grimaced. Everything about the whole sordid affair felt sleazy. Yet for Samantha, she would walk through Sleazeville and back, if it meant Sam and her kids were taken care of and treated fairly. "And Frank, as with everything else, send me the bill."

"Will do."

Roni heard what sounded like papers being ruffled in the background.

"I have one more item."

Her nerves went into overdrive. *Drake. Please don't let it be bad.* "What do you have?"

"I want to prepare you. The newspaper reporter in today's news was spot on."

It felt like acid had been poured over her stomach. She grimaced with the pain.

"They're looking at our boy, Drake, as the murderer. You can expect an arrest between now and Monday. Evidence, skin fragments under one of the nails believed to be Drake's."

"Thanks." She could barely push the word past her lips.

"No thanks necessary. I wish I had better news. But I'll continue looking. I'm bound to come up with something to keep our man out of jail."

"I appreciate all you've done. At the moment, I'm praying you'll find some way of proving his innocence, but until you do … keep this between us. "

After disconnecting, Roni gave the rocker a shove with her foot, the back and forth movement somewhat settling. Yet, her mind wouldn't stop worrying the problem of Drake and his impending arrest. If the authorities did a check of Drake's arm they would find the scratches. They wouldn't believe his excuse that it happened while Marcus was falling, and there would be no way to prove differently.

Marcus was the only one who could corroborate Drake's story. Hopefully, it's the killer's DNA and not Drake's, but highly unlikely.

CHAPTER 43

The quiet of the library, the late hour, even the storm threatening to cut loose, had Roni all keyed up. If their earlier plans hadn't fallen through, she and Drake would be sitting together right now watching a movie, holding hands.

Instead, Saturday night and almost ten o'clock, she was sitting home alone with the notion she needed to be doing something, anything, to prove Drake's innocence. Fortunate for them, the police hadn't arrested him or called him in for questioning again. But Roni figured it was just a matter of time though.

Her chaotic thoughts jumped from one thing to the next while she paced the library.

Nothing about Marcus' murder made sense. No leads, no suspects, nothing, which didn't bode well for Drake. And Geoff—that cheating, no good lowlife ... *Let it go.*

She huffed out a breath. Where was Drake? It was getting late and she should have received a call or text from him since he left the house around six to meet with the vet and his ranch foreman. He should have let her know what was happening, or at the very least, when he'd be coming home. But she hadn't heard a word from him.

She knew who to blame for her bad-tempered, and it wasn't Drake. Her grumpy attitude had everything to do with the murder, Geoff, and then, to add to the mix, Nick, and she could do nothing about any of them.

Roni had the sense something else was ready to burst upon the scene, but couldn't image what, unless it was Drake's arrest. She prayed it wouldn't take place at all.

At least the lunch yesterday turned out to be a good thing. It gave her a little more insight to Nick. And Drake seemed to think their meeting and day went well at the office. He had found and offered a position to Nick. All that was left, was for him to make up his mind.

Roni thought Nick seemed nice enough but was he trustworthy, or were they allowing a viper into their midst? If only Frank could uncover information to Nick's true character or who committed the murder, she'd feel more at ease. Whoever the killer was, had covered his tracks well, which didn't look good for Drake.

Samantha's dinner with Nick was tonight. Maybe if Geoff won at golf today—if he played golf—he would be less surly and more amenable. Maybe he'd be good and tired and perhaps fall asleep, giving Samantha and Nick a chance to become better acquainted. But then Geoff just might feel it his duty to be …

Enough.

To worry over what might or might not happen was a useless waste of time.

Roni grabbed the book she'd tried to read earlier in the evening without success. She slid back on the sofa, curled her legs up and got comfortable, determined to become immersed in the novel as the rain pelted the windows.

Her mind became absorbed in the suspense novel. The plot was plausible and well-written, enough so to keep her turning the page.

Startled out of the story by the *zitt-zitt zitt-zitt* of her phone, Roni dropped the book onto her lap and reached for the cellphone, her adrenalin pumping. *Hopefully, Drake is on his way home.*

I know who murdered Marcus—it wasn't Drake. Meet me 12 tonight at the old feed mill by the tracks. Come alone or I'll be gone with the info.

Her pulse quickened as she reread the message. Was the text a hoax or a nasty joke? Why text her and not the police? And if it was legitimate, why block the number?

In a quandary of what to do, her nervous fingers punched the button and reread the message. She owed it to Drake to at least check out the validity of the text, especially if the person had proof of Drake's innocence.

Glancing at the time, she knew she didn't have a minute to waste. The drive to the mill would take twenty minutes in this weather.

Where was Drake? She needed him, and he should be back by now.

A rumble of thunder rattled the window panes causing Roni to nearly jump out of her skin again. She moved to the window, brushed back the drapes, and then watched as the storm raged outside which contributed to her uncertainty.

The decision made, she rushed upstairs to change into a pair of jeans and boots, hoping Drake would be home before she left for the mill. She pulled her navy jacket from the closet, and then headed back to the library.

After a quick glance at her phone and seeing no message from Drake, she decided to call him. His phone went straight to voice mail. Her stomach churned as she left a message, praying he'd get it in time to meet her at the mill.

A meeting on her own wasn't the wisest decision she'd ever made, but she didn't have a choice. If there was a remote possibility of proving Drake's innocence, the trip and anxiety would be worth going.

She placed a call to Frank. When he didn't answer, she left him a message to meet her at the mill with instructions of how to find the place.

Surely, one of them would get her message. She could call Geoff, but she didn't need to deal with his surly attitude. Regardless how foolish, she'd rather face the unknown on her own than to face it with him.

As she left the house, Roni's stomach tighten, wishing she had another alternative. The rain fell in sheets as she drove causing her wipers to work hard to maintain a little visibility. By the time she reached the road, the weather had slacked up enough to see and she applied more pressure to the gas pedal, yet careful not to drive too fast.

According to the time on her dash, Roni figured she would get to the feed mill in plenty of time, barring no unforeseen problem. For once she was glad the road was deserted. The car became a dark cocoon for her dismal thoughts.

Though doubt wormed its way into her thinking, she felt this was the right thing to do. Even with a remote possibility this person wouldn't show or the text might be a prank, she couldn't afford to miss the opportunity to clear Drake's name. She would do whatever it took to prove his innocence.

Her mind fought with her to turn around, yet she countered with all the reasons why she had to continue. She didn't feel comfortable in meeting some unknown on her own, no protection, no backup, no way of knowing what was waiting for her. And she didn't dare alert the police. The person would vanish along with the evidence.

Roni approached the town square and stopped for the light, her heart racing. Dark, deserted store fronts mocked her as though they were in on the conspiracy. Henderson County Courthouse stood like a tall avenging shadow in the center of the square. The trees surrounding the building whipped and snapped with the wind as a fine mist swirled in the air.

The prospects of this meeting were growing less and less appealing. At least she wouldn't have to trudge through pouring rain.

A carload of teens crossed in front of her. One boy hung halfway out of the window, arms spread open. He hollered for her to come and get some. A couple of his companions pulled him inside as they sped around the corner laughing.

Shaking her head, she couldn't remember ever being that carefree and uninhibited. She was young when she faced the heartache of her parent's death. And now, the last few days seemed to pile on more trouble and sorrow for those she loved.

The light changed and Roni made a decision to approach the old feed mill from the west. She drove past the courthouse and down two blocks before making a right.

At the next block she made another right then slowed down. From the direction she traveled her headlights would illuminate the parking lot and she'd have the opportunity to hopefully recognize the informant's car. She needed every advantage just in case.

The quasi-industrial area at one time used to be a busy on and off railroad loading area and consisted of old buildings and houses either deserted and deteriorating, or locked down for the night. Roni knew this particular area had a reputation for being the seedier side of Athens, if there were such a thing.

She scanned the area carefully as she drove. During the daytime it wasn't too bad to drive through, but to venture into this vicinity after dark was a different matter altogether.

Again, Roni ignored her sixth sense pleading with her to turn around and go home.

Streetlamps were nonexistent and the clouds obscured the moon. Roni relied heavily on her headlights to keep her car out of the ditch or the abundant potholes in the road. The blacktop held the appearance of a war zone where landmines had been set off, leaving behind craters in the road to ensnare unsuspecting drivers.

Stopping at the corner, she looked across the street at the building, and then to her left then right. The area was deserted except for a lone dog running down the road. Glancing around again, more carefully this time, she still came up short as to who she might be meeting.

The clock on her dash displayed eleven-fifty-five, meaning she'd either arrived first or the person she was supposed to meet was the cautious sort, parking their car out of sight. They evidently didn't want to be seen at the building, which didn't bode well.

Nothing stirred except the tree branches and the tall weeds lining the parking lot. Four blocks ahead, she could see the occasional car headlights as they passed north and south on Highway 19.

Roni had never felt so alone or so scared in her entire life, except for the time in the principal's office when she was told her parents were dead. Funny, after all these years, she could still remember the officer's name … *Meeks*.

She relived the awful moment of her parents' death knowing even then she had no choice in the outcome. But she had a choice this time. She could leave, which her head told her to do, but her heart commanded her to take the chance to prove Drake was innocent.

The choice was hers, but both held pitfalls.

Maybe the person had changed their mind or perhaps … what? A prank? But why would someone play such an awful joke with something so serious and at this time of night?

Then again, maybe the person was afraid of getting caught, or didn't want to be involved in the murder for fear of reprisal. She would never know if they were in the building unless she got out of her car and went inside. The information could be vital to Drake's defense.

Roni drove across the street into the caliche packed parking lot. Her car bounced when she failed to see a huge hole filled with murky water. Gray mud spurted up into the air and sloshed down over her hood and windshield blocking sight of the warehouse. She pulled the wiper lever several times, adding clean water to the murky mess until she was able to see again.

Pulling in front of the door, Roni stopped, honked, then waited, as the noise of the horn echoed around her. When no one came, she tried again, with the same results.

She backed up until she was across the parking lot from the entrance, her headlights illuminating a good portion of the building. She turned off the engine and pocketed the keys then sat waiting ... for whom? Should she go in? Or as the logical side of her brain warned, turn around and go back home?

CHAPTER 44

Drake's night had turned out to be a complete disaster. Well, not really. He'd spent the entire evening in the barn with his foreman and the vet working to save his prize bull, which they did. The quiet evening he'd planned with Roni never materialized. Frustrated, he tromped the gas pedal, releasing the clutch with a snap. The Jeep's wheels began spinning as mud shot up into the air.

The vet had left minutes before.

The foreman was staying behind with the bull.

Drake was driving like a madman hoping Roni would still be up. His need to see her, talk to her, hold her in his arms before she went to bed, spoke volumes of how much he needed her in his world.

If he could have his way, they'd be married tomorrow. But until the suspicion of his father's murder was no longer a factor, he wouldn't ask. But the minute his name was cleared, he'd marry Roni.

Thoughts of her hadn't strayed far from his mind all evening long—her smile, her impish teasing ways, her caring, and sweet disposition. There were so many things about Roni he loved. He couldn't image his world without her.

Cellphone service, hit and misses in the country most times, was non-existent at the barn. Built in one of the lower lying areas of the ranch with rolling hills and trees surrounding the structure, Drake knew it was useless to call Roni earlier or even now. He knew he'd have to wait until he reached higher ground to let her know he was on his way. He hoped she had waited up for him. The need to see her, hold her in his arms, had Drake wishing they could get married.

When the Jeep topped the hill, he reached for his cellphone and noticed he'd missed a couple of calls from Roni and a voicemail. He played the message.

Hi Drake. I have a lead on your dad's killer. I received an anonymous text tonight to meet someone at the old feed mill at midnight. The message said to come alone. I'm headed there now. If I'm not back home by the time you get there, please come to the mill by the tracks. I sure could use you about now. This might be a prank or dead end, but worth looking into. Since I didn't reach you, I'm calling Frank also. Hopefully, he'll be able to meet me at the mill. I love you.

Drake's heart stopped as the image of Roni alone in a deserted building with some madman. His heart kicked into overdrive, violently pounding against his chest as his attempt to call Roni failed. The time on her message was 11:35. He threw the phone back into the catchall and with rapid precision shoved the gear in place and tromped on the gas.

The Jeep bumped over the holes and ruts at a higher-than-safe rate of speed. Drake prayed he'd reach Roni in time. He took the turn out onto the blacktop, swerving, then fishtailing. He knew he was at least fifteen minutes from town and ten minutes behind Roni. A lot could happen in ten minutes.

Who were they dealing with? What if it was the same person who killed his father? But why call Roni and not him?

Throwing caution to the wind, Drake tromped the gas pedal again, his wheels whining as they spun on the wet pavement before gaining ground. Water and mud shot up into the air leaving a rooster tail trailing the Jeep. Extra aware of his surroundings and the speed he traveled on wet pavement, Drake back off slightly knowing he'd be no help to Roni if he landed in a ditch.

He gripped the wheel tighter as visions of Roni hurt and lying helpless danced before his eyes. In his gut he knew something was terribly wrong about this meeting. Why midnight? Why alone? And why the old deserted feed mill where no one would be around if Roni called for help?

With his gaze on the road, he fumbled around for his cellphone. When he latched on to it, he punched in Roni's number hoping he could stop her before she entered the building. He sent up a prayer for her safety as he listened to the ring tone. *Answer the phone!*

When Roni answered, relief flooded him. "Roni, don't—" Just as quickly his elation dropped to the pit of his stomach when he realized it was Roni's voice mail. His gut tightened and worry ripped through him. A trip to the mill, even in dry conditions, would get him there past midnight.

Her voice flowed over him as he impatiently waited for the beep, causing him to realize if he lost her he wouldn't survive. He hoped against hope she would receive his voice mail, yet he knew by her not answering she was probably in the building at this moment facing only God knows who … *alone.*

When he heard the beep he said, "Roni, I'm on my way. Don't go into the building. Get back into your car. Go to the courthouse and wait for me. I have a bad feeling about this. Please wait for me. I love you."

Drake disconnected, let out a defeated breath before throwing the phone back into the console catchall. He slammed the steering wheel with his palm, the frustration inside him growing. Why wasn't he there to protect her?

Roni wouldn't back down if it meant finding the killer. Hopefully, Frank was there with her. But something in his gut told him she was in the building alone and without protection. Pictures of Roni meeting a madman played before his eyes as worry burned through his gut like a fire lapping up trees.

Who could have lured her? Maybe it was as she said. The person had proof of who killed his father. If so, why at midnight, why a deserted building, and why alone?

Drake entered town and knew he had at least five minutes before he would reach the old feed mill. It felt like he'd swallowed acid and his stomach was full of holes.

A lot could happen in five minutes.

CHAPTER 45

Thankfully, the rain had stopped, leaving behind a low ceiling of clouds. Roni debated whether to go inside or wait in her car for Drake or Frank to arrive. Her choice to meet an unknown had her rethinking her snap decision at the house. But the remote possibility the person had proof of Drake's innocence meant she would go in.

The clouds parted and for a moment Roni had a well-lit view of the deserted parking lot before the moon disappeared again. The lot appeared darker, more sinister than before as the shadows shifted and swayed playing tricks on her eyes. Roni reached into the glove compartment and grabbed the flashlight for those *just in case* occasions—flat tires, car trouble, wreck, or ... *like now.*

Another glance around told her there wasn't any sign of a car or person, neither any sign of Drake or Frank. She'd hoped one of them would have arrived by now, but it looked like she was on her own. And by the clock on her dash, she couldn't wait any longer to discover if this meeting was a hoax. She had to move now before the person left—if the person was even inside at all.

Roni got out of her car and quietly shut the door, her flashlight probing the shadows. A chill snaked up her spine as she moved toward the entrance. Drake would be angry with her, give her a lecture for such folly. Roni would gladly take the scolding and then some if the person proved to have the evidence to clear Drake's name.

The metal roof buckled and groaned. Somewhere along the street a door banged with the gusts of wind. The late hour, the deserted area, and the howling wind were working in unison to frighten her out of her wits. She should turn around and go back to her car, but she couldn't until she knew for sure no one was here.

She gathered what little courage she had left, stretched out her trembling hand, then turned the knob, halfway praying the door wouldn't open. To her dismay, the door swung in on rusty hinges, the screech echoing in the building.

The place reeked of mold, damp dirt, and other dubious things. She covered her nose, wishing she'd had the good sense to stay in the car. With her heart in her throat, Roni took a deep, nervous breath and almost gagged over the stench.

She swept the room with a beam of light, and found she stood outside a small empty office of sorts. The room had two doors leading into parts of the mill. Crossing the threshold, she was greeted by what sounded like moaning. Fear skittered across her skin, causing her hair to stand on end. She felt foolish when she realized it was the wind whistling through the rafters in the warehouse.

Once again her flashlight swept over the room but this time she took note of what it contained—a dirty, torn up couch pushed over onto its back, a desk listing to one side due to a broken leg, and the floor littered with broken beer and wine bottles and debris, no doubt a teens' hangout.

The peculiar feeling of being watched caused Roni to swing her flashlight around the room in a wide swath, but she didn't see anyone.

"Hello. Is anyone here?" She waited but received no reply. "Hello?"

Roni walked over to one of the open doors, shined her light inside before entering. It was the milling area as she suspected.

Wooden pallets were stacked dangerously in the center of the room. One shove would probably tumble and scatter them across the floor. Further in the building, gathering dust, was a bulky hammer mill along with other aging equipment, but no sign of the person she was to meet.

A skittering noise drew her attention. She clamped her mouth shut to keep from screaming. A large, fat-bellied rat with a long tail ran from behind the crates, stopped, sat on his haunches, and then stared at her, nose twitching. The little creature's round eyes sparkled like black beads of fire and seemed mesmerized by her light.

Roni hunched her shoulders, cringing at the sight.

"Shhh, little rat. If you come anywhere near me, I swear I'll run out of here. So please go back into the hidie-hole you came from and leave me alone." Roni had every intention of fulfilling her promise if the rodent took one step in her direction.

The creature's nose twitched again as though sniffing the air, then turned and skittered back behind the wooden pallets. Roni held the beam on the repulsive rat until it disappeared and her light landed on a pair of men's shoes, the legs bent at odd angles.

A man, on his side, his back facing her, wasn't moving. She walked closer. When the thin shaft of light landed on the body, even with the distorted shadows, she knew who it was.

Feeling like her heart had been ripped from her chest, she couldn't suppress the small cry escaping as she ran toward the body.

"Drake."

She pulled him over and shined the light on his face. Relief flooded her when she realized it wasn't him, then remorse set in.

Looking back at her with unseeing eyes was Nick Holdum.

Roni bent down, resting on the back of her legs. She searched for a pulse, but knew it was a wasted effort. Blood covered his shirt and a puddle fanned out on the concrete. There was a small, black hole in the vicinity of his heart.

Tears streamed down her cheeks for the man she barely knew. Nick didn't deserve to die here alone in this awful place. What a senseless waste and for what? One crime to hide another?

Standing, she swiped at her cheeks and then dug into her purse to retrieve her cellphone. It wasn't there.

Panic took over as she flashed the light around the room. A prickling sensation raced across her skin. She felt someone's presence and knew she had to get out of there, and get to her car.

She backed away from Nick on legs that didn't seem to want to work. Doing her best to calm her nerves and think logically, she froze in place when she heard the sound of grit being crushed beneath shoes. It came from behind. She prayed it was the fat rat making the noise, but knew the source to be human.

Sensing danger, she pivoted, bringing her flashlight around. Before she completed the turn, she heard a whoosh of wind. She couldn't react quick enough to move away from the threat. Something hard hit the base of her skull causing excruciating pain to shoot up through her head. She felt herself falling as bright lights flashed and the feeling of weightlessness took over her body, and then nothing.

CHAPTER 46

Damp cold seeped into Roni's consciousness making her aware of her surroundings. Excruciating pain pounded inside her head as a chill soaked deep inside her bones. Unable to control a violent tremor, her body shook, forcing the fog to recede further from her sluggish brain. The pain in her skull throbbed with each beat of her heart and brought her back to the dark reality. Someone had killed Nick ... tried to kill her.

Every fiber of her being cried out over Nick's senseless death as she marveled at her own stupidity for coming here alone in the first place. Roni didn't know how long she could stay in this prone position without alerting her attacker she was conscious. She didn't have any control over the tremors shaking her body.

The onslaught of other aches and pains materializing were minor compared to death. She willed her body to ignore the discomfort, even calmed her breathing to a slower more even pace as she listened to her surroundings and prayed for Drake's arrival.

Through her lashes, Roni couldn't see her assailant but instinctively, she knew the person was in the warehouse. Her flashlight, still lit, lay next to a man's leg, shining back toward the entrance. *Nick!* She was on the floor only a few feet away from Nick.

The agonizing pain in her head was nothing compared to his senseless death. At least she was still alive.

She realized her flashlight wasn't the only light in the building. Somewhere behind her, another stronger light illuminated the room. It grew brighter and wider as the crunch of footsteps came in her direction, and then into her line of sight. Through her lashes she could see shoes.

No—not shoes, boots. Cowboy boots. She recognized them.

"Don't try to fake it. I know you're awake."

The familiar voice caused the hair on the back of her neck to rise. Questions jumped to the forefront of her mind. Why would he want her dead? For some reason, she knew trying to convince him not to kill her would be useless. He'd killed Nick, so he'd have to finish the job—her. Had to be his ultimate goal all along, but why?

When she didn't move, he kicked her foot causing her to jump.

He backed away a few steps. "Get up!" His near shout had her doing his bidding.

Without a word, she gathered what little strength she had and rolled shakily to her hands and knees, then to her feet. Dizziness caused her legs to buckle, but somehow she caught herself and remained standing.

Woozy, her stomach churning, she wasn't sure which she would do first—faint or throw up. Hopefully, neither.

Roni steadied herself, brushed her hands together to free the grit collected from her palms and swallowed a gasp of pain. She took a deep, fortifying gulp of air as she felt around on her palm and found a shard of glass or rock partially embedded in her hand. With shaky fingers she managed to pull the object out, throwing it on the ground. Blood ooze through her fingers. She made a fist to stop her hand from bleeding.

Shoving the hair from her eyes with the back of her other hand, Roni stared into the bright beam focused on her face.

"Could you lower the light, please? I already have a blinding headache, which I can thank you for, and I know who you are."

Geoff's sadistic chuckle chilled her insides. She wouldn't say he sounded exactly unhinged, but close to the edge. He lowered the flashlight to shine on her torso.

"For a moment there, I thought I might have killed you with the blow to your head. If I had, my plans would have changed considerably. But thanks to your hard head I won't have to make any changes." He chuckled again, sounding more like the old Geoff.

"I'm going to enjoy this, Veronica *dear*. Do you know the best part about all of this?" He waved the light at large. "No one will ever suspect me."

His laughter chilled her already troubled heart, yet she wouldn't allow herself to show fear. She forced herself to act normal, yet strong, and above all, she needed to keep him talking to give Drake or Frank a chance to arrive, if they came at all.

"You'll never get away with this, Geoff? Any moment Drake and Frank will arrive."

He shook his head. "I'm afraid not. You hired a pitiful excuse for a PI. Couldn't see what was right in front of him. I sent him on a wild goose chase. He won't be here anytime soon.

"And Drake? To get him away from your side was easy. All I had to do was make his prize bull sick." He laughed again, the sound loud and alarming. "He's probably still out on the ranch nursing that stupid longhorn of his. Amazing what a shot of drugs will do to an animal.

"But you Roni, dear, you were the easiest," he continued. "I knew you wouldn't pass up a chance to save the day and prove Drake's innocence."

She'd been careless to fall into Geoff's plans. Again she shoved the hair from her face, this time tucking it behind her ear. Her gaze traveled past the gun pointed at her chest straight at the shadowed face of Geoff, a person so familiar yet so unrecognizable.

"Why?" Roni squared her shoulder willing strength in her arms and legs. "Why Marcus? Why Nick?"

He chuckled, if the hideous sound coming from his lips could be called such. "Why not?" The evil of his deeds belied the familiarity of his face.

Why hadn't she picked up on the small clues to his character?

"Marcus loved you as a son."

His grunt was both disdainful and spoke to his true feelings.

"It doesn't make sense. He was a sick man. You could have waited for him to die?"

"Oh, but it makes perfect sense. You didn't know the real Marcus Peters. Nobody did, except me. He exacted his pound of flesh daily, pushing, needling, and pointing out my failures on a daily basis." His voice grew hateful. "Nothing I did pleased him. I never measured up to the almighty Peters' men." The darkness caused his sneer to appear almost demonic.

"When he threatened to take away all I had worked for, I couldn't let it happen." He took a deep breath, his face contorted with hate.

"Marcus had the nerve to threaten me. Me! His own son-in-law. He demanded I break off my affair and tell my wife everything. If I didn't, he said he would and I wouldn't get a cent of his money. He was going to tie Sam's inheritance up in a trust where I couldn't get to it. I had to kill him."

So Marcus knew about the affair.

Roni figured her best plan of action was to agree with him, keep him talking. "I can understand killing Marcus, but why Nick?"

"Nick, the bastard son?" He spat on the ground. "What a joke. Marcus, a pillar of the community, a deacon of the church. And he had the nerve to point his finger at me when he'd done worse. At least I didn't leave any brats hanging around with their hands out. He was just plain stupid." He shook his head. "And then Marcus had the nerve to threaten me, said he would tell Sam and take away my kids and my money. I wasn't about to let that happen."

If Geoff wasn't already over the edge, it wouldn't take much to push him there. *Keep him talking. Focus on him.* "Yes, but you didn't answer why Nick?"

"I thought you were smart, Roni. Use your brain. Doing away with Nick made perfect sense. Marcus saw nothing wrong with giving Nick a part of the estate, granted a small portion, but it rightfully belongs to me. By getting rid of Nick, Sam's inheritance is bigger—therefore mine is bigger." He tilted his head, shrugging.

"You're right, of course. But why did you text me? I'm not keeping the money. It's going back into the estate for Drake and Samantha."

He shook his head. "Neither of them would have allowed you to give back the money. With you gone, everything—all the money and holdings, especially since Drake will be rotting in prison—will belong to me."

Roni wasn't going to tell him his reasoning was flawed. "You don't want to do this. Drake should be here any minute. If you put down the gun, I can help you."

"Like I'm supposed to believe you?" He laughed. "I'm not stupid. You and I both know with two murders I'm headed for death row. And this being Texas, probably execution."

"I can make an appeal to the judge. Ask for leniency due to your mental state and Marcus threatening to cut you off. A judge will take it all into consideration. I'll make sure you get help."

"Shut-up, you stupid cow."

The flashlight wavered. Eerie shadows danced on the graffiti wall, mocking her. A piece of the tin roofing banged somewhere behind her. The cacophony of sounds made a perfect background for a sinister end to her life. But she wasn't going to let it happen. She'd die fighting.

"Geoff, listen to me. Samantha and the kids need you. You don't want to do this. I know I can help. I'll explain everything to the police, how Marcus drove you beyond reason. They'll understand. You'll do no time at all once I build your case."

His face contorted into a sneer. "You'll help me?" He motioned about him. "If you look around, Veronica dear, I think you're the one in need of help. I would like nothing better than to avoid this, especially with you." A cunning sparkle appeared in his eyes.

She wasn't dealing with a demented man. She was dealing with someone who had worked out his plan carefully and executed his scheme down to the last detail.

"You know, at one point in time, I thought you and I could have something in common. We would have made a perfect couple—you with your survival instincts, me with my will to have the Peters' money." Geoff gave a laugh. "But when I saw how devoted you were to my *dear wife*, and how you wouldn't look at anyone but Drake, I knew it wouldn't work.

"A pity. We could have had some good times together. I like my women on the aggressive side. More fun taming them."

Roni did her best to keep her revulsion from showing.

"By the way, what did you do for dear old daddy for him to leave you an equal share? Warm his bed?"

She couldn't hold it back. "You're sick, Geoff." The words were pushed through clinched teeth. She was repulsed by his filthy mind and his hideous laughter chilled her bones.

"No matter. Your constant probing into what was none of your business landed you here. That, and knowing your one-third of the estate will go back into the pot and make my portion bigger. So you see, getting rid of you and Holdum works best all the way around."

"You don't have to do this."

"Oh, but I do." Geoff took a menacing step forward then stopped. "You're a liability I don't need. Without you or Drake around, Sam will do as I tell her, she always has. If not, there are ways to make her, or maybe she'll meet with an accident. But first, I'll siphon off the funds, sell off the holdings, and move the money to an off shore account while Drake rots in prison. No one will be the wiser."

"Someone will eventually connect you to the murders, Geoff."

He shook his head. "That's where you're wrong. I've planned it all out, down to the last detail. All the blame will point to Drake for Marcus' murder. He fought with Marcus and was angry enough to kill him. That night, he was the only one, besides you, at home."

He chuckled. "I saw how Nick looked at you. I also noticed how possessive and jealous Drake was. It'll be easy to plant the story you were meeting Nick, Drake followed, and found the two of you together. In a fit of rage, Drake killed you both. So you see, I just have one loose end to deal with—you."

Geoff raised the gun slightly, pointing at Roni's heart.

She knew it would only be a matter of seconds before she'd be lying on the floor next to Nick.

A noise from behind Geoff caused him to look around for the source.

Roni took advantage of the distraction. Head down, she lunged her body at Geoff's gut. On impact her head felt like it had split open.

Geoff grabbed at Roni as he stumbled backwards. He tripped over a two-by-four, and then landed on the ground, taking her along with him.

The crack of his skull hitting concrete resounded through Roni's head. She landed on top of him and felt the thud of his body reverberate through her as a whoosh of air from his lungs fanned her face.

Roni heard the gun as it skittered and scraped across the gritty floor. The flashlight rolled making a clacking sound as eerie flashes of light shot off the equipment and walls then came to rest by the pallets.

All sound stopped except for Roni's heavy breathing.

With only one chance to get the gun before Geoff revived, Roni scrambled off him, her gaze searching wildly in the direction she heard the gun slide.

The pistol, a few feet from her, had Roni pawing her way across the floor. Palming the gun, she twisting, then scooted into a sitting position. She aimed the unsteady weapon at Geoff, hoping she wouldn't have to pull the trigger.

He didn't move.

The gun shook in her hand. She reached out for the flashlight, shined it on him. "Geoff. I have the gun. Please don't make me use it."

She noticed a dark puddle beneath his head and saw the blank stare of Geoff's eye.

The rat who saved her life, sat by the pallets watching. The creature twitched its nose, as if to say, *I took care of him,* then skittered back into his hiding place.

She shuddered, still squeamish over the rodent. *If it hadn't been for you, my curious friend, I could have been dead.*

The adrenaline drained from her, zapping her strength. Sickened by the deadly events, she knew all of this could have been prevented if it hadn't been for greed.

Hearing a car engine and the crunch of tires on the gravel, Roni leapt to her feet and almost blacked out. Weaving on wobbly legs, she hurried from the warehouse into the small office.

Extremely unsteady, but determined no one else would catch her off guard, she aimed the light and the gun at the door.

God, let them be friendly.

Sparks dashed before her eyes and her weak legs begged to buckle. She was uncertain if she would faint or remain standing.

The screech of the door hinge caused Roni's finger to apply pressure to the trigger as she prayed she wouldn't have to shoot.

CHAPTER 47

Drake walked through the entrance. Frank close behind with his gun drawn.

Roni couldn't remember a more welcome sight. She flew into Drake's open arms, still holding the flashlight and gun. When they banged into his back, Drake let out a groan.

"Here, little lady, let me take care of these." Frank slid the gun and flashlight from her hands.

"I-I-I killed him. I didn't mean to, but-but I ..." She wrapped her arms around Drake, buried her face in his neck, and then broke down crying.

Holding her tight, Drake rubbed her back and spoke soothing words to her. His voice kept her from slipping into that dark place of no return. Tremors shook her body as reality hit—she had killed Geoff. Her best friend's husband. How would she be able to face Samantha or those little babies who loved their daddy?

Her sobs turned to hiccups, then to blubbers as words rushed out, running together. She knew she wasn't making sense. Her mind was full of images to horrible to express. Roni pulled back and looked Drake full in the face. "I didn't mean to, but I killed him."

"*Shh, shh*, that's all right. Don't think about it."

She grabbed the front of his shirt bunching it in her fists. He had to listen to her. "No! You don't understand. I. Killed. Geoff."

When she saw Drake's look of concern, she turned her gaze away in shame. "I didn't mean to. He was going to shoot me."

She heard Frank walk into the room. "He's dead and so is Nick. I've called the police."

Drake smoothed back the hair from Roni's eyes, cupped her cheek, and then gave her a gentle kiss on her forehead. "Did he hurt you?"

She shook her head then winched with pain.

"What's wrong?"

"The back of my head, it's a little sore." When she touched the spot, her fingers came away wet and sticky.

"Here, let me see." Drake gently turned her. "Frank, shine the light on Roni's head."

Drakes' fingers probed gently parting her hair.

She clinched her teeth to keep from crying out.

"Your head is split open. What in the world happened?"

"I didn't hear him come up behind me until it was too late."

"He who?" Both Drake and Frank asked the question looking around.

"Geoff, he caught me off guard. I'm not sure what he used, felt like a board." She tried to smile but winched instead. "Knocked me out. When I came to, he had a gun on me." She swayed.

Drake grabbed her, picking her up, holding her as if she weighed nothing. "I'd kill him if he wasn't already dead."

She placed her hand on his cheek. "No, you wouldn't, and I wish I hadn't. You're angry. I'm okay and feel a whole lot better since you came." She laid her head against his shoulder, feeling loved and protected, wishing sleep would come.

"At least he won't be killing again." Frank's gruff voice came from behind her.

"I'm taking Roni to the hospital to get her head stitched up. Tell the police where we are and give them my number."

"Will do." Frank strode beside them lighting their way out of the warehouse.

"Babe, where's your keys?"

She smiled at Drake's endearment. He'd never used it before and she liked the sound of it. "In my pocket." She leaned forward, dug out the keys, then nestled her head back against him. Her eyes heavy. The pain severe.

When they reached the car, Drake sat her down, then pushed her seat back into a reclining position. He placed something soft against her injury. "If you can, apply pressure to keep it from bleeding."

He no sooner finished his gentle care of her when flashing lights filled the parking lot. The lights bounced off the interior of her car. The whirl of the swirling lights caused Roni to feel dizzier than before.

"Roni, I've got to let the police know where I'm taking you so they won't try to stop us. Frank can fill them in on the details. Will you be all right?"

"I'll be fine. But shouldn't I go with you? Frank doesn't know what happened. They're going to want my statement." She tried to sit up.

He gently held her back in the seat. "Stay put. If they want to speak to you they can come to the car. You're not traipsing around with your head spit open and with the chance of losing more blood. Don't you dare move."

"I'm not sure I could if I tried." Head throbbing, heart torn, lethargy set in. Drake kissed her forehead. Her eyelids felt heavy as she heard the click of the door.

Roni woke with a start when the driver's door opened and Drake slid in behind the wheel.

"I must have dozed off." She stretched and couldn't keep from winching at the pain in her head—the vivid memory of the evening rushed back. She put her chair in the upright position, holding the red soiled towel. "Are we going home now?"

"No, I'm taking you to the hospital to have them clean and stitch up your head, then if *they* release you, I'll take you home."

Roni glanced around. She saw a couple of squad cars, the coroner's van, and other vehicles crowded in the earlier deserted parking lot. Frank stood talking with one of the officers.

"Didn't they want my statement?"

"Yes, but Frank and I told them what took place and that I was taking you to the emergency. They can catch you there or at the house in the morning." He chuckled.

"My guess is they'll come to the house tomorrow. I got fairly heated when one of them insisted on talking to you now. I told them I'd sue their sorry carcasses if they kept you here and anything happened to you." He chuckled again. "They didn't seem to have a problem with us leaving."

Roni, mind full of the night's images, wasn't sure she wanted to relive the event but knew she would have to in order to clear Drake's name.

"Drake, you do know I didn't want to kill Geoff, don't you?"

He gently squeezed her hand. "You didn't kill him. The coroner said when he fell, his head landed on a broken wine bottle. Killed him instantly. If it'll make you feel any better, I don't think he felt a thing."

She looked down at her lap. Her heart ached for what she had caused, but what couldn't be avoided, and couldn't be undone.

Reaching around her, he grabbed her seatbelt, and then fastened it in place. "Roni, listen to me."

Drake waited until she looked up at him.

"You did what you had to do to survive. This hasn't changed a thing between us. I love you and always will." Before Drake started the engine, he turned her toward him, than bent gave her a gentle kiss. His avowal and feather light touch gave her hope that she could face what was ahead.

Knowing he still loved her eased some of her guilt. Breathing in deeply she rested her cheek against the headrest, her gaze on Drake as he drove.

"There were several times tonight I didn't think I'd ever see you again."

Drake's dark glance was one of raw emotion. "When I got your voice mail, I was out of my mind with worry. Promise me you won't *ever* do anything like that again."

"Hopefully, I'll never encounter someone bent on murder again." A shudder ran through her. The nightmare resurfaced. What a senseless waste of life. She'd done her best to talk Geoff into surrendering. Oh, how she wished he had.

"Roni, I know you may baulk at this, but please don't go back to Dallas. Stay here. I don't want you far from me. I almost lost you tonight." He took hold of her hand, kissed the top of her fingers, and then, without releasing his grip, moved their interlocked hand to his lap. "I love you."

"I love you more than I thought possible. When I believed I was going to die, I thought of how we had just found each other and that I would miss having a lifetime with you."

"I almost lost you. If I had, I wouldn't have survived."

Drake pulled into the emergency drive, up to the sliding doors. "Stay here."

"I can walk." Roni reached to open the door.

"Don't touch that handle." He tried to look stern but missed the mark. "Either I carry you in now, which I figure will embarrass you more, or you wait in the car until I bring back a wheelchair." He cocked his brow showing her he meant business. "Which will it be?"

Reluctantly, yet not wanting to push Drake too far, she answered, "The wheelchair."

"Thought so." He climbed out of the car, stuck his head back inside, eye level with hers. "And don't you dare think about moving until I get back, do you hear me?"

Roni laughed because Drake knew what she was thinking. "*Roni*."

She chuckled again. "Oh, all right. I'll stay put. But really I can ..." She didn't finish her statement because Drake shut the door in her face, then jogged inside the emergency entrance.

For a moment, she almost succumbed to her obstinate nature. When she reached for the door handle, the motion made her dizzy. Drake was right, it would be best to wait for him and her carriage—even if it were a wheelchair.

CHAPTER 48

Three funerals in as many days—something Roni hoped she would never see again.

Roni rested her elbows on the porch railing, gazing out at the ranch. Taking in a deep breath, the smell of fall filled the air. She loved this time of year. The weather had turned cooler. The leaves were changing colors. But today, like the old Dickens' Christmas Carol, the ghosts of the past and what should have been, haunted her.

Regardless how much she tried she couldn't erase the horrible events from her mind. She didn't have a choice. The memories came and went of their own volition … like now.

Nights, in the bed alone, were particularly bad. Too often she would wake up, her heart racing, bedclothes drenched in sweat, in the throes of fighting for her life. Or sometimes she would wake startled waiting for her attacker to resurface only to realize she was safe, alone in her own room, in her own bed at the ranch. Only the shadows and ghosts remained.

Thankfully they were becoming less and less. However, with Geoff's funeral yesterday, she experienced another one last night. She hunched her shoulders against the cool breeze coming from the north.

His funeral was a particularly rough one for all concerned, especially Samantha and the children. Samantha had remained stoic and the boys were puzzled, crying some, but clinging close to their mother or their Uncle Drake, while Roni held on to little Ellie. The children couldn't grasp the concept their daddy was dead and was never coming back. And, unknown to them, they could thank their Auntie Roni.

Detective Jeffers was satisfied as to who and why, but Roni couldn't help but wonder if there was more to it than what Geoff had revealed to her.

One huge blessing came from the three senseless deaths. Drake wasn't a suspect any longer. Still, the question begged asking. What would turn a loving husband and father into someone no one recognized? Like all the other questions roaming around in Roni's head, she doubted they would ever know the answers.

She sensed Drake long before his touch. He bent over her back, wrapped his arms around her waist as he snuggled his head next to hers and breathed in deeply. His presence chased away the ghosts, replacing them with thoughts of him.

"*Mmm*. You smell good."

She leaned her head back against his shoulder and took in a deep breath. "So do you."

The miracle of their love never ceased to amaze her. What she had waited and prayed for so long was now a reality. Roni straightened and moved back into Drake's strong arms leaning into his chest. The depth of his love and affection he gave so freely, made her feel cherished and alive.

"Marry me."

His words, a mere whisper in her ear, were not a proposal because he had already asked and she'd accepted. She melted inside knowing he wanted to marry her now. She wanted to yell *YES!* Instead, she turned in the circle of his arms and gazed up into his loving eyes. Her breath caught at the sight of the raw emotions and need she saw in his face. His mirrored hers completely.

"Now?"

"Yes, this minute." He smiled. "I don't want to wait another day to make you mine."

Her heart sank, but she laughed to lighten the harsh reality of her answer. "Silly, we don't have a license yet. And I believe there is a little thing like a law that says we have to wait seventy-two hours after we apply for the marriage license."

He dipped his head and nuzzled her neck, then gave her a kiss strong enough to curl her toes and tie her stomach into delicious, little knots of anticipation.

"No prob." He raised his brow and gave her one of his persuasive, drop-dead, your-putty-in-my-hands smiles. "Las Vegas. We can fly out tonight and be married by morning."

The thought of doing something so wild and crazy was enticing. To leave all the ghosts behind and marry Drake tomorrow in Vegas sounded wonderful.

"You're impossible. What would people say?" She knew it didn't matter what people thought. It never had to him or her. She desired this marriage as much as Drake did. But ...

"Who cares? I want to marry you. The sooner the better, even if it has to be a private ceremony. And then whenever you say, I'll give you the biggest, most outrageous wedding anyone's ever seen." He gave her a sad little boy look, with a hint of a smile. "Please say yes."

Unlike Samantha, Roni had never wanted a big wedding. But the timing wasn't right even if it were just the two of them standing before the preacher. Everything had changed, and yet the world continued as if nothing had happened.

"Oh, how I'd love to but ..."

Roni knew what she had to say and she also knew it wouldn't be what Drake wanted to hear.

"If you can arrange everything, and Sam is okay with us getting married now instead of waiting, I won't marry you tomorrow, but I will marry you on Friday."

Drake pulled back astonished she had agreed. A teasing glint appeared in his eyes. "You sure I can't convince you about Las Vegas tonight?"

She smiled at him shaking her head.

Drake gave her a peck on the lips. "I guess Friday will have to do, if my fair lady won't fly away with me."

"I want this as much as you, but there are a ton of things I need to do first. And even if it is only the preacher, you and me, and a couple of our friends, I want to shop for a special dress for our day."

"The wait will drive me wild, but well worth it. I'll make it ... *barely*." He gave her a passionate kiss to show her how much he wanted the marriage now. He pulled back as shaken as she, took a breath, and said, "What can I do to speed things along?"

"We need to break the news to Samantha. I would like her to stand up with me, if she will."

"We'll talk to her tonight. What else?"

She glanced down at one of his buttons not wanting him to see the blush she felt flaming in her cheeks. "You can arrange a hotel room in Dallas, or wherever you choose for Friday and Saturday night. I would rather wait to go on a real honeymoon, maybe in a couple of months. I think we need to be close by for Samantha and the kids right now."

Drake lifted her chin and looked deeply into her eyes. "Thank you for being thoughtful enough to think of my sister and the kids over your own happiness." He kissed her forehead.

"Thank you for accepting my proposal of marriage." He kissed her cheek.

"Thank you for blushing when you thought of our wedding night." He kissed her other cheek.

"And finally, thank you for being you. I love the way you are. Don't ever change."

She anticipated the feel of his lips before they reached hers. What she didn't anticipate was the surge of emotions and love that flowed between them. Without Drake, her world would cease to exist. Why had they wasted so much time before realizing they were suited for each another?

He broke the kiss and pulled her up close, resting her head on his chest. "Have I told you lately that I love you?"

The deep rumble of his voice resonated through her, allowing her to feel the warmth of his embrace. He completed her in every way.

"Not in the last ten seconds or so."

"Well, then let me rectify that right now by saying, I love you, Ms. Veronica Luann Reeves, with all my heart, soul, and body. And I can't wait until I make you mine in word and deed."

"I love you too."

"Now ... is there anything else you would like to mention that I need to do before I kiss you senseless?"

"It doesn't take much to make me senseless where your kisses are concerned. And yes, there are a couple more things to discuss ..." She gave him an impish grin. "But they can wait."

She gripped his shirt, leaned up on her tiptoes, and pulled him close to her. "Kiss me, you big hunk, before I perish for the lack of your touch."

Drake chuckled then kissed her soundly, causing her insides to melt.

Roni's emotions took over. She was so thankful Geoff hadn't completed his mission. If he had, she wouldn't be here now to enjoy Drake, a man who meant the world and more to her. She looked forward to spending the rest of her life fulfilled by his love.

CHAPTER 49

"Are you nervous?" Samantha arranged the shoulder length white veil over Roni's head. Her hair had been pulled back flowing down her back with wispy curls framing her face.

"No." She wrinkled her nose. "Well, maybe a little. More excited than anything."

Earlier, Samantha had ushered Roni through a side door of the church, and then into one of the church Sunday school rooms to finish getting dressed. Brightly colored miniature kid-size tables and chairs were stacked and pushed back against one wall to provide room for their makeshift dressing area.

Roni stood before the full length mirror satisfied with how she looked. In a few minutes she would walk up the aisle of the church and commit her life to Drake, which thrilled her beyond imagination.

"You, of all people, should know this has been a dream of mine since the first day I laid eyes on your brother."

"Dream?" Samantha made a silly face. "More like an obsession. When we were younger it seemed like all you wanted to talk about was Drake. Drake this. Drake that. Until I was sick of hearing my brother's name."

Roni chuckled. "I wasn't that bad ... was I?"

Sam pounced her fists on her hips looking sideways at her.

"*Hmm*, I guess you're right. I did have it pretty bad."

"Tell me about it." Sam shook her head. "But on a more serious note, I want you to know how much I appreciated you being there for me over the past few weeks. You've been a true sister to me in every sense of the word. And I pray you much happiness, as much or more than you have given me. "

She gave Roni a hug then dabbed at her eyes with a tissue. "I can't imagine what my life would have been without you. I love you."

"I love you too." Roni grabbed a tissue. "Stop it or you'll have me crying. And then your brother will think I don't want to marry him."

Samantha snorted. "Not hardly. He wouldn't allow you to change your mind even if you wanted to." She smoothed out a nonexistent wrinkle on Roni's dress before glancing at her in the mirror. "You make a beautiful bride."

"Thanks to you and all your help."

"Nonsense. You needed no help from me." Sam's face turned serious. "My prayer for you and Drake is lots of love, which you already have, a long life, and ... a house full of kids."

"Thanks, Sam. However, I'm not certain about the house full of kids ... we'll see." At the moment, Roni wished her parents could have been here to celebrate with her and Drake.

"I think it's time for us to get down to the business of getting you and my brother hitched. This whole week, Drake's been an anxious old bear thinking something might go wrong to keep this wedding from happening. He even thought you might change your mind at the last minute."

"*Never.*" Roni shook her head, knowing she was as anxious as Drake to be his wife.

"He's got it bad. I've never seen my brother like this before."

"Well it's about time. I suffered how many years just wishing he'd notice me." Roni turned back and forth, making one final inspection in the mirror.

Her dress, a simple white, knee-length, formfitting dress with three-quarter organza sleeves, was perfect for a simple wedding. The sequins woven into the bodice, sparkled in the light with her movements. Tuesday, when she pulled the dress from the rack, Roni knew it was exactly what she was looking for.

Satisfied everything looked perfect, Roni reached for her bag and pulled out a slip of paper, then gave it to Sam. "This is where we are staying. We'll be back in town Sunday evening. But remember, if you need us for any reason before we return, call. We're only in Dallas, and we can be here in an hour."

Sam sputtered out a laugh. "And have the wrath of my brother down on my head. No thank you. I'm not that foolhardy. But if we don't get you out of this room and into the church, my brother will be knocking down the door to see what's happening."

"I think you're right on that score."

Opening a huge, white box, Samantha pulled out a bouquet of white roses with baby's breath trailing with honey suckle, then handed it to Roni.

"Oh, how beautiful. Did you pick it out?" Roni pulled the bouquet up to her nose and breathed deeply of the sweet scent.

"Can't take the credit. Drake was the one. He said you would like it."

"I do." The heady fragrance of honeysuckle and roses surrounded her. Roni knew the smell would always be a reminder of her wedding day.

~ ~ ~

Drake couldn't remember being this uptight before. His throat was dry, and he needed a larger space to pace. The pastor's study where he, his best man and college friend, Tom, and Pastor Johnson waited wasn't cutting it. Way too small and cramped for his liking.

To keep his mind off of the small room and the endless wait, Drake made a mental note of the various items he'd accomplished this week to furnish the wedding Roni deserved.

A white runner was purchased for the center aisle. He'd ordered flowers to fill the sanctuary and vestibule, rented candle arbors decorated with flowers and flimsy cloth, and more flowers were tied with bows from the same material and hung on the ends of the pews. He'd seen the church earlier before he was confined to *the box* and thought Roni would be pleased.

BJ, one of Roni's friends from UT, who was also a photographer, said she'd take the pictures which worked out well. Samantha got in touch with Madison, and between the two of them they contacted the other sorority sisters, many who were coming.

He still wasn't certain about Megan Reynolds, Roni's friend in Granbury. With such short notice, she wasn't sure if she'd be able to find someone to run the Primrose Tea Room and Antiques. And then there was the matter of their friend Jennifer Stanley who had gone missing a few years ago, she wouldn't be here. Roni and Samantha still worried about her from time to time.

However, with all of Roni and Sam's sorority sisters who were coming with their husband or friend, and his relatives and friends who were here, the church should be fairly full.

Of course, he couldn't take all the credit. He'd asked his sister's help, which Samantha was more than happy to do.

She assured him Roni would be pleasantly surprised. He just hoped he hadn't gone overboard.

"It's time." The woman he'd hired to make sure everything ran smoothly at the wedding and reception stuck her head inside the pastor's study.

Drake's heart kicked into overdrive. He hadn't seen Roni since she left for Dallas Sunday night. Talking over the phone several times during the day and night didn't compare to being with her, holding her in his arms. His first glimpse of her would be when she walked down the aisle to become his wife.

"We'll go through here." Pastor Johnson held open a side door motioning for Drake to follow.

Organ music played softly in the background as Pastor Johnson, Tom, and he walked out of the study. They faced the pews where a hundred or more of his and Roni's closest friends and relatives sat watching him expectantly.

He didn't like being in the spotlight—never had. But for Roni he would do just about anything to please her, even stand before a crowd with all eyes glued on him.

Before Roni left for Dallas, he told her he would take care of all the arrangements. She had told him to keep it simple. He tried, but looking around the church now, he knew he'd failed miserably. All he hoped and prayed for was that Roni would be pleased and not too upset.

She was expecting only Samantha and Tom to stand up with them. Now she would be coming into a fully decorated church from the vestibule to the platform and with a lot more people than she'd anticipated.

His other bombshell—the reception afterwards with appetizers, three course meal, cake, and punch—wasn't expected either. Hopefully she wouldn't be too shocked … *happily surprised would be nice.*

He tried to smile but his face wouldn't cooperate. His courage deserted him. And though he wore a suit to work every day, his clothes felt hot and confining. He wanted to tug at his tie that seemed to be chocking him. *What is it about a wedding that could turn a confident, successful man into a quivering lump of humanity?*

Where was Roni? She should be coming down the aisle now.

He stared at the closed doors at the back of the church—*nothing, no one.*

He hadn't been told him he'd be this nervous waiting for his bride.

The organist switched music.

The doors opened.

Drake saw his sister but didn't see Roni.

He wanted to leave the platform to go find her, but he felt the gentle touch of the pastor's hand on his arm.

"Steady now. She's coming next. And remember to breathe. I don't want you passing out on me."

For a second, he allowed his gaze to stray to the minister. Drake gave a nervous chuckle. Pastor Johnson's words helped to calm Drake enough that he remembered to breathe.

The rustle of people standing drew his attention back to the crowd and then to the door.

He saw her. *Roni.* His beautiful bride.

Everyone turned to gaze at the exquisite vision at the back of the church.

His heart beat like a hammer against his chest. He forgot to breathe. His starved lungs dragged in air as everything stood still.

Roni wasn't moving. Her lips formed a mute O as she scanned the church. Then her brilliant smile relieved his worries. He knew he'd both surprised and pleased her.

Her gaze locked on him and she began to move up the aisle in time to the music.

Roni. His eyes filled with moisture. His throat constricted. His heart stopped then leapt with joy.

He'd seen beautiful brides before, but none compared to his. Dressed in all white, a thin veil partially hid her face as it fluttered around her shoulders. Everyone faded into the shadows. He knew the image of Roni walking toward him would be indelibly stamped on his mind for as long as he lived.

The surreal moment had him shuffling his feet as time was suspended. Everything progressed too slowly for his liking.

Roni's leisurely, precise steps brought her closer yet tantalized him by deliberately making him wait. Her unhurried movements as she came up the aisle were almost too agonizing to watch, yet he couldn't take his gaze from the vision coming toward him.

It felt like he had waited forever for this moment and now … Roni was taking her time, drawing out his torture.

He wanted her to hurry. He wanted to tell her he loved her. He wanted Pastor Johnson to say the words to irrevocably bind them together for life.

The Pastor nudged Drake. He knew that was his cue to step forward and meet Roni before turning to face the minister again.

He walked down the three steps, stared into her gorgeous eyes and whispered, "You are the sunshine in my life. I love you beyond reason."

Tears brimmed at her lashes. "Not half as much as I love you."

Her sweet smile gripped his heart as her whispered words washed over him, thrilling him like no other. He would never tire of hearing her say those three simple words that meant so much.

Drake reached out and placed her trembling hand in his and witnessed the merriment in her eyes.

"And this is what you call a simple wedding?"

Her grin was infectious. "Anything to please my gal."

They both chuckled as they moved up the three steps to the platform where the others stood waiting.

"You may be seated." The minister opened the little black book where his finger had marked the page. When the shuffling of people settled down, Pastor Johnson smiled at both of them.

"We are gathered here today to unite Veronica Luann Reeves to Marcus Drake Peters, the third, in holy matrimony. It is not a matter to be taken lightly, or ..."

Time stood still as the words flowed over him. The solemnity of their sacred vows before God was something he would never take for granted. They weren't just words. He would cherish, honor, and protect Roni with all his soul, mind, and body, and take care of her as they grew old together.

Roni's gaze never wavered from his. Her eyes sparkled with unshed tears of love. The exchange of their vows and rings sealed the hallowed ceremony as they exchanged their single status for oneness and unity.

"... And I now pronounce you husband and wife. You may kiss the bride."

Drake lifted the veil from Roni's face. Her expectant gaze told him all he needed to know. He dipped his head to hers. Their lips touched sealing them as one.

Drake prolonged the kiss, lingering, savoring the sweet taste of Roni on his lips—the kiss lasting longer than expected.

When clapping and laughter filled the church, Drake pulled back and noticed his wife had turned beet red. He bowed which caused more laughter and clapping to which Roni shook her head and joined them.

Drake pulled Roni up closed and whispered in her ear, "Tonight you are mine in every sense of the word." He smiled as he gazed deep into her eyes.

"Mrs. Peters, have I told you lately that I love you?"

EPILOGUE

Drake scooped up his littlest nephew, Peter, and then rolled with him to the ground. Within seconds, Timmy ran and jumped on Drake's back, arms around his uncle's neck. Laughter and squeals filled the air while Drake rumbled with the boys.

"Looks like Drake has his hands full." Frank's lanky body momentarily shaded Roni from the sun.

Her hand shielded her eyes as she glanced up at him. "They've been at it for a while now. Drake will be worn out, but he loves to play with the boys. He gives them as much of his time as he can. They miss their dad even if he was ..." She shook her head, marveling how Geoff had fooled them.

Frank chuckled. "I know what you mean. But some people have a knack for living a lie."

"One good thing I believe about Geoff, he loved his kids." Placing the book she'd been reading face down on her lap, she motioned to the Adirondack chair next to her. "Have a seat. If you'd like a soda or water, they're in the cooler."

Roni continued watching Drake and the boys as Frank grabbed a Coke and then slid into the chair next to her.

"What brings you out our way? Do you need to speak to Drake?"

It wasn't a secret Drake had Frank looking into matters dealing with the Peters Corp which called for numerous reports.

"No. I'm here to see you."

"Oh?" Her brows furrowed as she tilted her head. "What's up?"

"Over nine months ago you asked me to look into your folks deaths."

Roni's pulse accelerated as her hand moved to her stomach. She worked to regain the calm of earlier.

"I completely forgot I had asked you to look into the matter. I'm sorry you went to all the trouble, but it's not important any longer. Send me your bill and close the file."

Her heart swelled with love as she watched Drake pick up Peter and fly him in circles, and then did the same with Timmy. He'd make a wonderful father.

She glanced back at Frank.

He shrugged, giving her quizzical look. "Okay. Do you want me to give you a short rundown of the report or just mail it to you?"

She wasn't certain if she wanted to know any of the details. Yet, with Frank's reminder, the questions resurfaced, hovering at the back of her mind, doing its best to dredge up the old hurts.

What did it matter? In her heart, she'd forgiven all who were or might have been involved the week before she married Drake. If she asked Frank for his report wouldn't she be dredging up old ghosts that might come to haunt her? Or worse, be plagued by unanswered questions Frank's visit had resurrected?

"Frank, will your report change anything in the large scheme of things?"

"It all depends on who's asking?"

"I'm asking."

"Then, yes. I believe it will give you peace of mind."

"I already have that."

Frank chuckled, his eyes narrowing. "Well, little mama—"

Roni's hiss of indrawn breath stopped Frank from continuing. "How did—"

"How did I know you are expecting?" He laughed outright this time. "That's why people like you and your husband pay me the big bucks. I'm good at my job, and I'm observant."

He raised his leg, settling his ankle on his knee. "When I mentioned my report, it disturbed you. Unconsciously, your hand moved protectively to your belly, where, if I'm not mistaken, the next little Peters is resting—am I correct?"

As she nodded, Roni could feel her whole face light up. She knew her pregnancy didn't show yet, but she could feel the small bulge beneath her palm. The joy of experiencing the miracle of new life was both thrilling and amazing.

"You're more observant than my husband. And I just found out for certain this morning. Tonight, I was going to tell Drake over a quiet candle light dinner. Now it looks like I'll have to tell him this afternoon instead." She felt Drake's stare. She looked up and waved.

When he noticed Frank, he waved back, then spoke to the boys before jogging in their direction. Peter and Timmy, at a full run, passed their uncle.

"Your secret's safe with me. Tell him tonight. He'll never know I guessed first."

Frank stood, then bent on one knee, arms outstretched, waiting for the boys to ram into him, which they did full force, almost knocking him over.

"Uncle Frank, Uncle Frank." Timmy and Peter wrapped their arms around Frank's neck. Though he was no relation to the boys, he loved the honorary title.

"Hey, buddies, I've missed you." He pulled them up tight.

When the boys unwrapped themselves, they gave Frank a high five. The youngest, Peter, latched on to Frank's hand. "Come play, please, please."

"While I'm saying hello to Frank, go get something to drink and cool down a bit first." Drake motioned to the cooler. "And Timmy, bring me back water please. Once we've had a chance to talk, maybe I can convince Frank to play four-man football."

Both boys hooted while jumping up and down.

Drake waved them on to the cooler before turning to Frank. "To what do we owe this visit?"

Frank glanced at Roni which drew Drake's curious gaze.

"Before we were married, I asked Frank to check into my folks' death. I forgot all about it. He's finished his report. However, I told him it wasn't necessary now."

Drake dragged a chair up next to Roni's, sat down, then leaned in close to her, resting his elbows on his knees. He gathered her hand in his.

"Sweetheart, I understand how you feel. But I think you need to listen to his report, otherwise, the uncertainty will trouble your mind."

His compassion moved Roni. Regardless what was revealed, she knew it wouldn't change anything between her and Drake. Nor would it bring back the hurt she'd released over a year ago.

Her decision made, uncertainties welled up as she turned to Frank. "What did you find?"

"That's my girl." Drake gently squeezed her hand.

"My research points to accidental death. Cause … brake failure. There was a factory recall for your father's make and model which he apparently didn't know about. Over a period of time, due to heat and stress, the brake line connection sometimes would break, allowing brake fluid to drain out. In some cases this would happen while parked, in others while driving.

"In your father's case, he had no way of knowing he didn't have brakes until he stepped on the brake pedal, then it was too late. At the rate of speed they were traveling, he couldn't make the curve." Frank looked down at the ground then back up at her, his gaze compassionate. "I'm sorry, but the car went down an embankment hitting a tree, killing both upon impact."

Roni's throat constricted. Tears stung her eyes. After so many years her heart still ached over their early death. But she was thankful to finally know the truth and put the questions to rest.

"Come here." Drake pulled Roni onto his lap.

He held her in his arms as she nestled her head in the crook of his neck and allowed silent tears to fall.

Everyone was quiet, even the boys.

Roni composed herself, wiping her cheeks. "Thanks, Frank. And though it doesn't matter any longer, it is at least good to know my father wasn't directly responsible for their deaths."

He shook his head. "You can rest assured he wasn't."

Frank watched her and Drake for a few seconds then shuttered his eyes, but not before Roni saw the raw hunger in his gaze. She knew the want of belonging and how it took the Peters' clan and their love and acceptance to rid her of the feeling.

Frank needed someone to care for him, to love him, as Drake and she loved each other. Maybe then he'd feel the contentment she had found. Until then, she'd make sure he was included in as many family gatherings as possible.

"Come on boys." Frank motioned to Peter and Timmy. "Let's play ball while these old folks take a rest."

"They're not old." Timmy, ever the grownup, gave Frank a strange look. "Uncle Drake doesn't look as old as you do."

"Oh-ho." He grabbed up Timmy and tossed him over his shoulder and carried him off. "You'll think I'm old when I get through with you, young man."

Little Peter scrambled after them, attaching himself to Frank's leg. He snatched up both boys under each arm, running with them before turning their rumpus into a free-for-all.

"Are you sure you're okay with Frank's findings?" Drake's brow was etched deep with concern.

His love never ceased to amaze her. She placed her hands on his cheek. "Yes. Even if he had found evidence to the contrary, I would still be fine." She gave him a quick kiss.

"Whatever happened in the past is just that ... in the past. Before I married you, I settled everything in my heart concerning Marcus and my parents. I didn't want anything standing between us that would undermine our marriage."

"I love you, Mrs. Peters, with all my heart, soul, and body."

Drake pulled her close and gave her a deep kiss leaving her shaken. Lifting his head, he leaned his chin on the crown of her head. His rapid heartbeat matched hers.

"I was going to save this for tonight, but I think now is the perfect time to tell you my news."

He pulled back, questions in his eyes.

"In seven months you're going to be a father."

Drake looked as if he didn't understand. Then she saw it dawned on him. A broad smile appeared. He lowered his hand to her belly and lovingly rubbed back and forth. "Are you sure?"

"Yes. Quite sure."

"Roni, you've made me the happiest man alive." He hugged her up tightly. "Have I told you lately that I love you?"

"Not as much as I love you."

He growled and kissed her again.

"Do you need me to take the boys for a ride while you two find a room?"

Frank's laughter caused Roni's face to do a slow burn.

Drake seemed unaffected. "Could you?" He raised his brows suggestively. "I find my wife and I have some celebrating to do."

"*Hmm.*" Frank cocked his head. "What's the occasion?"

Roni stood, allowing Drake to rise. His arm slid around her waist, pulling her close.

"Seems I'm going to be a father."

"Congratulations." He patted Drake on the back and gave Roni a wink. "Couldn't happen to a nicer couple."

"Thanks." Drake beamed down at Roni.

"Hey, when are you going to come play?" Peter ran up juggling the ball.

"Yeah, when?" Timmy chimed in.

Drake shook his head. "I—"

"He's coming now." Roni gave Drake a shove. "I'll go inside and be waiting for you."

Roni's look wasn't lost on Drake. "Fifteen minutes, boys, and then I've got to take a shower. You're Auntie and I have some celebrating to do. Uncle Frank will take you home. How does that sound?"

"Great!" Timmy walked off with Frank. Peter ran after them.

"Roni."

She glanced back at her husband.

He crooked his finger at her, his smile playful.

With a gurgle of laughter, she walked the three steps back to where he stood raising her brows. "*Yeesss?*"

Drake pulled her up close, nibbling her ear causing shivers to run up her spine.

"I'll be up in less than twenty." He grinned suggestively. "The Jacuzzi would certainly feel good, especially if you join me."

"Why, thank you for asking, Mr. Peters." She gave him a saucy smile. "I'd love to."

He captured her lips in a deep kiss. Roni's knees nearly buckled, desiring more, but knew this was neither the time nor place.

When he released her, she turned, knowing the effects of his kiss would linger with her for quite a while. "One Jacuzzi coming up." She sashayed up the small incline.

Drake let loose a wolf whistle, which caused her to exaggerate the sway of her hips all the more. In turn, it brought about a loud bark of laughter from her husband.

"Have I told you lately that I love you?"

Roni shot back over her shoulder, "Not in the last few minutes."

"Well, I do ... love you."

"Not as much as I love you."

Again, Drake's laughter filled the air and quickened her heart.

A love like theirs only comes once in a lifetime.

Run ... But You Can't Hide

Paradise Found – Fourth in the Texas Sorority Sisters' Standalone Series

When I am afraid, I put my trust in you. Psalm 36:3

Rick Stanley blames the loss of his Senate race to his ex-wife. He knows Jennifer is hiding. It's only a matter of time before he finds her and exacts revenge.

Living under a new identity wasn't something Aimee Hamilton envisioned when she married her ideal man. On the run and terrified, Aimee finds Ben Wheeler, Texas, the perfect place to hide, until her art brings notoriety and ... a killer to her safe haven.

Aimee has two choices. Run. Or convince her reclusive neighbor, medically discharged Special Ops Tom Branigan, to train her in the art of self-defense. Reluctantly, Tom agrees, but soon recognizes Aimee is teaching him to look beyond his anger to hope.

Now a skilled marksman and survivalist, Aimee is prepared to do what Jennifer Stanley would never do ... kill to stay alive.

www.ingramcontent.com/pod-product-compliance
Lightning Source LLC
Chambersburg PA
CBHW062109170626
46813CB00002B/376